BREATHLESS

As she shook out one of the pillows, Strider took her hand and pulled her down beside him on the bed. Before Laura could protest, he'd curled his hand around her neck and drawn her close. He kissed her on the lips, a sweet, lingering kiss that melted her bones and made her lose her bearings. Any will to struggle, or any protest she might have raised, died in her mind.

Her heart raced. She'd never experienced such an unbearable sweetness. His grip tightened, and she could feel his heart pounding as she braced her hands against his chest. Decorum dictated that she had to remove herself from this compromising position posthaste; sticklers for propriety would have had severe palpitations while viewing this spectacle.

She couldn't pull away even if she'd wanted to. Heat rushed over her skin, and she was aware of every nuance of his mouth against hers and the taut muscles under her hands.

"You're taking . . . advantage of me," she said, struggling to regain her breath.

"Yes . . . I am," he replied, just as breathless as she was. "I couldn't help myself."

"If someone discovered us here . . ."

"I would have to ask for your hand in marriage immediately." His eyes began gleaming anew.

<u>BOOK YOUR PLACE ON OUR WEBSITE</u> AND MAKE THE <u>READING CONNECTION!</u>

We've created a customized website just for our very special readers, where you can get the inside scoop on everything that's going on with Zebra, Pinnacle and Kensington books.

When you come online, you'll have the exciting opportunity to:

- View covers of upcoming books
- Read sample chapters
- Learn about our future publishing schedule (listed by publication month *and author*)
- Find out when your favorite authors will be visiting a city near you
- Search for and order backlist books from our online catalog
- Check out author bios and background information
- Send e-mail to your favorite authors
- Meet the Kensington staff online
- Join us in weekly chats with authors, readers and other guests
- Get writing guidelines
- AND MUCH MORE!

**Visit our website at
http://www.kensingtonbooks.com**

LORD SANDHURST'S SURPRISE

Maria Greene

ZEBRA BOOKS
Kensington Publishing Corp.
http://www.kensingtonbooks.com

ZEBRA BOOKS are published by

Kensington Publishing Corp.
850 Third Avenue
New York, NY 10022

All Kensington titles, imprints and distributed lines are
available at special quantity discounts for bulk purchases for
sales promotion, premiums, fund-raising, educational or
institutional use.

Special book excerpts or customized printings can also be
created to fit specific needs. For details, write or phone the
office of the Kensington Special Sales Manager: Kensington
Publishing Corp., 850 Third Avenue, New York, NY 10022.
Attn. Special Sales Department. Phone: 1-800-221-2647.

Zebra and the Z logo Reg. U.S. Pat. & TM Off.

First Printing: August 2003
10 9 8 7 6 5 4 3 2 1

Printed in the United States of America

Prologue

Miss Laura Endicott dabbed at the tears misting her eyes as she watched her best friend—the sister she'd never had—pledge her vows to Laura's erstwhile fiancé, Sir Richard Blackwood. She could've been the one to stand in front of the vicar and next to Richard, but she was glad that she'd opted out of the marriage earlier in the year. Richard had turned into a good friend and the brother she'd never had, and now she was witnessing her two friends' happiest day as they smiled at each other under the rose arbor at Eversley, Richard's estate. Anyone could see how besotted they were with each other.

Laura wondered if she would ever get married, but so far offers had been elusive. Meager feeling had fueled Richard's courtship of her, and she'd felt no romantic attraction toward him. She might not have had Richard's proposal at all except that he'd promised his father, and hers, to take care of her.

She needed no one to take care of her.

She knew she could fend for herself and Endicott Keep, and all the kind souls who depended on her for their livelihood. Her cousin Edwin, to whom Endicott Keep had been entailed, lived in the Colonies and had no intention of returning to England until his children were grown. She acted as his steward of sorts, and he trusted her implicitly. She enjoyed the challenge, and everyone helping her had become like a big family to her.

Independence was one of her strengths, but she missed someone at night as she sat alone in front of the fire, or on the back terrace, as was her wont on warm summer nights. She loved gazing out to sea, the breeze playing across her face, her kittens and dogs gamboling around her feet.

The animals never strayed far, but even as she loved her four-legged friends, she missed two-legged companions. Mind you, her animals might turn out to be the most intelligent and certainly the most loyal of all, she thought as she sneaked a glance at the man at her side, Viscount Sandhurst, who had escorted her to the wedding in Sussex.

Julian stood tall and proud beside her, his blue eyes enigmatic and his handsome face remote. She'd known him most of her life, but she could not tell what he was thinking today. His expression gave away nothing. He had shown a renewed interest in her in the last two weeks, one that spoke of more than friendship after she gave Richard his *congé*. Still, he had made no mention of a joint future with her. In fact, he acted more like the old friend he was, as if his recent amorous attentions toward her meant nothing. It bothered her that he appeared to be able to turn his feelings on and off, or conveniently forget that he'd shown some ardor.

Besides being her friend, he was her closest neighbor. Almost every morning he visited her at Endicott Keep, but ever since Richard's courtship ended earlier in the spring, he had adopted a formal note in his voice and kept any warm gestures to himself—until these last weeks. Strange, she thought. Why the change?

She didn't have a lot of experience and didn't know

how to read his behavior. Once, he'd kissed her with passion during a dinner party at Sandhurst, and she'd responded, her senses aflame. Perhaps he'd realized that he had no real interest in her after all, or perhaps he couldn't make up his mind.

It was hard to tell as he would not speak of it, and she dared not broach the subject due to the possible outcome of humiliation. She liked to keep the status quo. It wasn't her place to bring up the future, but she could easily see the merging of their adjoining properties, the Endicott land that was not entailed, and which had come to her upon her mother's death. The question was, could he?

She believed he could. What gentleman would turn down the opportunity to extend his property handsomely with little effort? But she wanted more than to give her hand away to seal a business agreement. She would only marry for love as her friends had done.

She turned her attention back to Jillian and Richard. Jill looked beautiful in a cream silk dress embroidered with seed pearls and a crown of cream roses that accentuated her shiny black hair and dark eyes, and Richard in his dark blue coat and cream waistcoat stood as a perfect foil to her beauty.

They looked so happy as they gazed at each other, warm light in their eyes. As she watched Richard kiss the bride, a feeling of emptiness washed through Laura. Would she ever be as close to someone as Jill was to Richard? The prospects looked bleak, but hope springs eternal, she thought and tossed a glance at Julian. His expression bordered on boredom, and she could've sworn he was smothering a yawn as the ceremony came to an end.

One

Pain pierced him with every breath and his leg ached with a viciousness that left him exhausted. One of his arms lay useless and throbbing in the rough grass beside him, and the white clouds careened across the sky above his aching and gritty eyes. He needed to throw up, but couldn't find the strength to turn over onto his side. *I'll die here now. I struggled to come back for naught. How could I be such a nincompoop as to fall prey to an ambush when all I had to do was to practice caution?*

He burned and throbbed more with every second. He swore under his breath as the most intense wave of pain singed every nerve ending of his body. He heard himself whimper, but when had he started to sound like a dog?

A wet tongue slathered his face and foul breath filled his nostrils until his stomach rebelled and heaved in a giant wave of nausea. He turned his face away, sharp-bladed grass pricking his skin as he threw up over a stand of bluebells.

Humiliating and hopeless, he thought, disgusted with himself. The smell of the dog still lingered, and another wave came over him.

Hands moved over his body, pushing hard until he got onto the side that wasn't torn to shreds with pain. Every move sliced like knives down his leg and arm, and he couldn't find his breath. He heaved once

more, clearing obstacles to his breathing, and sweet
air flowed into his lungs. Sweat streamed down his
face and scorched his eyes.

His head throbbed and his eyes ached as he lifted
his gaze to the owner of the small pushing hands. A
woman's concerned cornflower blue eyes met his and
something warm wound around his heart, easing the
pain for a moment. A curling fringe of gold-tipped
eyelashes framed the lovely, kind, and honest gaze.
She seemed familiar, but his tired brain could not find
any clues to her identity.

I want to die, he thought.

But those hands would not leave him alone, and
that disgusting slathering tongue, which evidently belonged to a large brown dog, kept washing his ear and
his neck. Blast the mongrel!

He tried to find his voice, but could only muster a
croak. A frog sounded better any day.

"Don't move," the female said unsteadily. "You're
covered with blood."

He wanted to soothe her fear and make light of his
wounds, but his voice still didn't obey him.

"What happened to you, and what are you doing in
my meadow?" she asked.

He moistened his parched lips with his tongue. "Accident," he managed to squeeze out.

She tut-tutted, her trembling hands slowly moving
over his aching limbs. "That's a blatant untruth, unless you were trying to shoot yourself and only
managed to mangle your leg and then your arm. Your
aim is dismal."

He tried to glare at her, but couldn't find any power
behind the effort. Thank God his attackers had ex-
hibited poor aim, or he'd be standing before his
Maker this very moment. The next second he longed
to die as pain tore at him like starving wolves.

She had beautiful pale blond hair that curled around her face and hung over her shoulders where it had escaped the confines of her frayed and faded straw hat. He felt an urge to touch one golden hank but couldn't move.

"I'm going to fetch help," she said with deepening concern in her voice.

He tried to protest, but still his voice failed him. Under no circumstances did anyone need to discover his whereabouts. "Don't . . ." he whispered, but she'd already left. The dog with the foul breath still remained, lying by his side, its brown gaze trained on his face and its tongue lolling out of its gap. The canine looked friendly enough and he could hear the tail slapping against the grass.

I'm watching over you, so relax. I take my duties seriously, and I'm very good, the dog seemed to say.

I'm losing my marbles, he thought. Dogs did not talk. The blood poisoning had probably reached his head by now. His eyes closed as he could no longer keep them open, and he drew a painful sigh. Bone weary. Beyond redemption, no doubt, but he'd made an effort at justice—albeit rather clumsily.

The next thing he knew, several pairs of hands manhandled him onto a cart padded with horse blankets. The cornflower-eyed woman had returned, and with her two older men who looked like stable hands. They smelled of horses and the sea.

Through the forceful red haze of pain, he noticed the black nag pulling the cart, and the threatening rain clouds gathering in the distance. He had no idea where he was, but the sun beat down on his face and the grass rustled in the wind, and he was sure he could smell whiffs of the sea. The old men muttered under their breath.

"A large 'un, this 'un," the man at his feet said as he

struggled under the weight. "Looks like a furriner to me."

"'Em clothes—a gypsy, mayhap?" the other man replied. "If we're not careful, 'e'll put a curse on us."

The other man shook his head. "Not when we're so kind as to help."

"Make sure ye don't jar him, Ollie."

You're right, the wounded man thought. *You are kind.* Not that he could conjure spells, but his loose blue shirt of embroidered silk did not spread confidence around here. The bright colors of the Orient probably disturbed the English brown-gray sensibilities. Pain consumed him as they laid him on the cart, jagged shards rubbing against his nerves. He moaned.

The horse moved restlessly, and as the equipage jolted forward, the ruts in the field jostled his wounds to a point where he wanted to scream. He didn't. He bit down on his lower lip so hard he thought he'd punctured it. Why did such agony exist at all? It would be better to fly free of this tormented body. Why, God?

He discovered that freedom from pain was not to be his as they jostled him through some creaking back door set in an ancient gray stone wall thicker than his waist. His fevered mind traveled through many scenarios, one more gruesome than the next. They were going to carry him to some torture chamber and have all his fingernails pulled out. He tried to sit up, but his limbs had the substance of jelly, and continuous pain knifed through him.

"Do not struggle, sir," the woman said. He noticed she had the most melodious and kind voice. "We are only here to offer our help. You're badly wounded and you've lost a lot of blood."

The two men crossed themselves before carrying him into a chamber lit with oil lamps. The grim stone walls were circular, as in the towers of old. Somehow the woman was connected to this ancient building. She looked very much at home and very confident. He knew where he was, but couldn't quite grasp the situation.

"Do you have any laudanum?" he croaked.

She nodded. "Yes, but I have to clean you, and the doctor has to take a look at these wounds before we can give you a sedative."

"Have mercy," he said, his voice lengthening into a groan.

"Miss Laura is the most merciful lady ye could ever 'ope to meet, and if an'one can 'eal ye, she can," one of the old men said. "Don't you give 'er any lip, or you'll 'ave to deal with me!"

The woman spoke. "Jethro and Ollie, thank you for your help, and please keep this event to yourself as we don't know what transpired."

He watched as they touched their forelocks and bowed. "Yes, mum is the word, miss. Ye know ye can trust us, and ye know where we are if ye need 'elp."

They left, and she turned to him. "Who are you?"

He thought for a moment. Under no circumstances could he reveal his real identity. "Strider Hunt," he said.

"An unusual name," she said. "You're from these parts?"

"I'm a world traveler, but I once had connections in Cornwall. We *are* in Cornwall, aren't we?"

She nodded. "Most surely. Did the ship on which you arrived anchor in Plymouth?"

"Yes . . . some time ago."

"Well, you're not particularly fortunate if footpads set upon you shortly after you returned to your homeland, Mr. Hunt. By the looks of these wounds, you were attacked. You didn't just fall off a horse."

"Yes . . . footpads . . . no, highwaymen." He fueled

her assumption so that she would ask no more awkward questions. "And you, ma'am? Since we've not been formally introduced, can I ask you who you are?"

She smiled, which made his heart leap and accelerate. He suspected he'd gone to heaven and that she was one of the angels, but then renewed pain stabbed through him as she touched his leg. This was truly hell.

"I'm Laura Endicott, and you're at Endicott Keep."

Damn, he thought. Endicott Keep. Miss Laura had grown up; he remembered only a small shy girl with long curls who had clung to her mother's hand. Dogs and cats had always adhered to her, and that hadn't changed, he noted as he threw a sideways glance at the mongrel that had stood guard over him in the meadow. The ugly if endearing face with floppy ears still hovered right there at his shoulder.

"Would you mind removing that dog? His breath . . . well, I don't want to be indelicate. . . ."

Her laugh brightened the gloomy room. "Ah, I understand." She snapped her fingers at the dog. "Leo, go outside." The large brown mongrel obeyed, his tail between his legs. "Oh, don't play the martyr!" she cried after him.

She turned back to the bed. "Leo likes to be at the center of attention."

"Leo?"

She smiled ruefully. "He is a lion, brave, fierce, but lazy."

As he protested, she began cutting away the fabric of his trouser leg. "This wound in the thigh has stopped bleeding. You're fortunate. Your arm is still bleeding, but not as much as when I first came upon you in the meadow. I'll staunch the flow with spiderwebs."

"Spiderwebs?" He doubted he'd heard right. "I've no desire—"

"They will help to save your life."

He couldn't argue, but doubt filled him. The woman seemed to have more hair than wit.

She threw him a curious glance. "I'm surprised there are highwaymen around these parts. There haven't been rumors of any for a long time."

"I traveled some way after the footpads set upon me," he replied, grimacing with pain.

"Footpads? I'm astonished you could travel any distance at all," she said, and ripped the last of the fabric, baring his entire leg.

Damn!

He wasn't about to argue the finer points of his adventures. No one needed to know the truth until he could prove the injustice committed against him. That is, if he ever could.

"It's not common for footpads to carry pistols; from the stories I've heard they're more likely to carry cudgels and clubs. There's no doubt this is a bullet wound." She peered closely at his throbbing leg.

"These did carry pistols," he said defensively. "Highwaymen . . . footpads, I don't know." Coldness was seeping into his bones and he began to shiver. His skin was on fire as if lying bare under the India sun, but his insides ached with cold. He suspected he would not survive this damage. If he did, it would be a miracle.

The bullet still sat lodged deep in his thigh, and he doubted he would be able to use his arm ever again. So close to his goal, but he might have bungled his mission, damn it all. A wave of despondency overcame him and he closed his eyes. He might not get another chance. Surprise would have been the best strategy.

"You'll be right as rain, Mr. Hunt. Give me two weeks; my herbal concoctions are wondrous healers."

"As long as there are no frog eyes or lizard toes or raven innards involved, I'm game," he said with a groan as she cut open his shirtsleeve. He drifted off into a wave of pain and the very air swirled around and around until he lost his bearings. He must have fainted. When he came to, he heard the sound of a woman sighing heavily.

A knock sounded on some door in the room, and she put down the scissors and went to answer it. A tall bony gentleman with spectacles on his nose stood in the opening. His dark hair had sprinkles of gray at the temples, and his kindly eyes sat in folds of wrinkles. He took one look at Strider and marched across the room with his black bag at the ready.

"He's rather poorly and running a fever," Miss Endicott said. "The wounds are becoming infected."

"We have to remove the bullet," the doctor said. "No more time to waste."

Strider closed his eyes and gritted his teeth. Fear ran cold through his veins. He didn't want a sawbones to dig into his flesh with filthy instruments. "I don't want it," he said hoarsely. "Stop it now."

The doctor and Miss Endicott exchanged worried glances. She moved out of the room.

"You will have to—if you want to live, sir," the doctor said kindly. He took off his coat and rolled up his sleeves, and then proceeded to wash his hands in a basin that Miss Endicott carried into the room when she returned.

"I don't care at this point if I live or die. Too much pain," Strider said, speaking the truth.

"Any one of my animals shows more fortitude than you do," Miss Endicott said with a sniff of disapproval.

"'Tis not proper that you attend me unchaperoned," Strider said to avoid the challenge to his courage.

"In a matter of life or death, I daresay decorum can be set aside temporarily. I am by far the most experienced healer in this household."

"You're hardly out of the schoolroom, if I judge correctly." His teeth had begun to chatter, and she placed a thick quilt over the unharmed parts of his body.

"That's neither here nor there, sir." She turned up her nose slightly, and he fought a desire to laugh. He must be delirious, and the room seemed to fade in and out of his vision.

"She's the most experienced horse doctor in these parts. No one can rival her success with the animals," the sawbones said.

"It must be a poor area indeed to have to rely on young women to heal ailing animals."

"Some have a knack, that's all," the doctor said simply and laid out his instruments on a clean linen towel.

"That's right," she said.

Strider wanted to halt the proceedings, but his tongue wouldn't form the words, and he felt an overpowering urge to sleep. He might truly draw his last breath tonight, and a blessing it would be.

All these years he'd wanted to get back to Cornwall. He'd burned with desire to see justice done for an old crime, but now that he was here, he wondered if these last fourteen years had been worth all that fire in his belly. Justice might be served—or not—depending on if he survived, but did it matter any more? He'd carved out his own life, a wildly successful enterprise at that.

He drew a painful breath as he pondered the dilemma. Deep in his heart he knew that justice would have to be served, or he would never rest. As that thought faded, he fainted.

"Just as well," Dr. Turner said. "The man is obviously out of his mind with pain."

"He looks familiar, but I can't place him," Laura said, as she cleaned around the ragged thigh wound with brandy. She watched as the doctor poured some over his long pincers, and took a long breath. She prayed the patient wouldn't awaken during the procedure. At least the doctor had deft fingers and a good eye, unlike his predecessor who'd been a drunkard and a fool.

The doctor lifted the stranger's leg and looked at the bruised underside. "The bullet went in at an angle or it would've come out on the other side. I'd say it was fired from rather a distance. Someone is a very good shot to find his target at all."

"The villain must've aimed at the heart."

"Yes, possibly, but this gentleman is equipped with a great measure of luck."

"Or nine lives, just like my cats."

The doctor chuckled as he began working on the wound. Laura held her breath as she watched him gently probe. Perspiration broke out on her forehead and she found it hard to draw another breath. It was as if the pain were hers, but how foolish! She didn't even know the stranger.

"Oh, dear," the doctor whispered and probed gently.

The world seemed to have stopped, and she waited as the doctor searched. She had only felt such tension when her beloved animals suffered. The doctor breathed as if facing difficulty. The minutes trickled by, and Laura could hear the sound of the candles dripping on the table nearby.

When the pincers finally came back out of the wound with the bullet at the tips, she inhaled deeply with relief. The patient cried out, but didn't awaken. His face glowed red, and sweat dampened his forehead. He looked as if he wanted to toss and turn, but couldn't quite manage. She pressed him down with all her strength as the doctor cleaned the wound free of blood, sprinkled basilicum powder over it, and bandaged it.

"No bones are broken, but he won't be as he once was. I'm certain some muscle was damaged." He glanced at the swollen leg. "And he might never walk as well as he once did, but at least he's alive."

She glanced at the stranger's handsome face so close to her own, and she felt strangely protective and drawn to him. "I'll nurse him to the best of my abilities," Laura said. "I don't know why, but I think it's important."

The doctor grunted something as he worked on the arm, and Laura prayed during the whole procedure.

"The young man is lucky indeed. No shattered bones, and only part of his flesh has been torn. I've repaired the wound as well as can be done, and if he overcomes the infection, he'll live and walk."

Laura felt relieved and wondered why a stranger would have such an impact on her senses. She didn't know the man, and by the looks of him, he must be a gypsy, as Jethro had implied earlier. She stroked the stranger's wavy dark hair, which stuck to his forehead with perspiration. His eyelashes fluttered, but he remained asleep.

She couldn't understand his attraction. No one would ever approve of her forming a *tendre* for a man that she knew nothing about.

She watched as the doctor finished sewing together the long jagged edges of the wound, and she tore strips of clean linen for bandages. He sprinkled the wound with a thick coat of basilicum powder. "The scars won't be pretty. The bandage will have to be changed every morning and evening."

Laura nodded. "Yes, I'll be diligent."

"He'll heal in no time under your care," the doctor said, smiling.

She glanced at the patient and a strange worry took hold of her. What if she didn't succeed in her nursing? She couldn't bear the thought that she might lose him, and she'd never seen him before.

"Who is he?" the doctor asked as if echoing her thoughts.

"He says his name is Strider Hunt. A stranger traveling through, but something about him triggers vague memories."

"I don't like the idea of you spending any time unguarded with an unknown man. Who knows——?"

"Don't worry, Dr. Turner. He's not in any shape to take advantage of me, and when he recovers enough, one of the menservants can take care of him. I could not abandon a wounded person, even if he were the worst kind of criminal."

"It's commendable, Miss Endicott, but also somewhat foolhardy."

Laura shrugged. "Please don't worry about me." She covered the patient with a sheet and then folded the quilt around him. He lay in a protective cocoon. "I'll have to find some new clothes for him."

The doctor cleaned off his instruments and put them in his bag. "I'll come in late tonight and see how he's faring." He handed her a packet of medication. "Fever powders. You're likely to need them."

"Thank you, doctor. I know we have a long day and night before us."

She accompanied the physician to the front door of the Keep, and as he left, she momentarily felt at a loss. It was a great responsibility to nurse the stranger. No virile—and possibly dangerous—young man had ever lain incapacitated in one of her beds, but surely it wouldn't be much different from nursing a sick horse.

She sensed an underlying dark tow, as if some current had flowed into her life that would change her forever. Just as she turned to go back into the east tower, Julian Temple, Lord Sandhurst, arrived at the front entrance. He kissed her cheek politely. His manners were impeccable, as always.

"Laura, you look dazed, as if jolted out of a dream." He took her chin and studied her face. "And your skin is so pale. Are you feeling poorly?"

"No . . ." The story about what had happened hung on the tip of her tongue, but somehow she couldn't get it out. Why she felt a need to protect the stranger she couldn't explain, and why she would keep secrets from the man whom she was likely to marry was a mystery. She remained silent.

Julian's blue eyes narrowed as he studied her face. "Is there something the matter? What is going on?"

She glanced away and swallowed hard. "Nothing . . . nothing at all. You're imagining things. I'm just a trifle tired."

He gave her a long look, but she didn't meet his gaze. She didn't like to lie; she mostly never did. It was wrong to lie to the man who should be her closest confidante.

But he wasn't, when she thought about it. Jillian was. Just as soon as Julian left, Laura would write a note to Jillian at Eversley. A month had passed since the wedding, and Jill would have some time to write a note of advice.

Julian wanted to partake of tea and cakes, and she sent word to the kitchen for a tray. They went into one of the parlors where rusting coats of armor stood sentinel by the door. She sat on the wide cushioned stone casement by one of the windows and he sat in a green damask covered wing chair near her. The room was cold despite the sunshine outside.

"How is your grandmother?" she asked, knowing full well what the answer would be.

"Fine, under the circumstances. Nothing has changed." He crossed one leg over the other. "But it's kind of you to ask."

Laura had known Julian's grandmother all her life. Until dementia set in, the Dowager Lady Sandhurst had been an imposing woman, a matriarch of the neighborhood. Everyone had turned to her for advice, but now she mostly spent her time in an upstairs suite at Sandhurst, her nurse-cum-maid in attendance.

"Where my mother failed in her parental duties, Lady Sandhurst was like a mother to me. I miss her, and yet she's not gone."

He nodded. "Yes, she was like a mother to everyone in the area before she fell ill. A pity, really, what happened to her mind."

"There are times when she's lucid, I believe."

He shook his head and his lips turned downward. "I'm afraid not. She has not said one word of sense in the last two years."

The door opened and a footman carried in a tray. Aunt Penny, Laura's companion and chaperone, followed. She greeted Julian cheerfully.

"Brumley said you'd come for a visit, Julian. I have to hear the latest gossip."

"And make sure I behave with utmost decorum." Julian gave her a wry smile and a peck on the papery cheek.

Aunt Penny's faded blue eyes twinkled, and she patted her white hair, arranged in a tidy chignon at the nape of her neck. "You rogue." She gave Laura a smile. "Did he behave, then?"

"So far, so good," Laura said with a nervous laugh. She wondered if Julian would behave in any other way. He'd been even more withdrawn since Jillian's wedding, and Laura couldn't understand it. What was wrong with him?

No one except the two stable men and Brumley, who had met the doctor at the door, knew about the stranger in the tower room, and Laura decided to keep it that way until she'd found out more about him. She knew that's what he wanted.

"Not that I fear any ruthless and uncouth behavior from you, Julian, but we act with decorum at all times, don't we?" Aunt Penny poured the tea and handed Julian a fragile, gilt-edged cup. Steam curled out of the golden liquid.

"I heard there have been visitors to this area, which is unusual since Cornwall is hardly on any of the main roads," the older woman continued. "Someone saw an Arab dressed in one of those long gowns and turbans they wear, and horses—ten beautiful Arabian horses."

"That is odd," Laura said, remembering the clothes the wounded man had been wearing. "They must be foreigners." She turned to Julian. "Do you know anything about them?"

"No . . . someone might have decided to add on to their stables. It wasn't me, however much I'd enjoy an Arabian stallion."

"I heard gypsies are in the area," Laura said.

"They always are," Aunt Penny said. "That old woman, Tula—the one they say is a witch in Pendenny—is one of those."

Laura recalled when she'd once met the witch during a ride with Jillian. The old gypsy had told her she would marry a man named Julian. She threw a troubled glance at Julian, sitting so at ease in her home. She didn't know any other Julian, but this one acted more elusive every day.

As if to confirm that observation, he said, "I'm going to London on business for a few days."

"When will you be back?" Laura asked.

He shrugged. "I don't know. When I'm ready."

"We ought to plan a dinner party here soon. You would attend, wouldn't you, Julian?" Aunt Penny asked.

"Yes . . . I'll be here unless I'm detained in London. I have some business transactions that have to be taken care of immediately."

Laura had no reply to that, but a wave of disappointment rolled through her. She couldn't force Julian to stay at her side and pledge his devotion, and she never would. They finished their tea mostly in silence.

"When you go out, Julian, try to discover as much as you can about those foreigners," Aunt Penny said.

He nodded. "I will, but I doubt there will be any kind of salubrious gossip involved."

"A pity, but I'm certain you'll discover some new gossip in London to bring back," Aunt Penny said with a small smile on her lips. She set her cup delicately on its saucer. Her thin hands fluttered to her hair, where every strand lay meekly in its place. "Every day seems to run into the next without much happening, like pearls on a string."

Julian rose. "Yes, it's rather quiet around here."

Laura escorted him to the front door. "I'll miss you, Julian," she said, and rose on her toes to give him a kiss on the cheek.

He grabbed her shoulders suddenly, and before she could protest, kissed her on the mouth hard. Shocked by the unexpected move, she lost her breath and could not really enjoy his seductive attack. Her head spun, and she tried to back away. When he let go of her, she staggered back. "I'm . . . surprised," she whispered.

"Did you think I'd lost interest in your fair person?"

"Most certainly you've taken me for granted. No compliments or sweet nothings have crossed your lips, and if you think my feelings thrive on nothing, you're sadly mistaken. As surely as flowers need water, I need encouragement from you."

"Mea culpa. I've been preoccupied, but that doesn't mean I feel less for you." His blue eyes revealed nothing but faint amusement.

"I'm not a plaything or a new horse, or an *old* horse for that matter."

"No." He laughed and touched her chin with his fingertip. "You're a vibrant young woman, someone a man would be fortunate to call his own."

So why aren't you asking for my hand in marriage? she asked silently. Something had gone very much awry in the last month, and she had no idea how to bring up the subject. Deep inside she knew he wouldn't give her any explanations, and any declarations of love would not be forthcoming.

Laura had never felt lonelier. When he left, she hurried to her room to compose a letter to Jillian. She needed to tell someone about her misgivings and her find in the meadow.

Two

The stranger's skin burned under her hand, and worry gave her a prickly feeling under her skin. He'd tossed off the heavy quilt, yet he shivered uncontrollably. His arm looked doubly swollen and red, as did his leg. She wondered if she'd be capable of nursing him alone, yet she dared not tell anyone about him. If she did, she knew something horrible would happen, she just *knew.*

The doctor returned at nightfall. He shook his head with concern when he rebandaged the wounds. "These look sadly inflamed. 'Twill be a miracle if he survives this ordeal."

Laura shuddered, more than anything wanting to save the man. No one deserved to die such a painful death. "I'll nurse him night and day."

"He'll have a better chance if we amputate."

"Both the arm and the leg?" Laura looked at him, flabbergasted.

The doctor nodded. "He might have only half a life, but he would survive. As it is, he's likely to die before the sun rises twice."

She glanced at the feverish face with its high cheekbones and hooked nose. "He's too young to die," she cried.

The doctor didn't reply. He washed the wounds with brandy and rewrapped them with clean bandages. As he tied the last knot, the stranger awakened. He looked lost and struggled to sit up, but cried out with pain and fell back down against the damp pillows. Laura bathed his forehead with cold water, and he gripped her wrist with his hand. His strength surprised her.

"Who are you?" he rasped.

"You don't remember?"

He shook his head. "Where am I?"

"You're at Endicott Keep, in the tower room with its threadbare carpet and bare walls. I'm your hostess, Laura Endicott, and you're badly wounded. Dr. Turner wants to amputate your leg and your arm."

His grip hardened around her wrist. "Never! Do you hear me? Don't let any sawbones touch me. I'd rather die than to live like a cripple for the rest of my life."

"If that's your decision." Laura tried to pry his fingers away, succeeding only as he relaxed. She exchanged a glance with the doctor. "You heard what he said, Dr. Turner."

The old man nodded. "A fool is born every day." He closed his bag, and after shaking his head once more, left through the back door where he'd entered earlier. He'd promised to keep the whereabouts of her patient confidential until she gave him permission to speak. He disapproved of her decision, but didn't argue. She didn't quite understand her own actions in the matter, but she had to keep the man hidden or something dire would happen. She always trusted her intuition, no matter how outlandish the issue.

The oil lamps went out. Laura lit some candles in the iron sconces around the room, which was sparsely furnished with a rusty bedstead and an old worm-eaten armoire, three wooden chairs, and a washstand. The window high in the wall let in a stringent beam of golden evening sunlight.

She noticed that Strider Hunt's eyes followed her every step, but he wasn't moaning, as he had been when they brought him in.

Strider drank in the view of the slim and graceful figure of Laura Endicott as she moved around the room. Her long hair had partly fallen out of her chignon and tendrils cascaded down her back like pale gold. Most improper in a true lady, but she didn't seem to notice. She carried an unworldly air that he found endearing. Most young misses would never have dared to approach him in his current condition, but strife and illness did not repulse her. His angel. She'd found him. He knew that if she hadn't, he'd be dead by now. Pain and weariness overcame him, but he struggled to remain focused on her. It was the only way to stay alive, he thought.

She returned to the bed, now winding her hair back into an untidy bun, securing it with pins. "You have to be strong, Mr. Hunt." She mixed a powder into a glass of water and held it to his lips. He sipped obediently, knowing that she would not tolerate any protests. The mixture flowed bitter over his tongue, and the simple movement of drinking exhausted him further and aggravated his pain.

He threw a quick glance toward the door as something scraped against it.

"It's one of the dogs. You're safe here," she said simply. "I have refrained from broadcasting your whereabouts, but I suspect you're connected to the Arab with the exotic horses that has been seen in the village."

He nodded. "That's Abdullah, a friend and a very clever fellow. He knows everything about horses."

"Did you come here to sell steeds?"

He held back his response and she sensed there was more to his sojourn in Cornwall. "Yes . . ." he began. "I'm very tired."

"You're burning with fever. Sleep is the best cure at this juncture."

She placed a cool cloth on his aching forehead and he closed his gritty eyes gratefully. "You truly are an . . . angel, aren't you?"

She laughed. "No, you're delirious."

Pain crashed through him and sweat covered his body in seconds. He'd never felt this kind of agony, not even that one time when he'd broken his leg in two places. "I don't want to go through this," he whispered, his mouth parched from the fever. Cool water trickled over his lips and he drank with difficulty. "I'm exhausted yet restless."

"It shall pass," she said simply.

He thought her hands were as soft as down on his skin, and where she touched he felt better. She had the most soothing presence and her kindness was evident in every touch. His arm burned abominably and he could barely feel his leg, only a massive throbbing ache where his leg should've been. Mayhap they had cut it off already!

He fought to open his leaden eyelids, but he couldn't look beyond the edge of the bed cover. He was too weak even to lift the blasted quilt. "Did you . . . ?" he asked, too weak to finish the sentence.

She laughed, a high melodious sound. "Cut your leg off while you were asleep? No, we did not."

He relaxed and stopped fighting the pain. Nothing but a losing struggle anyway, and he couldn't do anything that would alleviate the agony. "Damned criminal," he muttered to himself as the face of his enemy stood before his inner eye. "Damn you to hell."

"What did you say?" she asked, leaning closer. He

could smell the clean, sweet fragrance of her skin, and he longed to press his nose against her, perhaps forever. The fever made him think strange but wondrous thoughts.

"What?" He struggled to look at her, but he could only see the flickering light of candles against her silhouette, and the room lay in darkness. Light and shadow. If you could see light, you could always count on a blasted shadow lurking somewhere. Anger fueled even more pain.

"Don't you have loved ones who'll worry about you?" she asked. "Do you want me to send word to someone?"

He indicated a "no" with his head. His business endeavors and his plans for revenge had consumed his entire life. "Abdullah will find me," he whispered.

"Are you related?"

"No, but he's been more like a brother than a friend. He'll find me, and when he does, let him in."

She nodded. "Very well. I hope he doesn't worry about you."

"Abdullah has lived a life of hardship. He doesn't worry about anything, and he knows I can take care of myself." He pointed one finger at himself. "Just look at me."

"I'd daresay accidents happen sometimes. Do not blame yourself."

"I don't like lying here helpless."

"Yes, a big, strong gentleman like you. It must irk you no end."

Her teasing voice soothed him. If he were whole and hearty, he would make her pay for such a comment—with kisses. He seemed to have lost his wit as well as his health. "To be incapacitated is a rather humbling experience." Even his lips were tired now. He had to rest, and for a moment there was a lull in the pain. For one precious minute he felt almost normal, and then he slipped into nothingness.

No one had ever fascinated Laura as much as this stranger. Strider Hunt brought a breath of different cultures, a sense of adventure, of danger. She could almost smell the exotic spices of the Orient on his clothes, but that must surely be in her imagination.

He slept restlessly and his arm looked even more swollen under the bandages. She sensed that she needed to inspect the wound, and with dismay she noted the angry red edges and the streaks. If she didn't do something the man would die.

The doctor may not have approved, but she would gather a handful of plantain in the meadow and wrap it over the wound. The leaves were known to draw out infections, and she knew she didn't have a lot of time to help the man. Part of her wanted to know him better; she didn't understand his attraction, but some things one just couldn't explain. Part of her was afraid of him and the truth about his arrival, wounded, on her property. There was also the fact that he didn't want his whereabouts known.

Some of the servants knew, of course, but she'd spoken to them and explained that Mr. Hunt's presence had to be kept a secret until the perpetrators could be found. She wished she could confide in Julian, but if he found out, he would immediately contact the authorities and see to it that Mr. Hunt would be removed from the Keep.

Her need to protect the stranger baffled her. With a heavy sigh, she went outside. The full moon sent a brilliant silver light over the earth, reflecting on the restless water of the Irish Sea below the cliffs onto which the Keep had been built centuries ago. Had some long ago ancestor stood on this spot admiring the same moon over the sea? Had the soldiers of old walked the battlements and stared across the water? It was silly of her even to ask that question. Of course they had. No one could resist the beauty of the natural wonders. She glanced toward the spinney at one side of the Keep. On the other were masses of gorse and a path winding down toward Sandhurst. In the front of the ancient gray stone fortress stretched small hills and the moor, except for various clumps of trees and shrubs that had been planted over time.

For a moment she felt a cold loneliness, but she shook that feeling off and went in search of plantain. It was easy to spot the fairly large oval leaves in the moonlight, and soon she'd picked two handfuls. Returning to the sick room, she closed the tower door carefully behind her.

She crumpled the leaves in her hands and placed them right on the wounds, holding them down with clean strips of bandages. Her patient moved restlessly and she struggled to finish her ministrations. He muttered something in his sleep, which sounded like "Sand . . . damned curse," but she wasn't sure.

When she had completed her task, she washed off his face with cool water. Very hot to the touch, he lay there in utter vulnerability. He was completely at her mercy.

The night grew very long as she kept bathing his face and torso with cold water. She feared he would burn up from his fever. Finally, pulling one of the chairs away from the bed, she closed her eyes and leaned her head on a pillow against the wall. She didn't think she would fall asleep, but she did.

Early morning sunlight slanted into the room from the windows high in the wall and awakened her. Stiff from her awkward position, she got up and stretched.

Her neck ached abominably, and she glanced at Mr. Hunt, fearful that he had died during her sleep.

He still breathed, albeit laboriously, his face red. She hurried to untie the bandages and was pleased to see that the wounds looked much better from the plantain treatment. Elated, she hurried outside and gathered some more.

The dew still lingered on the ground, wetting her feet. As she gathered the plant, she glanced up at the gray wall towering above her. Her maid would wonder where she was. She sometimes slept in the barn with the horses, but only on rare occasions when she was nursing a sick animal.

She would see to the wounded man, then go upstairs and take a bath and change. She must look a fright, but she rarely thought of her appearance. Touching her hair, she noticed that her chignon had fallen apart and the thick tresses hung loosely over her shoulders. Botheration. Her hair never obeyed any combs or pins. She'd deal with it later.

The stranger had awakened by the time she returned. He was staring at her intensely, and she suspected she looked like a complete spectacle. Her cheeks grew hot and she looked away.

"How . . . er, are you this morning?" she asked.

"Feeling less pain, thank you." He looked down at his arm, which she'd left unbound at his side. "An ugly wound to be sure."

"Indeed. I started wrapping it with plantain and it's drawing out the poison." She placed the bundles of leaves on the bed and felt shy about approaching him. In broad daylight, he looked a lot more dangerous than in the gloom of nightfall. His beard stubble had grown a dark shadow over his jaw, his hair straggled in all directions, his lips had become chapped from the fever, and his eyes were unnaturally bright.

"Did you stay up all night to nurse me?"

"Perhaps," she said, and busied herself with the plantain and the bandages. As she tried to lift his arm, he winced. She jumped, but he took hold of the fabric of her gown and helped her by bracing his arm. She saw that he clenched his jaw and that sweat broke out on his forehead as he battled the pain.

"Thank you," he said hoarsely. He looked at her the whole time she rebandaged the wounds, and his intensity confused her. Never had she met a gentleman like him before.

"I'm sure your admirers tell you your hair reminds them of spun gold," he said when he'd overcome the wave of pain of her ministrations.

She shook her head, feeling self-conscious, and wrapped her hair into a bun. Her hands trembled, and her legs weakened under his gaze.

"I'd rather give you a compliment about your smile. It's like sunlight glittering on the sea."

"That's very . . . kind, sir, but there's no need . . ."

He grinned, even if it was more of a grimace than a smile. "Don't deprecate my words, Miss Endicott. First thing you learn in polite society is how to appreciate a compliment."

"I'm sadly lacking, as I've taken very little part in polite society. We're not sticklers for convention in these parts."

"Refreshing, to be sure, but people judge harshly."

She nodded. "I know. That's why I've lived somewhat like a recluse here at the Keep."

"A pity. You have great kindness and sweetness of character. Why hide that under a bushel?"

"I don't, really; it's just that opportunity rarely comes knocking on my door. I do attend local gatherings regularly. The people accept me for who I am."

"As they should!" He looked outraged.

"Well . . . er, I'm considered somewhat of an outcast. 'Tis whispered the Endicott women are witches. It has gone down through the bloodlines for generations. I had a magic pendant once, but it's now gone as it helped a friend. Not that I practice anything untoward, or magic."

He pointed at his arm and leg. "You're healing these, aren't you? I'd say there would be some magic involved, because last night I knew my feet were close to the grave."

"I hope and pray that you're on the mend." She finished knotting the bandage on his thigh and noticed a red, leaf-shaped birthmark on his thigh. So as not to appear as if she were staring at his bare flesh, she pulled the covers back over him. "It's highly irregular that I should be touching you in any way."

"Yes, but do you hear me protest?"

She laughed. "No, but maybe you should send for your manservant. I could assist him."

"His hands would not be as soft as yours," he said.

"Hmm," she said, and washed her hands in the washbasin. "Where is he? Surely it can't be Abdullah."

"No. My valet is in London at the moment." He didn't elaborate, and she didn't ask.

"In your sleep you muttered the words 'sand, and a curse,' or perhaps 'Sandhurst,' and I found it odd that you would know that name."

"It's the neighboring estate, isn't it? The owner has enquired about some horseflesh I sold to Squire Hanfield, but I have yet to meet him as my luck took a turn for the worse."

"Julian said he wasn't looking to increase his stables. He's an old friend of mine. When you're better, I'd be happy to introduce you."

His face clouded over. "I would not want to put you

in a compromising position. He would wonder how you know me and ask you probing questions."

"That's simple. We were introduced in the village. After all, you *are* a gentleman, not a pariah, surely."

He chuckled. "That's as may be. I never got the patina of a sterling education, but with some willpower and talent, you can create an empire, no matter what your position is from the beginning."

She didn't know how to reply to that. "My animals are my world," she said.

"And they are wholly besotted with you, surely."

She smiled. "Mayhap."

He drifted off to sleep just as he was about to comment. Dark rings under his eyes spoke of his exhaustion.

She tiptoed out of the room and went upstairs to bathe and change her clothes. She returned to the sickroom later and watched Mr. Hunt sleep, and the following night she went through the same procedure with the healing herb. Her own fatigue overcame her late that night, and she slept, her head falling toward her chest.

The next morning, the door leading to the house opened and two dogs bounded through. They assaulted Laura with happiness, yapping and licking her hands. She roused herself from her uncomfortable position and stretched. "Toby and Bonnie, desist!" she ordered the overjoyed canines.

To her surprise someone stepped through behind them, and happiness surged in her chest. "Jill! You must've traveled all night."

Jill nodded and swept Laura into a hug. Her flowery perfume wafted around her. "Your letter came by special messenger—an act of urgency in itself—and I felt the agitation between the lines of your letter and hurried here posthaste. Literally."

"Is Richard with you?" Laura glanced over Jill's shoulder to the door.

"No, he had business in London." She threw a curious glance at the stranger in the bed. "Who is your latest wounded bird?"

Laura glanced at her patient, who'd awakened at the sound of the dogs. The intensity of his gaze made her breathless.

Three

As the dogs bounced around them, Laura introduced the stranger to Jill. "Mr. Hunt is from foreign parts, but has recently returned to England."

Jill looked beautiful in a modish blue traveling dress and cloak, her plumed hat set jauntily upon her black curls, her dark eyes full of life. Laura had missed her friend, and she could see that Jill had blossomed as Lady Blackwood. She had no doubt that Jill was happy with Richard, and no doubt Jill had brought the winds of change into his life.

"You look rather poorly, sir, but of good constitution. If you don't mind me saying so, I believe you'll live," Jill said as if looking past him and into the future.

He chuckled. "I'm eternally grateful to you, Lady Blackwood, for that observation."

"And there's no need to feel sorry for yourself."

For a moment he looked outraged, and then laughed. "I like a woman who speaks her mind."

"I don't understand what business you have getting yourself wounded on Miss Endicott's property, but here we are, so let's make your healing come about quickly—so that you can go on."

"The last thing I wanted to do was to bother Miss Endicott, and I can leave now if you so demand. I probably have enough strength to drag myself onto someone else's property."

"That would be a blessing, but how a one-legged man can walk without aid is a puzzle I have yet to solve."

Laura laughed. "It's good to have you back, Jill."

Jill discarded her gloves and her cloak. Evidently she'd come straight to the sickroom without bothering to freshen up. Laura knew she'd been worried.

"Cornwall holds very special memories for me. I met my husband here, for one, and you, Laura, my very best friend." She set down her hat on top of the other garments on a chair, and gently patted her curls into position.

"I have acquired several more dogs since you last saw me," Laura said, scratching one of the dog's ears. "But these scamps you already know. Bonnie! Not now!" She pulled the dog down from dancing on her hind legs in front of Jill.

The other canine had jumped onto the bed and was busy licking the sick man's face. Mr. Hunt protested, but the dog didn't understand the word "no" and continued in happy ignorance. Laura finally had to drag Toby off to give the patient some peace, and then the dog tore around the room trying to get everyone involved in a game.

"I get exhausted just looking at him," Jill said with a sigh.

"I shall have Brumley deliver a tea tray to the parlor. I need something to give me strength," Laura said. "I have no energy."

"I apologize if I've worn you down, Miss Endicott," the patient said.

"Well, I had to watch over you, or I wouldn't have slept a wink in my bed wondering about your progress."

"Thank you . . . for your . . . kindness." Clearly it had taken great effort to keep up a conversation. His red-rimmed eyelids closed, and within seconds he'd drifted off.

The women went out of the sickroom and Laura led the way through the cavernous hallway with its icy flagstones to the front parlor. A vase of yellow roses adorned the white marble mantelpiece that had been added to the room centuries after the Keep had been built. Two surly coats of arms stood on each side, rusty and faded shields in front of them as if expecting an attack at any moment.

Jill stepped up and studied the visor of the one closest to the doors. "These always make me think someone is inside, looking out at us. They frighten me."

Laura sat down on a faded sofa from the last century and laughed. "You're right, but I'm so used to them they don't bother me. When I was a child I saw bloody battles in my mind's eye, men in armor like these. I always wonder if they—the souls—are somehow trapped in these suits, but it's pure nonsense."

"How very ghoulish of you," Jill said with a nervous laugh.

"*Something* frightens you, as well."

She waited for Jill to make light of it, but her friend remained thoughtful.

"This is of course a place where lots of violence occurred in the past," Laura continued. "The very walls are imbued with it."

Jill nodded. "I always felt that, from the moment I stepped inside for the first time. But how morbid we've become! Tell me about the handsome wounded stranger in the tower room."

Laura described how she'd come upon him in the meadow and what little she knew about his life. "I may be thimble-witted to harbor him here, but he intrigues me."

"What if Julian finds out? He'll be mad with jealousy."

Laura shrugged. "He won't find out, nor will he suffer jealousy. Once the stranger has recovered enough, he'll have to leave the Keep, with no one the wiser. I couldn't very well abandon him to bleed to death. If we discover that he's a villain, the authorities will take over his care."

"You and your tender heart, Laura. Despite your compassion, you have a core of steel. A more squeamish woman would've succumbed to a fit of the vapors at dealing with the wounds."

"Julian was here yesterday, and I worried that Brumley's tongue would slip. He's so fond of gossip, but Julian left none the wiser."

"Hmm. Just as well. I've decided I don't like the man. There's something underhanded about him; he's very secretive, always off to London on his mysterious business. I thought he would've declared his intentions to you by now."

"Oh pooh, 'mysterious.' Doesn't Richard have business to attend to, as well?"

"Yes, but he explains the nature of it, and I never have to wonder. "

"He's an honorable man," Laura said. "But so is Julian, and he doesn't have to answer to anyone."

"You're only interested in Julian because there have been no other suitors kneeling at your feet. Then there was that old wise woman in the forest who said you were going to marry someone named Julian. Well, the village is small, and everyone knows that Viscount Sandhurst would be a good match for you, and as far as I know, no other eligible Julians live in these parts."

"Listen to you! So matter-of-fact. Of all the people I know, I thought you would be the one to believe in magic, that anything can happen. We have both witnessed magic, and you descend from a lineage of people who practiced magic."

Jill nodded. "Yes, I realize my father knew unusual things, but that doesn't mean that old woman has any special powers."

Laura felt disappointed. "I'm not going to argue about it."

Uncomfortable silence followed until Brumley entered with a footman carrying a tray. Cook had made a fragrant apple pie with lemony yellow custard in a silver dish on the side. Dainty cakes and a bowl of bonbons teased Laura's appetite, but the events of the last two days had taken her focus from all mundane things. No pangs of hunger assaulted her as she viewed the delicacies, but when Brumley handed her a cup of golden tea, she drew a sigh of relief. She sipped the hot liquid, letting the smoky but sweet flavor fill her mouth.

"Ahh, just what I needed to strengthen myself," she said to no one in particular.

Jillian agreed. When Brumley had left, she chose two glazed cakes and bit into one with evident relish. "Now that I'm married I intend to have gatherings at Eversley. You'll be invited to come for a lengthy stay, of course, and with some luck, we shall find the perfect husband for you. Someone named Julian."

"You sound like a dowager duchess already," Laura teased.

Jill made a moue. "I don't mind. Someone has to help you conquer the Marriage Mart."

"Marriage Mart?" Laura set her cup down. "Of all the hare-brained—you know me better than that! I won't be paraded in front of pinch-nosed and sour-faced gentlemen just because I'm unwed and rather a catch. I'm not desperate."

"You need someone, a loving companion, in your life."

"I agree, but there's no hurry, and I have no lack of companions."

"We all know that, but they speak in dog language, which is rather limited and rustic," Jill said firmly. "No polite conversation there, surely."

Laura laughed. "You made me spray tea all over my gown!"

Jill giggled. "How hoydenish of you. Julian would be outraged at your behavior, don't you think?" She had to set down her cup before she spilled her tea, as well. "That is, if he could take his focus off himself long enough."

"You are very wicked, Jill. Your tongue has not softened with marriage."

"But I'm right. He's not a gentleman capable of great love. His desires would always come first, Laura, then his horse's desires, then his mistress's."

"What? You must be jesting."

"I may be wrong, but I've come to understand that young gentlemen have . . . well, female 'friends.' Cousin Alvin rudely informed me of that once, and he certainly is a good example of a man who doesn't mind indulging himself."

Laura put her hand to her mouth as she digested the sordid information. "I . . . er, daresay the procreation of mankind is at the bottom of this, just as it is in the animal world."

"You're always so kind and tolerant, Laura."

"It upsets me that you would speak badly of Julian."

"Yes, it is rather ill-mannered of me, and I apologize. My long journey to this point in my life has brought me a certain degree of cynicism, and I'm fortunate that Richard had enough faith in me to look past my flaws."

"Richard would never think of only himself. He's solicitous, and I suspect he doesn't need special 'friends' when he has you." Laura felt her face grow hot, and she put a napkin to her mouth as she started laughing.

"Our conversation is beyond the pale," Jill whispered. "Aunt Penny would be highly distraught to hear us talk like this."

"Anyone would," Laura whispered back. "Our conversations are never boring, are they?"

Jill shook her head and served her friend a wedge of apple pie. "You must eat something. You're nothing but a ghost of your former self."

"That's an exaggeration, to be sure, but I shall eat something." She placed a hand on Jill's arm. "I'm so glad you're here."

"Where is Aunt Penny, by the way?"

"She's visiting her sister in Plymouth for a week. Thank God for that, or she would be poking her nose into my business."

Strider Hunt awakened later, when the sun slanted at a sharper angle through the windows. Unfortunately he couldn't look out, and he was still too weak to move, but some of the pain had subsided. A dull throbbing still paralyzed his arm, but his leg felt much better. Miss Endicott had magic hands, and she knew about herbs, which in itself was unusual. He pictured young English gentlewomen as mainly weak and full of vapid innocence, but then he'd not been in England for a long time.

The brown dog, Leo, was back. He lay on the bed now, a warm comfortable shape along Strider's undamaged side. Leo elevated one crinkly eyebrow as if asking how he felt, and Strider lifted his good arm and petted the dog. Leo rewarded him with a blast of foul breath as he panted with delight. Strider's hand trembled with the effort of the caress. By God, he was weak as a kitten!

"Aarrgh," he cried out. "I don't want to be laid flat

and powerless like this, and with you breathing on me."

Leo now wiggled both his eyebrows as if saying he was sorry but that patience was indeed a virtue.

"Look at something else, will you!" Strider commanded, glaring at the dog. "And put a paw in front of your ugly maw."

Leo held steadfast. Nothing could really shake this dog, Strider thought sourly. He wanted to get out of bed and stretch himself, but couldn't. He wondered how long he'd have to stay like this. Much longer than he wanted, no doubt.

He glanced at the thick, scarred oak door. That was all that separated him from freedom, unless he counted his disability as a hindrance. Blast and damn! How could he expect to get things done while lying in bed all day?

He dozed off just as he was becoming really riled, and when he awakened it was dark. In the glowing orange light of candles, two female faces hovered in his vision. Their eyes looked concerned, and he immediately recognized Miss Endicott's cornflower blue gaze. Then he recalled her friend, a wholly different kind of person—bold and striking, but kind, as well.

"Good evening," the friend greeted.

He bowed in his mind, but only managed a curt nod with his head. "Ma'am . . . I'm sorry to say I can't remember your name. Everything is a haze."

"You are rather ill, so such minor details may be excused," the woman said.

"Thank you," he muttered as he struggled to stay awake.

"Your wounds are healing. The infection seems to be halted," she said.

They changed his bandages, wrapping them over yet another batch of plantain leaves. He felt so tired and irritable, part of him wanted to lash out at them. But they least of all should be blamed for his misfortune.

Leo's patient gaze challenged him once more. Blasted dog!

He swore under his breath when Miss Endicott knocked against his wounded leg unwittingly. "Damn," he muttered, and then apologized for his language. "It's just that I'm beyond myself with boredom. I'm not used to being immobilized like this."

"You'll soon be back on your legs," Miss Endicott assured him with a warm smile.

Her smile made him even weaker inside. He so wanted to touch her soft cheek and wrap his hands around her hair.

"Isn't there someone we should inform?" the other woman asked.

He shook his head vehemently on the pillow. Abdullah had stayed away, which surprised him. The man could track just about anything in the desert. It was just as well. The tall Arab would only raise questions with the locals.

"Well?" Laura prodded.

"No." He didn't need Abdullah to come looking for him and drawing attention to his hiding place. "There's no one that has a particular interest in my whereabouts."

"That's sad," Laura said, her eyes filled with concern.

"No . . . it's freedom from obligations," he contradicted. "I like my freedom."

Four

Later that night, before Laura and Jill went to bed, they stood outside Laura's bedchamber, discussing the events of the day and the fact that the stranger had improved even if he still suffered from great pain and a racking fever.

Jill said, "If he were any more secretive, he might as well be mute."

"He's just very private." Laura was not really clear on why she needed to defend him.

"We don't know anything about him. I don't know how wise it is to harbor him here."

"Jill, do you truly believe there's danger? He appears to be a decent kind of fellow."

Jill nodded. "Yes, but sometimes appearances deceive."

"You have more experience than I have."

Jill looked closely at her friend. "I suspect you've developed a *tendre* for him. Under normal circumstances, he would be a very charming fellow. Devilishly charming, I believe."

"Yes, I think he would be, but I have no real interest in him. I only care for Julian. You know that. I don't care if I ever find out about the stranger's business. I wish him to get well, and when he leaves, I won't miss him."

Jill squeezed her friend's arm. "I'm glad to hear it.

Anyhow, I'm rather intrigued by him. There's a very interesting story behind all of this, I'm sure, and I don't believe for one minute that highwaymen set upon him. He has left many details out of his explanation; he's deliberately holding back."

"Yes, but that's his right. I shan't pry."

"You are so accepting. Aren't you a little bit curious?"

Laura laughed. "I'd be lying if I said no, but it wouldn't be right to question him."

"I have no qualms about that, but I also know he won't tell me anything. A more slippery fellow I have yet to meet."

"You're cautious, which is good, but any suspicion of foul play is unfounded."

"On *his* part perhaps, but what if someone wants him dead?"

"Oh, pooh. That is melodrama of the worst kind, Jill. I understand you have a flair for that, but that kind of skullduggery doesn't happen in these quiet parts. In London, yes, but the countryside of Cornwall is rarely the setting for high drama."

"Unless you're a smuggler or a ship wrecker."

"Jill! Those things took place in the last century."

"It's not that long ago," Jill said with a grimace. "And smuggling still goes on, I'm sure."

"So you believe the patient in the tower is a smuggler or—heaven forfend—a ship wrecker?" Laura couldn't believe her ears.

"Well, you're situated on the coast. It wouldn't be wholly far-fetched."

"Oh, yes," Laura said, "I can see him now, rolling kegs of brandy across the beach at midnight."

"Sarcasm doesn't suit you. I'm certain the excise patrol is still active in these parts."

"More so on the Channel side of Cornwall, I suspect."

"He could've been hunted all the way here," Jill said. She began pacing back and forth, her blue gown swishing against her legs.

"Fiddlesticks. And all we would get in these parts is potatoes shipped from Ireland, and that is if they could land among the craggy cliffs. The ports are few and far between."

"You always give people the benefit of the doubt. He could be a thief and a murderer, for all we know."

"One that speaks with a gentlemanly accent?" Laura folded her arms in front of her. "I don't think so. You're letting your imagination run wild." Annoyance gave her voice an edge. "I don't want to argue over this."

"You're right." Jill placed her hand on her friend's arm. "I'm sorry. I would do better if I were more trusting, like you. I won't bring up the subject again unless I see a desperate need for it."

"Thank you. I'll take the first watch downstairs, and I'll wake you in a few hours. I know the trip must've tired you."

Jill nodded. "A short rest will restore me, and then it's your turn."

"And don't hammer him with questions if he's awake, " Laura said sternly.

Jill laughed. "I just pictured myself holding such a tool aloft and threatening him to tell us everything."

Laura giggled. "You're incorrigible. Life is never boring when you're around. You attract excitement."

"Life's not meant to be boring."

Laura went downstairs and slipped into the tower room. The stranger was tossing as much as he could with one side immobilized by the two wounds and Leo glued to the other. She made the dog get down. Strider Hunt looked uncomfortable, his hair stuck to his forehead with sweat, and the quilt bundled into a heap at the bottom of the bed. He was burning again, and Laura gently sponged him off with cold water. The nightshirt stuck to his muscular frame with perspiration and she really noticed how handsome and well-formed his body was, with its wide shoulders and long, powerful legs.

When well, she was sure he could run fast. A proclaimed lover of freedom, he would if he could, but it would be a long time before he had all of his movement back in his leg. Her heart bled with pity, but mayhap Jill was right, that she was feeling compassion for a ruthless criminal. No, it couldn't be. She would *know* if there was a reason to be afraid.

She dozed in a chair by the bed, and in her dream she heard voices and running footsteps. Dogs started barking everywhere, and Leo growled deep in his chest as he stood by the door. Startled, she opened her aching eyes. It hadn't been a dream. Someone was hurrying up the steps that ran from the tower to the main hall.

Gasping with fear, she got up to find out what was happening, but the patient's hand gripped her wrist hard. "Don't," he whispered.

"What is going on? Do you know anything about this?"

"No, but someone might be looking for me."

"But why?" she hissed, trying to pry herself free. He let her go as the steps died down in the distance.

He didn't reply. His face looked grim in the light from the candle on the bedside table. The flame flickered eerily in the gloom.

"Why don't they come to the front door like regular visitors?"

"I have enemies, but that's all I'm going to say."

"They are aiming to kill you?" She bristled, her

shoulders tensing. "It's the outside of enough. I won't be part of any underhanded dealings."

He didn't loosen his grip. "I swear to you that I have done nothing criminal. Just trust me this once. You're not in any danger."

She stared hard at him, her whole being rebelling against his refusal to explain. "You can trust me with any secret. I don't gossip."

"But can you trust me? Right now I can't speak of the issues at hand." He struggled to sit up, every movement obvious agony.

Her mind fought with her heart. She knew she shouldn't trust some stranger who wanted to keep his whereabouts a secret at all costs, but at the same time she knew he was in danger, and if she expelled him from the Keep, he could possibly get killed. How could he fend for himself with only one working arm and one leg?

Still, it wasn't her responsibility to keep him hidden. Filled with indecision, she stared at him. His intense gaze burned into her, pleading, but also pitiless, telling her she could not suggest any compromises.

As the debate raged within her, the door flew open, and Brumley, dressed in a boldly red dressing gown and nightcap, stormed into the room. Jill followed, also shrouded in a voluminous dressing gown.

"We've been chasing burglars through the house, but they got away," Jill shouted, panting.

"Miss Laura, are you unharmed?" the old retainer asked, his voice tight with concern.

"Yes, no one came in here."

"We heard a disturbance in the hallway, but when we got downstairs, whoever entered clumped through the house and was gone in a flash," Jill explained. "One of the windows by the front door had been broken."

"How very . . . odd, to be sure," Laura said breathlessly. "Who would break in without any concern for stealth?"

"Well, they did."

"I . . ." Strider Hunt's grip hardened around her wrist, and she succumbed to the pleading in his eyes. "I didn't hear a thing," she continued. "I was asleep and then the patient needed a drink of water. Probably someone broke in, desperate to find some food."

"No one raided the larder. We looked," Jill said her voice tinged with suspicion. She glanced at the wounded man, then back at Laura, and his hand around her wrist.

Blessed darkness that hides my embarrassment, Laura thought. "I have no idea who it was."

"You don't seem too worried," Jill said. "This is now a matter for the authorities." She gave the stranger a meaningful glance, and Laura knew her friend was right.

"I don't want the constables here, not yet," Laura said.

Heavy silence fell over the room, and Brumley heaved an exasperated sigh. "If only your cousin would return from the Colonies," he said under his breath. "He would not stand for this."

"Since he isn't here, what I say is law," Laura said with more conviction than she felt. She motioned to Brumley. "Thank you for protecting me, but go back to bed. Ask one of the footmen to board up the window until we can have new glass installed."

Brumley bowed, his face heavy with disapproval. "I shall sleep with a blunderbuss by my pillow."

Jill closed the door behind him and they waited until his steps had faded.

"What is going on here?" Jill asked, her voice tense.

The patient let go of his grip on Laura's wrist.

"We are not going to bring in the authorities," Laura said. "Not yet. I intend for Mr. Hunt—or whoever you are"—she directed this at the wounded man—"to heal and then he'll be on his way. Until then, we'll keep him here, quietly. Justice, if need be, will come to him in due time."

"Have you lost your senses?" Jill asked, her eyes filled with worry.

Laura shook her head, still wondering if she had chosen the right path. What if the stranger only brought chaos and destruction? That certainly appeared to be the current course, but she pushed away the disturbing idea. As she worked on his healing, she felt responsible for him, as she did with all of her patients, whether they be two-legged or four-legged. She also realized that she trusted him, however dimwitted that was.

"He needs me," she said simply.

She heard him draw a deep sigh of relief, and he seemed to deflate against the pillows. Two red spots glowed on his cheeks, and the rest of his face looked bilious, as if he wanted to throw up.

She sensed an argument forming on Jill's tongue, but to her relief, it was never spoken.

"I trust you know what you're doing, Laura," Jill said, her voice filled with heavy foreboding.

No, I don't, Laura screamed in her mind, but only smiled.

"I'll be here to help you." Jill turned to the patient. "You're very fortunate to have such a staunch supporter."

He nodded, his voice raspy. "I know." He turned his gaze on Laura. "You won't regret this. I owe you my life, and I'll never forget. If you ever need help, I will turn heaven and earth to come to your assistance."

"From exotic lands, that might be somewhat difficult," Laura said dryly. "And you like your freedom."

"There's Irish blood there somewhere," Jill said. "He knows how to turn a phrase into a grandiose statement."

He looked riled. "Let me ask you, how can someone so young be so cynical?"

Jill took on a superior expression. "I am not cynical. And Laura is most definitely not."

He managed a small laugh. "I have already come to that understanding. Miss Laura is most tenderhearted."

Laura thought the words "and gullible" hung in the air, but she pushed them away. "I'm patient and tolerant. If you break my trust, you're the one who loses the most," she said staunchly.

He looked at her for a long moment, as if digesting her words. "You're right," he said at last. "I believe you're the sweetest person I've ever encountered." He turned to Jill. "But you're another kettle of fish altogether," he added with weak banter in his voice.

"I'll pretend that I didn't hear that," Jill said. "You'd rather not get on my bad side, Mr. Hunt, because I think Laura is the kindest person I've known and if you harm her in any way, I'll avenge her to the end of my days."

Mr. Hunt laughed. "Now *you* sound as if you have Irish heritage. Anyway, you would be a fierce protector, Lady Blackwood. I realize you're a gently bred lady, but do I detect some gypsy heritage in your blood?"

"How very uncouth of you to speak with such familiarity to my friend," Laura admonished.

"He's right, of course," Jill said with a sigh, and sank down on the nearest chair. "And the Endicotts hail from an ancient line, as well. This was once a stronghold and mayhap one of the oldest keeps in these parts."

"Yes, my forbears were a bloodthirsty lot, and one

of them, Lucinda, is said to have been from Hungary or Russia," Laura explained. "But she didn't last on these cold and damp shores."

"She left you the legacy of healing," Jill said, and eyed the bandages and bottle of basilicum powder on the table by the bed. She seemed oblivious to her state of dishabille. "The ancient lore of herb is carried down through the centuries from people like her and my father."

Laura nodded, her eyes twinkling with mischief. "We need to put our minds together to concoct a strengthening elixir for my patient."

"No," came his quick reply. "I was too weak to question the greenery piled on my wounds, but now that I'm more like myself, I shall protest if you take liberties with my injuries. I won't drink any herbal concoctions."

"Liberties? That's gratitude for you," Jill said with a grimace.

Laura laughed. "I believe you won't be able to fight back for quite some time to come, Mr. Hunt."

"Call me Strider," he said curtly. "The name reminds me of when I could stride along the lane with speed and grace."

"Strider . . . your mother must've been about in her head when she christened you," Jill said. "Why would you want to saddle an innocent babe with such a name?"

He didn't reply, and perhaps there was no reply to that, Laura thought. "We all have our crosses to bear."

Jill burst out laughing, and the man in the bed looked uncomfortable.

"At least your recovery is making *strides,*" Laura continued. "Before long, you'll be striding right along."

He sighed and glanced at her with unexpected tenderness. "I'm glad you're showing such an optimistic view, Miss Endicott."

"I always view things favorably—just ask Jill." Laura straightened out some towels over the iron rail at the end of the bed. She wrung out one in the washbasin and joined it to the others.

He remained silent, as if embarrassed to ask such personal questions.

"I understand if you don't want to interview a matron in dishabille in the middle of the night, or an unwed lady who is compromising herself every time she enters this sickroom alone. We must seem very peculiar to you, but you have to remember that we're very far from the Capital."

He chuckled, and then grimaced as if the movement created great pain in his body. "Yes, I'm shocked speechless," he said, his voice threadlike with pain. He threw his head against the pillow and swore under his breath. "I'm sorry to display such foul language, but I'm deeply frustrated."

"It's understood," Laura said kindly. "My poultices of herbs will quicken your recovery."

He peered at her through half-closed eyelids. "I'll have to trust you in that."

"I guess it is a matter of trust on both sides," she said simply, and busied herself with changing the bandages once more.

Jill assisted, but she looked tired. It had been a long day, and none of them really wanted to think of the danger that had approached in the night. That was the first and the last time, Laura thought, and decided to set some of her more assertive dogs to stand guard inside the Keep. No one would be able to step past them.

"Are those intruders that came here liable to cause . . . harm to whoever steps in their way?" she asked as she knotted the last bandage together.

"No, if they weren't common burglars, they were

looking for me. They want me, not you. But I know we're dealing with very ruthless people, so we have to eliminate any chances of their returning. Just as soon as I get strong enough, I'll leave you alone. It can't be soon enough."

Laura felt a stab of disappointment. She'd grown attached to her patient and wouldn't want him to leave and never come back. There was something beguiling about him, and she enjoyed his banter. In health, he would be a most attractive and witty man, she thought. As it was, he was still frail but could find moments of humor. He displayed great strength. "I daresay you'll make a full recovery."

They made sure the patient was comfortable, his quilt pulled to his chin. Jill hauled Laura outside.

"It can't be soon enough that he leaves the Keep," Jill whispered as they walked into the main part of the building.

"Be that as it may," Laura said evasively.

"No need to protect him," Jill said. She stared closely at Laura, who found it wise to change the subject.

"Jill, one of the servants brought over an invitation from Sandhurst for a dinner party on Saturday night," she said. "I forgot to tell you. You'll be going with me—as my chaperone."

"Does Julian still come for a visit every day?"

"Almost, but lately he seems distracted. I don't see much of him; it's almost as if he's avoiding me again. For a while, he spent more time here than at home."

Jill nodded. "While Richard was courting you," she said in a cool voice. "Mayhap he was afraid you would marry Richard. Just think of all that fine land being lost to Julian."

"Your cynicism is showing again, Jill. Just remember that I intend to marry him."

"He's rather a slippery fellow. He appears to

change his course suddenly, as the fox in the fox hunt."

Laura frowned. "How can you liken Julian to a fox? That's uncharitable of you. I appreciate your candor, but sometimes you go too far. You have to remember that I've known Julian for a long time. You only just met him."

Jill pointed to her nose and her eyes. "I have good instincts."

Laura threw her gaze heavenward. "Give me patience. You're wrong."

"Only time will tell."

Five

The broken window had been boarded up, and no more intruders dared to break in. Still, Laura and Jill stayed on high alert, and Brumley looked as if he hadn't slept for days.

Strider Hunt's recovery was going well, but slowly. He struggled to regain his strength, but even if the wounds appeared to be healing, he kept falling asleep and staying asleep most of the time.

On Saturday night, Laura and Jill were ready for some change. Laura looked forward to seeing Julian again. She had not seen him since the day he'd kissed her in the foyer of the Keep.

Julian's beautiful estate, Sandhurst, sat peacefully among the trees of the parkland awaiting the arrival of the guests. Candles glowed in every window. Climbing roses and ivy thickened more every year over the brick façade, and the plantings of flowers bloomed in their full summer glory in the twilight. Reds, pinks, and yellow roses filled the air with sweetness, and the gravel in the drive crunched under Laura's evening slippers as she walked from the carriage to the front steps.

Footmen greeted her and Jill at the door and took their evening cloaks. Laura wore a pale yellow silk gown adorned with embroidered white flowers at the hem and the neckline. Matching fabric held her hair up in an elegant arrangement of curls that her maid had taken hours to accomplish, and she wore pearls at her throat and in her ears. In one hand she waved a fragile filigree fan. The finery made her feel feminine and attractive.

She thought Jill looked beautiful in a midnight blue Empire-style gown that brought out her dramatic black hair. Garnets at her throat and in her hair combs shot dark red fire in the light of the many candles in the candelabras.

Sandhurst welcomed Laura as on so many other occasions. The beautiful Oriental carpets of red, gold, and brown softened her steps, and the eighteenth-century damask-covered sofas along the walls invited her with their comfort. Not one suit of armor in sight, she thought. Distinguished Sandhurst ancestors stared down at her from the walls lining the curving staircase that led to the upper regions.

She saw a movement in the shadows on the landing above and recognized the old Dowager Lady Sandhurst. Her white hair stood out against the dark wall. Laura waved, but the dowager pulled back, her eyes darting across the hallway below. Then she was gone.

"Did you see her, Jill?" Laura asked.

"Who?"

"The lady on the landing. That's Julian's grandmother."

"I haven't had the pleasure to meet her, but perhaps I will this time."

"She's not coming down for the meal; she never does."

They heard sudden raised voices from the parlor beyond, and the door flew open. A gentleman that Laura vaguely recognized as a squire from one of the other Cornish villages across the moor came out. His demeanor barely held back the storm that battled within him, but he bowed politely and then left, snatching his hat from one of the footmen. He hadn't said a word.

"Who was that?" Jill asked.

"I don't know him well, but he's a local squire."

Julian exited the parlor and closed the door, his face grim and set, but when he noticed the guests, he came forward, his extreme anger gone in a flash. His smile didn't quite reach his eyes, though, Laura thought. He always seemed to be in control of himself. She wondered what the argument had been about.

He took Laura's hand in his and kissed it tenderly. She shivered with pleasure at his attention, but when he did the same to Jill, some of that special glow faded within. It was just in course with his charm to treat all ladies with the same courtesy.

"You look splendid, Laura. Your hair gleams of gold I didn't notice before, and your blush is very becoming."

"Oh, stop teasing me, Julian." She slapped him with her fan.

He turned to Jill. "Marriage becomes you, Lady Blackwood, but how is it that you've left your recently wedded spouse to join us here in godforsaken Cornwall?"

"Richard may join us shortly," Jill said evasively.

That was news, Laura thought, but perhaps Jill hadn't thought to tell her.

"I look forward to seeing him again," Julian said. Clearly, his previous ill humor had dissolved, as he was all smiles.

Laura thought about what Jill had said yesterday about Julian, and she watched him closely. She wished Jill hadn't sown seeds of doubts in her. She'd known Julian practically forever and he had never hid anything from her—that she knew. Poor Jill must've been overwrought with everything that had been going on.

If Julian has nothing to hide, we certainly do, Laura thought.

He threw open the doors to the library that joined the formal dining room. Masculine accents of deer trophies and swords hung on the wall over the mantelpiece, and the brown upholstery and dark bookcases lent a comfortable air to the room.

"Sherry is served in here," he said, and fetched two glasses for them from a tray on the table. He poured himself a hefty measure of whiskey from a decanter, and Laura realized he needed that to still his nerves. As he drank the whiskey, he said, "Maureen, Lady Penholly, will join us shortly, and Vicar Johnston from Pendenny. But Rupert drones on quite a bit, so it might've been a mistake to invite him."

"Maureen will find a way to interrupt, I'm sure," Laura said dryly. "She knows how to carry a conversation."

"Then there's Lord and Lady Larigan."

"The gentleman who left . . . is he coming back?" Jill asked.

Laura's gaze flew to Julian's face to see his reaction. He shook his head, his face bland. "No, Squire Norton only came on business."

Then why the argument? Laura wondered.

Lady Penholly arrived, a striking woman in a gown of bronze taffeta and a matching turban on her brown locks. Her quick gaze moved from one face to the other. She swept Laura into a perfumed embrace. "You look . . . well, not older, but more experienced, my dear. And Jill!" She took Jill's hand and squeezed it. "I'm delighted to hear that you and Sir Richard married. You're so suited. I never thought Sir Richard would come to his senses and see the truth." She turned to Laura. "I'm sorry, my dear."

"Oh, just whip me with your unadorned statements," Laura said, and smiled. "It's clear for all to see that Jill and Richard are the perfect match. I hold no grudges."

"That tender heart of yours is as deep as the ocean," Lady Penholly said with a sigh.

She went on to kiss Julian lightly on the mouth. "This rapscallion has been hiding from me lately. Where have you been, Julian?"

"I have a lot to take care of, Maureen. I'm not sitting idle, if that's what you believe."

"You don't have to sound so put off, naughty boy."

"I'm not put off," he defended himself. The perpetual smile had gone from his face. "I do, however, object to your reducing me to the size of a child in short coats."

"Oh, pooh, don't turn prickly. You *were* in short coats once, and a delightful child you were."

"Don't bring that up. I'm trying to appear mature and responsible in front of these ladies."

"And you're doing a rather good job," Laura said in defense.

He looked cornered, but Maureen only laughed. "How silly! Pride is man's downfall." She glanced around the room. "Is your grandmother well enough to join us?"

He shook his head, all animation leaving his face. "Unfortunately not. She has been poorly lately, and her memory is gone, alas. I would not want to burden you with her presence."

"Lady Sandhurst was a sharp-witted woman in her heyday. It's sad to hear that her deterioration is complete."

"Very much so," he agreed.

The elderly Vicar Johnston arrived, wearing an old-fashioned wig and a gray coat over a fine, embroidered waistcoat of red silk. He was quite taken with Jill as she chatted with him about Devon and East Sussex, where he'd been born.

The Earl of Larigan and his wife arrived last. The older man full of dignity, and Lady Larigan, the most celebrated beauty in her youth, greeted everyone warmly. The earl and countess lived closer to the Devon border, and rarely visited. The earl was a busy man acting as the magistrate of the district.

"Laura, you must come and spend some time with us," Lady Larigan said. "I need some young people around me."

"Thank you. When the summer harvest is over, I shall accept your invitation."

The butler announced that dinner would be served without delay, and two footmen held open the double doors to the dining room. The aromas of fish and cooked beef filled Laura's nose, and her stomach moved with hunger. Julian's cook always offered the guests fine meals, and this time they were served clear beef broth, turbot in aspic adorned with sliced hard-boiled eggs and sprigs of dill. The second course consisted of sliced beef with a smooth brown sauce, new potatoes, and peas. She tasted morsels of the second and third courses, saddle of mutton, fine veal, and mushrooms. For dessert the footmen served pears in brandy with clotted cream. The conversation flowed smoothly, the vicar's intolerable ramblings interrupted as soon as he started.

"I've heard rumors of strange foreigners in these parts. Gypsies, mayhap," Lady Penholly said. "People with horses, lots of horses."

Laura gave Jill an uneasy glance.

"Yes, they have been staying in these parts," Julian said, "but I have not had an encounter. If I ever find them on my land, I'll evict them posthaste."

"Why would they want to stay here? We're far from

any trade routes," the vicar said. "They are heathens, to boot."

"Perhaps they like the quiet of this area," Jill suggested.

Julian shook his head. "No, I believe they're here to sell their horses. Rumor has it that one of them was wounded in an ambush. I'd say we should have the authorities get to the bottom of the mystery. The local constables are useless." He turned to Lord Larigan. "Please don't take offense, but what we need is a sharp Bow Street Runner to solve the threat that these men might pose."

"I've heard of no threat," the earl said, clearly surprised. "No incidents have been reported to me."

"Threat?" Laura asked, placing a trembling hand on her heart. "I doubt we're in any danger."

"You never know," the vicar said, sounding almost offended. "I certainly don't sleep peacefully at night wondering what villainy might be afoot in the village. The gypsies are prone to theft."

"I'm only a feeble female, but I certainly don't worry at night," Laura said. "I suspect it's wrong to judge the people as villains because they're foreigners."

Uneasy silence fell and even the servants seemed to slow down.

"You're right, of course," Lady Penholly said in a loud voice, and laughed nervously. "Because gypsies have a rascally reputation doesn't mean that the ones who are camped by the village are villains."

"That's right," the earl said. "I believe in treating everyone fairly."

The vicar moved in his seat, his eyes flashing. Laura noticed that Julian hid a smile behind his napkin before he put it down. The atmosphere still hung leaden over the dinner party, but he did his best to lift it.

"No matter," he said, "we're not here to judge anyone

or try to make a drama out of something that might not be one."

Laura felt warm inside at his words. Julian had a great amount of common sense; he'd just proved it. He was everything she'd ever wished for in a husband, but she doubted that he had the same opinion about her, even though he'd renewed his interest. She suspected that he judged her as a country hoyden compared with the polished ladies in London. She wondered where her insecurity lay, but as she thought about it for a moment, she realized she felt comfortable with herself.

"Rarely does anything happen in these parts that is worth discussing," Lady Penholly said.

"That's right," Julian concurred. He turned to Laura. "Though to get back to the issue of strangers in the neighborhood, I heard some rumor that you had a break-in at the Keep. I surmised that if there were any truth to it, you would've contacted me."

"Of course I would have. Nothing untoward happened." Her cheeks started burning, and she cursed her fair skin. He could surely read the lie on her face.

"Why such a rumor would start is beyond me," Lady Penholly said, and forked the last piece of pear on her plate. "People are seeking excitement where there is none. The servants are forever gossiping."

"Everyone wants to know everyone else's business," Jill said.

Laura met her steady gaze that urged her to reveal the truth while the magistrate was present, but Laura could not. In her heart she knew that Strider Hunt was not related to any criminals.

"There has been strange hearsay lately," Julian continued. "There has to be some modicum of truth behind it, but everything gets blown out of proportion.

Not too long ago, it was said in the village that some stranger had been shot in the woods. That might have been one of the gypsies, as I said earlier."

"Really?" The vicar raised his eyebrows.

"No one discovered a body, so it's safe to say there was none." Julian looked around the room as if expecting someone to contradict him. The silence thickened, and the vicar moved uneasily in his chair.

"I daresay we're pitiful, as well," Lady Penholly said, her eyes flashing. "We're as caught up in the rumor-mongering as the villagers are. Isn't there something truly interesting to talk about?"

Julian shrugged. "Of course, but if there's any truth behind the rumors, we should protect ourselves." He turned to Laura. "I couldn't sleep a wink if I thought you were in any kind of danger, Laura."

She smiled, her lips stiff and her face tight. "You're very considerate, Julian."

Jill glared at her across the table, and Laura looked away. An urge to return home posthaste overcame her. Her nerves were all a-tangle, and her mind a fog of confusion.

"There are the highwaymen," the earl said, shaking his wispy white hair. "We've been hunting a group of three men who have struck on the moor, but so far they've proved to be elusive."

"Yes. Who knows if they are in any way connected with the rumors, but if someone was shot, they would be the most likely culprits," Julian said. "They are a ruthless breed."

"You're right there. If I knew they were in the area, I would hunt them to ground," the vicar said.

Laura shivered, every word torturing her nerves.

The rest of the evening passed in a blur, but before it was over, one strange thing occurred, something that took everyone by surprise.

Six

When everyone had gathered in the foyer to leave the dinner party, Laura heard a commotion upstairs on the landing. At first she thought one of the footmen had dropped something, but to everyone's obvious surprise, the old Dowager Lady Sandhurst came down the stairs, her white hair in wild disarray and her tall body swept into a faded, pearl-gray satin dressing gown that had been elegant in the previous century. She stopped in the middle of the staircase.

Julian hurried toward her, but she held up her hand as if to stall him. She looked out over the assembled guests and pinned her blue gaze on Laura. As far as Laura could tell, the old woman looked alert, her eyes clear.

"You!" she said in a stentorian voice. "You have grown up. You look just like your vapid mother. How is she?"

Everyone gasped, and Laura put her hand to her open mouth. The dowager remembered her. Julian had said on various occasions that she had no memory left at all. "Lady Sandhurst," she said, and moved forward with outstretched hands. "How very delightful to see you! It has been a long time, and I miss you."

Julian stopped her at the bottom of the stairs by

stepping in her way. "It's just a strange coincidence that she would recall—"

"Mrs. Endicott was rather sickly, last I heard," the dowager went on, her hands gripping the banister hard. Her knuckles stood out like bony knobs against the dark wood.

Laura could've sworn she saw pleading in the old woman's eyes. "She passed on, my lady."

The dowager seemed to be processing that as she stared intently at Laura. Julian ran up the stairs and started leading his grandmother away, but she struggled against his restraint. "And your father?" she directed at Laura even as Julian pulled her upstairs.

"Also passed away, alas—a long time ago," Laura said, her heart beating hard.

The dowager gave a sad smile and waved as Julian pulled her into the shadows of the corridor. The guests stood in silence and stared at each other.

"She's not altogether lost," Lady Penholly said at last. "I haven't seen her for a long time, and I believed she was beyond help."

"According to Julian, she is," Laura replied. She heard his rapid footsteps above and waited until he'd come downstairs. He looked rather annoyed.

"I apologize for this unsettling show," he said. He put his hand protectively around Laura's elbow. "I had no idea. My grandmother doesn't realize she made a spectacle of herself."

"Clearly, she's not as befuddled as you thought, Julian," Laura said.

He gave a shallow laugh. "That's nonsense. She has her lucid moments, but they are far between. She's an exasperating—"

"Surely she's not," Laura said tightly. "She's a lonely old woman who can't help that she's afflicted with confusion."

Julian bowed his head. "You're correct, as always. I lack in patience, and I didn't want anyone to be embarrassed by her comments. Your mother—"

"She didn't offend me in the slightest, Julian." Laura removed her arm from his grip. "I'd like to talk to her some more, to reminisce."

He shook his head. "Oh no, I don't think that's a good idea at all. She's only going to frustrate you."

"She might enjoy the exchange with a younger woman. She must not see many at all, and as far as I know, few of her friends are still alive." Laura looked at Lady Penholly.

"You're right, Laura. Not many of her generation left now," Lady Penholly said. She turned to Julian. "It's rather a pity to have her closeted upstairs. I shall come and entertain her with singing and pianoforte."

Julian's voice held a sharp edge. "I'd appreciate it if you wouldn't meddle, Maureen. She's too weak to have visitors, and it might shake up the status quo. I don't want her to fall ill from undue excitement."

"Balderdash. A half-hour visit won't make her ill," Lady Penholly said with a hint of disdain. "There's no need to be . . . er, ashamed of the situation."

"Ashamed?" Julian repeated, his expression surprised.

"It is as if you're hiding her away here. With the right companion, she could still enjoy a ride in the barouche when the weather permits."

He nodded, but didn't brighten to the idea. "We shall see how she progresses. You have to remember that I watch her every day, and I know what is best for her. I shan't allow for any upheavals."

Lady Penholly nodded. "Yes, of course."

Silence followed and Laura went toward the front door. Jill followed her closely. They said their goodbyes to everyone, and it was with a sigh of relief that Laura leaned back against the squabs of her carriage.

"An eventful evening, don't you think?" she asked her friend.

"Yes. It was rather startling to see the dowager come down the steps and stare at you as if she'd seen a ghost," Jill replied.

"As a child I spent many hours in her company. I'm willing to wager that her kindness hasn't changed," Laura said.

"You could be correct on that score." Jill leaned back in her seat and fanned herself. "It's close tonight. I think we're going to have a storm."

"Yes."

"I'm surprised that you haven't confided in Julian about the stranger or the intruders at the Keep," Jill said.

"You shouldn't be surprised. You told me not so many days ago that you don't trust him."

"But you do." Jill flapped her fan faster in front of her face.

"Yes . . . but I promised Mr. Hunt to keep his secret, and I haven't told anyone even if I were tempted to make it known to Julian. I'm torn in my loyalties."

"I see no reason why you would show loyalty to the wounded stranger. He has done nothing for you."

"No, but I suspect he would under the same circumstances."

"I don't doubt you on that score."

"I trust him, believe it or not."

"He appears to be an honorable man, but appearances can be deceiving." Jill heaved an exasperated sigh. "What if the intruders were in truth looking for him and not valuables?"

"They were singularly stupid to break a window and raise the dogs. Thieves with any talent for cunning would have entered elsewhere and in the quiet of the late night hours."

"There's nothing that says they had to be crafty. Perhaps they wanted to locate the stranger and finish him off. Burglars would be going through the silver, not clumping through the house with the dogs in pursuit."

"Yes, but according to Mr. Hunt, highwaymen set upon him. They would not break in to locate him."

"You're right. That is, if he's speaking the truth about them attacking him."

"Let's pray that whoever broke in doesn't come back. It frightens me to think that we could be attacked."

Jill continued, "The Keep is so large they would have to search for some time to find Strider Hunt. I doubt that they would have a chance to discover us before the dogs attacked them. I doubt we have anything to fear unless Hunt turns out to be a traitor to the country. Then we would be persecuted for assisting him."

"It won't come to that," Laura said with conviction. "He'll leave shortly and we'll get on with our lives. I'll never forget this episode, though."

"He is rather a rogue, and with all of his faculties intact, he would be dangerous to your senses. Thank God he's incapacitated."

"That's a cruel thing to say, Jill! What if you were in his position? Would you want people to turn their backs on you?"

"I would never be in that kind of a position," Jill said with a sniff. "If you entertain danger, you have to reap the consequences."

"All these theories make my head spin," Laura said, and closed her eyes. A stabbing headache had started behind her eyes, and she longed to lie down. She hadn't had a good night's sleep since before she found Strider Hunt.

They returned to the Keep, where all was quiet. She said good night to Jill and went to change out of her silk gown so that she could go downstairs and check on the patient's bandages. Fifteen minutes later she stepped into the tower room.

Candles burned low where she had lit them earlier. Mr. Hunt sat in the bed, his back leaning against the pillows, a bowl of soup balanced in his lap. Brumley must've assisted him. It delighted her to see him eat. He was truly on the mend.

"You look beautiful with your hair all in curls," he greeted her.

She'd forgotten her hair arrangement, but was pleased with the compliment. "Thank you. I'm pleased to see that you're sitting up, and eating, no less."

"There's a first for everything. Your cook's broth is very tasty." He dipped a wedge of bread into the bowl.

"If you called Francois a cook, he would bludgeon you with a skillet."

The patient laughed. "'Struth, you have a French chef? That's the outside of enough."

"But true nonetheless. He came to these parts after the French Revolution."

"Brumley helped me change my clothes and gave me a shave, a hairbrush, and some tooth powder. I feel much improved, almost like my old self."

"No pain?"

"Yes, but I'm becoming accustomed to the agony, and I'm working on getting my movement back." He gave her such a warm smile that it made the skull-duggery of the situation worthwhile. "Seeing you tonight, Laura, is like balm to my torn senses."

"And your muscles?"

"Very sore, but improving, I hope." To show her, he lifted his wounded arm an inch, winced, and dropped it gently onto the quilt. "I'm too full of pride," he added, "and I have to pay the price as I try to do something I'm not ready for."

"You'll recover in due time."

"With your help." He motioned for her to sit on the chair by the bed.

"I have to change your bandages."

"Brumley did as he helped me. By the way, I've never met a surlier fellow. It was as if he held a personal grudge against me, and I sensed he wanted to throw me out and lock the door."

"He does hold a grudge—for all the upheaval you brought to the Keep. He's very protective of me."

"As is Leo," he said as she heard a scratch on the door. "That pesky dog barely ever leaves my side."

"He knows his duties. He's to protect you and to calm you."

Strider Hunt grimaced. "He smothers rather than protects me. He almost pushes me off the bed to get the most comfortable spot on the mattress."

She laughed. "A more loyal friend you could not find." She went to open the door and Leo bounded inside. He gave her a quick lick on the hand and leaped onto the bed, unheeding of the jarring he must be giving the patient. He pressed his big muscular body up against Strider's side as he made himself comfortable.

"You see what I mean?"

Laughter bubbled within her. "I think he's taken a great liking to you. I trust Leo, he's a good judge of character."

"So am I," Strider said, and ruffled the dog's floppy ears.

Leo eeled forward across the mattress, hopefully sniffing the soup bowl, but Laura told him to stay away from the food.

"I have found that he eats almost anything," Strider said.

"He's a supreme opportunist."

"A kindred spirit. I like his character." Strider patted the other side of the bed. "Please sit and talk to me. I'm going addle-brained with boredom."

She obeyed, pulling the hard chair closer to the bed. If anything, she wanted to know something about him. Perhaps he would confide in her now that the fever had stopped addling his brain.

"This is my only home," she began. "I haven't seen much of the world. You must've had many homes over the years, in foreign parts."

"What makes you believe I didn't spend my days abroad in one home?"

She thought for a moment. "You seem to be the adventurous type, not staying long in one place."

"When you've lost your roots, you don't care where you live," he said, more to himself than to her.

"My cousin has lived most of his life in the Colonies and doesn't consider England his home. That's why he hasn't taken the reins of the Keep."

"He saddled you with the responsibility."

"That has worked out well. However, I don't want to talk about me. I know nothing about you and that isn't fair." She gave him a long stare. "Surely you have nothing to hide."

"Obviously I was born in England, and my parents were from these parts, but they died young."

"How sad."

"Yes. My aunt raised me from a young age. I really miss her; she passed to her just rewards just after I turned fourteen. After that, I had few close family members to rely on."

"So you learned to be strong and fend for yourself at a young age."

He remained silent for a moment. "Yes . . . I'd have to agree with that."

She sensed his uneasiness. "From adversity comes strength of character," she said.

"I found myself on a ship bound for India, and once there, you worked and ate, or you starved. Fortunately, I knew of old friends of my father, the Ashleys of London. Bankers. One branch of the family had left London for Bombay. They owned a fleet of ships with business spanning as far as Arabia, and Theodore Ashley trained me in his business. I met Abdullah on one of our trips to Arabia and we began breeding and trading in horses."

"You're too young to have experienced all that."

"Sometimes you have no choice but to grow up fast, especially if you find yourself with nothing but your own resourcefulness."

"I admire you for that. I've lived a sheltered existence, but I've learned to manage an estate and our farms are thriving. I'm studying animal husbandry, and that is my greatest interest."

He smiled. "You certainly have a knack with the creatures. It's almost as if you keep a conversation with them."

"I do! From their expressions I know what they are thinking—"

"And *saying?*" His eyes gleamed.

She slapped his healthy arm. "You're teasing me."

"It's rather easy. You have rather weak defenses."

"But if you go too far, I'll bite you or set one of the dogs on you."

He laughed. "It won't be Leo." He patted the snoozing mongrel's head.

"No, you're right." She sighed and started refolding an extra blanket at the foot of the bed.

"Would you plump up the pillows for me?" he asked, and she gave him a measuring glance.

"As long as you keep your comments to yourself. I am somewhat miffed with you."

"I promise," he said, and placed his hand over his heart. With some difficulty, he put his soup bowl on the nightstand.

She leaned over him and smelled the freshness of the soap that Brumley had used to shave him. As she shook out one of the pillows, Strider took her hand and pulled her down beside him on the bed. Before she could protest, he'd curled his hand around her neck and drawn her close. He kissed her on the lips, a sweet, lingering kiss that melted her bones and made her lose her bearings. Any will to struggle, or any protest she might have raised, died in her mind.

Her heart raced, and she'd never experienced such an unbearable sweetness. His grip tightened, and she could feel his heart pounding as she braced her hands against his chest. Decorum dictated that she had to remove herself from this compromising position posthaste; sticklers for propriety would have had severe palpitations while viewing this spectacle.

She couldn't pull away even if she'd wanted to. Heat rushed over her skin, and she was aware of every nuance of his mouth against hers and the taut muscles under her hands.

With difficulty she lifted her face from his. "This . . . highly brazen . . ."

"Highly delicious," he whispered.

"You're taking . . . advantage of me," she said, struggling to regain her breath.

"Yes . . . I am," he replied, just as breathless as she was. "I couldn't help myself."

"If someone discovered us here . . ."

"I would have to ask for your hand in marriage immediately." His eyes began gleaming anew. "By the way, what is your cousin's name and address in the Colonies?"

"Surely there's no reason why you would need that."

"He's your closest male relative, isn't he?"

"Not very close obviously, but yes. I don't understand what you want with him."

Strider Hunt looked up at the ceiling. "I never thought I did, either. The ways of fate are incomprehensible."

"*You* are incomprehensible." She pushed away from him and rearranged a wayward curl that had fallen across her face.

"Never mind. I have lots of thoughts, and my mind may not be altogether balanced after my recent ordeal."

"Jill calls you a rogue."

"Yes, I daresay she might have even harsher things to say about me. She's only trying to protect you."

Laura nodded, feeling strangely vulnerable. "This is so sudden, and I don't know if I should be in this room at all now. From now on, perhaps Brumley can take care of you."

"I was drawn to you from the very first time I looked into your eyes in the meadow. If it hadn't been for the pain I suffered, I might've kissed you then."

"Fustian. Besides, *I* would not have kissed you back."

"But you did tonight."

"Only because I left my reasoning outside the door." She stood, her knees like jelly and her cheeks burning with embarrassment.

His face glowed in a way it hadn't during his worst fever, and she took notice of the admiration in his eyes. "Tell me, why aren't there more suitors at your door, Laura? Is there one at all?"

"Well . . . yes and no. Someone has shown his interest, but he hasn't come forth with an offer for my hand."

"I'm willing to wager it's your neighbor."

Surprised, she stared at him. "How would you know?"

"Logic says your land abuts to his, and any such union is a fruitful one."

Silence stretched between them. He was right, of course, but was that the sole reason Julian had shown interest in her? Part of her knew it to be true, but there had to be more or Julian would not have singled her out for his amorous attention. With Julian she wasn't sure; he still was her old friend, and he'd always been affectionate to a point.

"Spoken like a true businessman," she said. "But yes, you're right. Julian has shown interest in me. Tell me, how do you know about him?"

"Drat it all." He cursed under his breath, ignoring her question. "I pray you haven't given him any indication about your feelings?"

"There hasn't been a reason to, and he knows me very well. I'm sure he believes I would accept his offer on the spot."

"Would you?"

Laura thought about that for a moment. "Probably."

"You're jesting, surely."

If Julian had proposed yesterday, she would have said yes immediately, but now she wasn't sure. Nothing had touched her the way Strider's kiss had touched her, but she wasn't about to tell him that. Not that his advances would lead anywhere. "Your comment is offensive and arrogant, Strider."

"In a love match, there are no doubts. You wouldn't reply 'probably'—you would be jubilant and eager to plan the wedding."

His air of confidence needled her in a way it hadn't done before. "You are the expert, I take it."

"I certainly know my own feelings, and I wouldn't expect a 'probably' if I were courting the woman of my heart. I would make sure there were no doubts. If you want my opinion, I believe your neighbor takes you for granted."

"It's just that I've known Julian all my life. He probably looks at me as his little sister."

"There's that word 'probably' again. It's clear he hasn't assured you about his true feelings, the cad! If he were here, I would call him out for his shabby treatment."

Laura gave a crow of mirth. "How dramatic. No, I daresay he will declare himself when he's ready and not a moment before."

"A cold fellow, indeed, if he's that in control of his emotions." Disdain shaded Strider's handsome face. "I have no patience for such a cod's head."

Laura kept laughing. "It's obvious you don't know Julian's character at all."

"I don't *want* to know more. I've heard enough, and I instinctively don't like him."

"Well, I'm learning that you're rather judgmental, which surprises me. Someone as much traveled as you should be more tolerant, don't you agree?"

He laughed, and Laura liked the deep sound. "You have me there, Laura."

"Miss Endicott to you, sir," she said breathlessly. She couldn't recall when she'd had such an amusing time.

He bowed as far as his head could reach without moving his body. "Ma'am, I apologize from the depths of my heart."

"You're doing it too brown, Mr. Hunt." She went to straighten out the medical implements and refold the bandages. Not that they needed the improvement, but she needed something to do.

"Your cruelty wounds me deeply," he said, a catch of mirth in his voice.

"You'd better go to sleep before you become completely delirious. You're dangerously close as it is."

"I'd rather be delirious with happiness than dull with boredom, and without you, *Miss Endicott,* this room would be terribly dull. No insult intended, Leo," he aimed at the dog. "I can't wait to get out of this bed."

"When you do, you'll be well enough to leave this dull chamber and rejoin your colorful life, and you'll forget about us backward people in Cornwall."

"No, I won't. How could I forget you? You saved my life. I'm at your feet forever, and besides, I'll never forget those heavenly blue eyes."

"An exaggeration, I'm sure, but I'm glad you appreciate my help."

"Without you life would be over, and with you, it's just begun."

She stared at him, fumbling and dropping the bandage in her hands. "That sounds as if you're planning to see me again—after you've recovered."

"I would not let you go, Miss Endicott. I've only just found you."

"It's Laura to you, sir." She laughed, feeling silly with happiness. A bit of heaven had manifested here tonight, she thought.

"Aha! I'm back into your favors. Laura it is, from now on."

"You're very silly, and I don't think I can trust any of your promises. 'Tis clear you have wanderlust in your blood."

"I have 'wandered' far longer than I ever wished for. It's time to settle down and see to my business, my future, perhaps set up my nursery."

"You could marry an Indian princess or some such exotic lady."

"I could have, but no one was the lady of my heart. Not until you. Besides, I would have to fall in with their foreign habits, and I'm still British at heart."

She couldn't believe she'd heard him right. He had practically declared himself tonight, but she still felt as if she didn't know him. Her heart seemed to, though, and it made her nervous.

Part of her adored his adventurous spirit; part of her knew it was impossible to hope for any future with him, due to that spirit. If she didn't want to suffer heartache, she'd better guard herself closely.

Seven

Laura didn't sleep well that night. She couldn't get Strider Hunt out of her mind. If she fell in love, she suspected he would ultimately hurt her. He would leave her and take her heart with him. She was convinced his desire for adventure sat in his blood. It would be foolish to hope for anything more than a short dalliance with him. The thought made her feel low.

After a solitary breakfast in her room, she dressed in a simple blue serge gown and a lace fichu at her throat. Taking a deep breath to steady herself, she went downstairs. Her feet automatically turned toward the tower room, and she couldn't have stopped herself if she'd wanted to. With a sigh, she stepped inside.

Strider Hunt was walking! His good arm braced against the wall, he was taking tiny steps. Sweat stood on his forehead and his face had turned red with the exertion. He had a green tinge around his mouth as if nausea plagued him. His eyes glowed with pain, and he couldn't even force a smile to his lips when he saw her.

She hurried toward him, but he shook his head vehemently. "I'm going to walk the perimeter of this room even if it kills me," he said between gritted teeth.

"I'm impressed with your determination, but—"

"I have to get back on my feet posthaste. Nothing happens while I dally away the days in bed."

She gripped his arm. "Of all the totty-headed notions! If the wounds reopen, you're going to be ill again with fever, and the wounds will take longer to heal."

Before she could protest, he'd slung his arm around her shoulders. "Now you can support me, though I believe I'm rather heavy," he said, his breathing labored.

"I . . ." His closeness made her forget what she was about to say.

He pressed forward, leaning on her and bracing himself against the wall, and his proximity flustered her no end. Before she could utter another protest, he'd managed to walk around the room. Exhausted, he leaned against the wall and pulled her into his arms. He was taller than he'd looked lying down. Her nose touched his neck, and his beard stubble scratched her. It was the most intimate feeling, she thought, embarrassed at finding herself in such a compromising position, yet loath to let go. He nuzzled his face against her hair.

"Mmm, you smell so sweet and so fresh, Laura. Just like a dewy rose."

She stared at him. "Such flummery. Your tongue is too devilish by far."

He looked down at her face, various expressions of joy, pain, and regret passing across his features. "You're cruel when I'm only trying to articulate my impressions."

"You don't know me very well, yet you say the sweetest, most personal things. I can't trust that."

"Because I *do* know you. I could bet my last groat that you would never turn into a harpy."

She laughed at that, and he silenced her with a warm, breath-stealing kiss. Again he made her weak and unable to think about anything at all. This was all very dangerous.

She pulled away. "You must not kiss me! Please don't do it again." Utterly confused by her raging emotions, she went to pick up a pile of towels that had fallen to the floor. Her face burning, she kept her back turned toward him.

With a groan, he sank down onto the bed.

"'Tis a sad day when a young man can't walk across a room without aid," he said with a deep sigh.

"But it's progress, however foolhardy. If you relapse, I shan't nurse you," she said, angry that he would taunt fate. Then again, his action of impatience didn't surprise her.

"I regret to hear it. Your soft hands brought me back from the brink of death."

"Mayhap, but now you're doing everything to ruin what we accomplished."

"Don't look at it from a perspective of failure, my dear. You're too pessimistic. I'm stronger than I look." He glanced down at the loose white shirt covering his body, and one of the footmen's homespun knee breeches. "My flesh is melting away, alas, but after some hearty meals, I shall regain my strength."

She looked anxiously for fresh blood seeping through the bandages on his arm, but they remained pristine. She could not see his thigh, which was just as well, she thought, and blushed.

"You're very quiet, Laura. Did I offend you in any way?"

She shook her head. "Only that you . . . er, kissed me."

"I should say I'm sorry, but I can't lie. However, I shall do my best to—"

"Don't promise anything you can't uphold," she warned. "I know you mean well, but I truly can't trust you—I can't pin any hopes on you for the future."

"That is the saddest statement I've heard in a long time. Surely you have no reason to mistrust me."

"No, but I trust my intuition. It rarely ever fails me." She smoothed down the sheets at the bottom of the bed, and when he managed to lift his injured leg onto the mattress, she spread the quilt over him. He looked tired from the exertion, and his eyes shone as if overcome with fever.

"I trust mine, too," he said, but didn't elaborate.

"I'll leave you now, as I have many things to which to attend. Jill will surely sit with you for a while." Laura heard him plead as she hurried out of the room, but she couldn't face him any longer. Her emotions in much turmoil, she ran out to the stables and proceeded to talk to every cat that greeted her there. The horses gave her appreciative snorts when she curried their hides, and Ollie gave her a long searching stare under his forelock as he mucked out one of the boxes on the opposite side of the aisle.

She pretended that she didn't notice his unspoken question. Life was too complicated with humans, she thought as she caressed one soft horse muzzle. When she'd finished she went outside in the sunshine. Hector, one of the old horses that had been put out to pasture, greeted her in the stable yard. His gray muzzle nudged her face as if to reassure her.

"Oh, Hector, did you get out again? We'll have to put a sturdier lock on the gate so that you can't open it."

He neighed as if in protest. If left to his devices, he would follow her around like a puppy. He didn't realize he could not fit through the doors at the Keep. As she walked toward the small pond behind the stables, he followed, as did four puppies and three kittens. Sitting in the grass, she played with the rambunctious animals, and found that her world was tilting back to normalcy.

The sun was shining from a clear blue sky, and swallows darted above in search of insects.

She heard Jill's voice from across the yard. "There you are! I've been looking for you."

"I'm enjoying a day away from the sickroom," Laura said as Jill joined her.

"I don't blame you. I went in to see Mr. Hunt, and he acted wholly despondent. I read from a poetry book I found, but he wasn't listening. Besides his sour mood, he seems much improved."

"He is." Laura told her about the morning, but left out the details of his amorous attention. "He'll be leaving the Keep shortly; he only has to regain some more of his strength."

"Your tone of voice holds regrets," Jill said, her dark gaze sharp. She looked beautiful in a rose muslin gown with a white lace scarf over her shoulders. The long silk fringe trailed over her arms. Her maid had arranged Jill's black curls into a crown on the top of her head, some tendrils curling onto her shoulders.

"You're imagining things," Laura said, heavyhearted.

Jill sat down next to her. "You can't fool me. I believe you're more attached to the rascally Mr. Hunt than you care to admit."

"It makes no difference, does it? He'll be gone shortly, and that'll be the last we see of him."

Jill nodded. "You're right, of course. I don't see why I even worry. He's no threat to you, or us. If he were, he would've robbed us blind and slunk away in the night."

"I don't think he could 'slink' any time soon—rather, he'd hobble," Laura pointed out.

Jill laughed.

"'Tis no laughing matter. I don't think he came to us with the scheme to rob us. In my opinion it would be rather self-destructive to injure yourself severely just to gain entrance to the Keep."

"Yes . . . my suggestion does not make sense. It was feather-witted to even suggest it. I simply worry about you."

Laura did not respond. She could not deal with any more recriminations. "Just worry about yourself. I was ever so grateful that you would come to support me, but if you so desire, you can return to Sussex any time. I shan't hold that against you. I daresay you miss Richard."

"Yes, I do, but it's out of the question. I have to stay until the patient leaves the Keep. Only then will I draw a sigh of relief."

"You're overly protective, Jill."

"No crime in that, surely." She stood and brushed pieces of grass off her dress. "Do you care to take a ride on the moor? I'd love to, but I fear getting lost."

Laura shrugged. "That would be wonderful. It's been a while since I had the chance to ride for pleasure."

"You could delegate some of the care for the patient to someone else."

"We have to keep his whereabouts a secret for a while longer."

"I don't like it. There's definitely something strange going on."

They walked together to the Keep to change into their riding habits. Laura would have to agree with her. "Yes, but we've kept the secret this long. I won't change now."

Jill shrugged. "It is your home, but if he doesn't leave soon, I shall write to Richard for advice."

Laura nodded. "At least we know we can trust him."

They dressed and met downstairs a half hour later. Laura wore her mint green outfit with gold braid along the hem of both the tight-fitting jacket and the wide skirt. Jill had donned her red Hussar-inspired habit adorned with black braiding, and a matching hat with an ostrich feather curling over the brim. It felt good to ride side by side down the sunny, winding path.

A few trees dotted the meadows, casting leafy shadows across the path. The village of Pendenny lay one mile to the south. On one side it faced the moor, and on the other grew a small forest that held at bay the sometimes sharp winds from the sea. If the breeze came from the sea as it did this morning, one could smell the salt on the air.

"I'd forgotten how beautiful it is here," Jill said as they entered the muted greens of the forest. "And how magical."

"Yes, it always spurs my imagination and I find herbs to collect for my salves and tinctures. But today we ride for pleasure."

"The village looked very quiet."

Laura nodded. "Everyone is taking a nap."

"I saw no foreigners with horses."

Laura laughed for the first time that day. "You're right. I'm certain they have delivered the horses and left the area."

"Without Mr. Hunt?"

"He can join them later, can't he?"

"They would leave without knowing what happened to him?"

"Jill, as far as we know he might have sent out a messenger pigeon, or perhaps he's a master at telepathy, or his friends might not care about him. And as far as we know he has only *one* friend, Abdullah."

Jill had no comment to make about that. "It's all so secret."

"That's because we haven't had any contact with the mysterious Abdullah. He might not be as tight-lipped as Strider Hunt. For all we know, everyone else is privy to all the secrets. We've been secluded at the Keep, out of contact with the local gossip."

They moved deeper into the woods, and the trees filtered the sunlight. Green and gold splashed across the path, and before long they'd reached the last clearing before the forest ended and the rocks and the moor took over. Taken by surprise, they saw movement among the saplings lining the clearing.

"A horse! Look, it's a purebred," Laura said.

The dark brown horse turned his magnificent head and looked at them, neighing softly. Behind him stood a man in a long white shirt, with a turban on his head. His narrow face and blade of a nose had a swarthy complexion and a dark beard curled in a wild tangle around his face.

"That must be him," Jill whispered. "The mysterious Abdullah."

They saw another person move in the gloom and Laura recognized the old woman Tula, the village witch. She sat on a rock, her brown rags pulled about her, a basket standing at her feet. She gave them a sharp glance as they moved closer to the clearing.

"Good morning," Jill greeted cautiously. Her mare pawed nervously, as if afraid of the large stallion.

"Good morning." Tula greeted them without much conviction.

The foreign man nodded curtly. Not much town bronze there, Laura thought. "We heard there were strangers in the village," she directed at Tula.

"I've seen stranger things than a man from the Orient," Tula said coolly.

"Does he speak English?" Jill asked.

The stranger bowed. "I do, if not . . . er, good. I'm Abdullah, humble servant of Allah."

Laura introduced Jill and herself. "You bring horses?"

"I have . . . sold them," Abdullah replied hesitantly. "No more. None for you."

"We aren't asking to buy horses," Jill explained. "But what about that one?" She pointed at the splendid Arabian stallion.

"No for sale, no for sale," the Arab said with vehemence.

"Ye hear what he says," Tula said. "He won't sell that one, the most superb of them all."

"What's his name?" Laura asked.

"Strider, ma'am."

Both Jill and Laura gasped and looked at each other.

"Strider?" Laura echoed.

"Yes, ma'am." The man caressed the black muzzle and the horse stomped and snorted. The forest smelled of moss and rotting leaves around them, and Laura wondered why her world could change at the sound of one single word. *Strider.* She knew immediately that the stranger in the tower room had been leading her by the nose. How stupid could she be? Red with embarrassment, she stared at Jill. Her friend would say "I told you so," and Laura couldn't bear it. She had believed in Strider Hunt, or whatever his name was. Feeling broken inside, she bowed her head to the Arab and Tula and wheeled her mount around on the narrow path.

Hopeless. She was hopeless beyond belief! She wished the earth would open up and swallow her. How could she be so gullible?

She heard Jill follow her, and Tula's raspy voice. "I know who you are. You're still going to marry that man . . . Julian is his name. Don't forget."

Yes! Laura cried within. She was ready to marry Julian now. At least she knew him; there were no surprises there even if he wasn't the most forthcoming lover. He would change, and hopefully he would never find out about this humiliating disaster.

"How awkward," Jill said behind her.

"He lied to me all this time," Laura cried out. "How could I be so stupid?"

"Don't berate yourself, Laura. It's entirely his fault. You did nothing except assist him through his life-and-death struggle, and for that you deserve a medal."

"I should've listened to you." She kicked her heels into the mare's flanks and they flew through the rest of the woods and out onto the moor. She could ride away and never come back. After this, she could never face the liar again, but she would like to know the truth. Not that he would ever tell her.

"We'll have him leave the Keep just as soon as we return. I don't care if he's still crippled. He has stayed under false pretenses and he's preyed on your more tender feelings."

"I don't blame him for taking advantage, but it'll never happen again." Laura rode until she felt hot and breathless. The mare had a smooth gait and great endurance, and the ride soothed her agitated feelings.

"Do you want me to ask Julian for help?" Jill asked. "Perhaps we need a gentleman to handle this."

Laura shook her head hard. "No. I shall deal with it myself. I don't want to involve him; neither do I want him to know about my stupidity. He'll detest me."

"A real gentleman would not blame you. He would only be eager to help."

Laura doubted that Julian would act in such an understanding manner, and the thought worried her. Why couldn't she predict how he would react? "Julian won't have time for such trivial problems. I would never ask him."

"Trivial?" Jill shouted and pulled in the reins so that they rode side by side. "This is a serious matter. You don't know who you're truly hiding in the tower room."

A brisk breeze had stirred and blew through the

heather below and the horses' manes. Laura wished her heated cheeks would cool. "You're right. The stranger might truly be a notorious criminal. Mayhap someone shot him in self-defense."

The horses jostled and stomped, eager to continue the fast pace, but Laura held back. She needed a plan to deal with the stranger in the tower.

"I think we should ride over to Sandhurst and confess the whole to Julian," Jill suggested. "Oh, how I wish that Richard were here!" She addressed the skies. "There's no fairness in this; why would such an angel as Laura have to deal with such deceitful people?"

"No, I don't want to involve Julian just yet. Let's confront the liar at home. I can't wait to hear how he's going to try to eel out of this." Laura pressed her lips together firmly. Anger burned within her, and she was ready to confront the villain.

Eight

Laura hurried into the Keep after handing over her mare to Ollie at the stables. She didn't care about her appearance and her flustered face. She needed answers *now*. How could Strider Hunt have taken such advantage of her and pretended a depth of feeling for her when all she'd done was help to cure his ills? Evidently, he was an inveterate liar.

She tore open the door to the tower room only to find the space empty. Jill came right on her heels, and Laura heard her gasp.

"He's gone!" Jill cried. "Why, the oily so-and-so. I was so looking forward to speaking my mind."

Laura took the pillow, which still bore the imprint of his head, off the bed and threw it across the room. It hit the wall with a thud. The wooden bowl that had held his morning porridge followed. It cracked into two pieces and Laura wanted to cry with frustration.

"It's as if he knew," Jill said. "Just as we were getting too close to finding out something about him, he disappears."

"I'd like to speak with that strange Abdullah again, but he might only tell me lies. They are two of a kind." Laura longed to kick something, preferably Strider Hunt's leg, but since he wasn't available, she struggled to regain her composure. "I am so very angry!"

"It's time we set Julian and his men on his trail."

Laura looked at Jill. "What will that accomplish other than provoking Julian's ire over my actions? In his eyes, I've flown in the face of decorum."

Jill's eyes widened in surprise. "You don't mean to say you're aiming to keep this a secret still?"

"No . . . but my embarrassment is too deep to bring out for his inspection. I could not bear Julian's contempt."

Jill placed her hands on her hips. "If he shows contempt where compassion and understanding are needed, he is cut from the wrong cloth and I shan't have anything more to do with him, and neither should you."

Laura sank down on one of the chairs and sighed. "I never thought it would come to this."

"Let's send a messenger over to Sandhurst and ask Julian to join us. It's about time he knows the whole. I can only hope he cares enough about you to act in the proper manner."

Laura nodded, unable to speak. She dreaded facing Julian, whose eyes would narrow and whose expression would harden. She was certain he would comb the countryside for Strider, and even if she was infuriated with her erstwhile patient, she didn't wish him any harm.

Jill left the room, and Laura knew Julian would come as soon as his horse could carry him across the parkland.

She waited uneasily in the parlor by the front door, but to her surprise the servant whom Jill had sent came back with the information that Julian was in Plymouth on business and wouldn't return until the following day.

"There's not much we can do at this point," Jill said, her face filled with annoyance. "Except contact the local constables, but I don't know what that would accomplish. They would ruin your reputation as they bandied the story about."

"We could ride out and look for the foreign blighter ourselves." Laura had made up her mind to find her erstwhile patient and confront him with his lies. She didn't need some man to deal with her mistakes; she could handle them herself. "I shall get the truth out of him! Come, Jill."

Laura took her gloves and riding crop from the table in the hallway and marched outside. She could hear Jill protest behind her, but her friend followed. At least she could count on Jill to support her wholeheartedly.

They rode back into the woods behind Pendenny, and searched every path, but there was no sign of Abdullah or the horse. Tula had disappeared, as well. It was as if they'd never been there at all.

"Aarrgh," Laura cried and flung a stick that clung to her sleeve across the clearing. "They can't just vanish into thin air."

"No, but listen, do we know who bought the horses from them? We could start investigating there."

"Strider didn't say, but we could inquire in the village."

They turned their horses back through the woods and went into Pendenny. The wind had churned up a cloud of dust on the main road, and in the distance they could see even more dust. A chaise and four was arriving quickly, a wall of dust following it.

Laura saw two men drinking ale at one of the rough-hewn tables outside the local inn, the Duck and Arrow. She asked them about Strider Hunt and Abdullah but they knew nothing.

"I wonder who that is," Jill said, pointing at the approaching coach. "Could be Richard, but I doubt it."

"Julian drives his own equipage, but there are other

members of the gentry in the area. Coaches to Padstow and Newquay usually stop here to refresh their horses."

They waited until the carriage had stopped, and Laura immediately recognized one of her more distant neighbors, the elderly Squire Hanfield, and his son, Mr. Benjamin Hanfield. She knew at that moment where the horses had gone. Benjamin Hanfield had a great penchant for the turf, and entered several of his horses at Newmarket and other venues.

Squire Hanfield bowed to them with a smile, and greeted Laura by name. The haughtier son bowed, but didn't give them any attention. "I'll order a tankard of ale for you, Father." He proceeded into the inn, but the older man stayed to exchange some pleasantries.

"A fine day it is, Squire," Laura said. She introduced Jill and they exchanged pleasantries.

"Me old bones are too old to be jolting along the road in a coach," he said with a sigh as he stretched his rather stooped back. "A pint of ale might alleviate some of the ache, though."

"How are your horses these days?"

"All in fine fettle ever since you healed that large tear one of them suffered, Miss Laura. You must come and see them soon. We're working with the colts now." The old man leaned on his walking stick and viewed the ladies as they sat on their mares. "In fact, my wife and I are having a small tea party on Saturday afternoon at four. Would you two like to come?"

Laura and Jill accepted gratefully. "I look forward to seeing your horses, Squire Hanfield. Did you acquire any new members to the stables? I hear there were foreign horse dealers in the area."

"Aye, wait until you see the magnificent Arabian stallion and two mares I purchased. I might start a breeding program if they are cooperative. They will cause an uproar on the turf."

"The dealer? Is that someone we all know?" Laura held her breath waiting for the answer.

The old man shook his white-haired head. "Not from these parts. I had correspondence with people in London who knew of these breeders in foreign parts. On their word that the dealer was honorable, I took a chance and secured the steeds before they even arrived in England."

"The men were seen in Pendenny, and I saw one of the horses myself, a black stallion named Strider."

"That's the dealer's personal horse. I could have paid my entire fortune to get my hands on that magnificent animal."

Laura nodded. "Do you recall the owner's name?"

"Hmm, that's the strange part. As English as any one of us, he is, but foreign. He calls himself Mr. Hunt, the head representative of the company, Arabian Investments. Never saw a better horse trainer; I have some colts at this time that are difficult to rear. I offered to hire him on the spot, full-time, but he said he would not stay long in these parts. When his business is over, he'll return to those hot Arabian deserts." The old man rubbed his chin. "As far as I know, his business in this area should be over. No one else is purchasing horses, but they might want to when they see my acquisitions." He chuckled. "My neighbors will be green with envy."

"Yes, that wouldn't surprise me," Laura said.

"Tell me," Jill put in, "is that horse trainer at your stables now?"

"No, but he's supposed to be. The strangest thing is, I thought I saw him very early this morning, and he was limping badly when he got off his horse. Then he was gone, and I went to see my brother with Ben. I haven't seen the horse dealer or that foreign servant of his since. What puzzles me is that Mr. Hunt seemed injured. It's only been a few days since I last spoke with him about the progress of the colts, hale and hearty. Very odd business."

Laura gave Jill a glance full of frustration.

"I would've liked to have met him," Laura said, anger burning within. And if she did, she would clout him good.

"I'd say he almost has as fine a hand with horses as you do, Miss Laura, but I daresay he knows not as much about healing their ills." He tipped his hat. "I'll see you on Saturday. I know Jenny will be happy to see you, too. She's always asking about you and that fancy lord next door."

Laura blushed. "That's excessively kind of her, but I have no news to share. Everything remains the same."

"Well, we thought you would get married off earlier this year, but—"

"Sometimes the best laid plans don't work," Laura said with finality.

"Yes . . . by Jove." He peered more closely at Jill, but Laura didn't feel like explaining the situation here in the dusty street.

"Good afternoon, Squire Hanfield," she said, and turned her horse around. Out of earshot of the old man, she said to Jill, "Let's ride over to Hanfield Farms. We might catch a glimpse or an indication of Mr. Hunt's whereabouts."

"Laura, that's clutching at straws." But Jill fell into step with Laura's mare. "Is it far?"

"Only about three miles. No hardship at all. Should be a beautiful ride," she added automatically. Laura imagined various scenes in which she would deal with the ramshackle Mr. Hunt, or whatever his real name was.

They rode in silence, but it ended up to be a futile

trip, because the stables at Hanfield Farms were deserted except for three sleepy stable hands. The horses were all out in the pastures.

"He's not here. I *knew* he wasn't here," Jill said. "I should have objected to this trip."

"We might as well go back to the Keep. Racing around the moor won't bring him back to us." Laura raised her voice. "I shall take a piece of his hide if I ever lay eyes on him again."

"That's after I'm finished with the dratted man," Jill said.

They returned to the Keep, and Jill went upstairs to compose a note to Richard. Maybe he could help in some manner.

Thirsty and tired, Laura changed out of her riding habit. She resented that she hadn't had the chance to vent her anger at the villainous stranger. After drinking two glasses of cold lemon water, she donned a simple white muslin gown with a blue sash and went downstairs.

Too angry to occupy herself with anything useful, she steered her steps toward the tower room. Perhaps Mr. Hunt had left some clues behind, but she suspected that he was halfway to Plymouth by now.

She stepped into the tower room, and her jaw dropped when she found the wounded man sound asleep in his bed.

Nine

"Of all the ramshackle here-and-therians," she shouted, and started shaking him, not caring if she jarred his wounds or not. "You're a liar and a cheat, and no doubt a lothario of the worst kind." She took one of the extra pillows and hit him hard over the head.

"What in the world—?" He protected his face with his good arm, but she got in a few well-aimed blows.

"Desist, woman! Have you gone completely demented?"

"I hate you, you low, conniving worm."

"That's not what you said this morning," he shouted. As the pillow burst and millions of feathers covered him in a white drift, he laughed helplessly. "What are you trying to do? Suffocate me with feathers?"

"You deserve a much worse fate, you lummox."

"Blister me, what has gotten into you?" He gripped what was left of the pillow and ripped it out of her hands.

She sank down on the chair by the bed, leaning her head in her hands. "You've done nothing but lie to me since you came here, and I'm infuriated. After all I've done for you."

"Calm yourself, Laura."

"Calm myself?" She stood and leaned over him,

anger burning in every pore of her body. "What is really your name? Just tell me that without lying."

"What brings all this about?"

"I found out that you have a horse named Strider. I'm certain you took his name in the spur of the moment because you couldn't think of another in your pain-ridden state."

"What if I named the horse after myself?" He looked so calm she wanted to slap him again. She hadn't thought of that, but she didn't believe him.

"You're full of slippery evasions. I don't believe a word you're saying, and I know there's something going on that you won't talk about. And you left the Keep today. You claimed that when you were well enough you would return whence you came. Yet you're back here."

"I'm not well enough," he replied with a sigh.

"I think you are. You went outside on your own accord, and according to Squire Hanfield, you *rode* today, as well. Your wounds must be much better if you can ride."

"Sometimes we have to force ourselves to do things we aren't really fit to do." He touched his forehead. "The fever might be returning."

"You liar! I hope you burn up—in hell."

"You can't be that cruel."

"I don't get angry very often, but when I do, brace yourself. I abhor deceit." Laura's vision filled with a red haze and she would've pummeled him again if there had been another pillow. His head rested on the remaining one.

"There's no reason to get into a pelter over small details."

"Details? You still haven't told me your real name."

"'Tis not important at this point. You'll find out in

due course, and the truth doesn't affect you in any way."

"If you can't find the courtesy to tell me the truth, I see no reason why I should harbor you under my roof. From the very beginning, you've been hiding something and I honored your wish for secrecy, but now you're making a fool out of me. I can't abide disrespect."

He did have the decency to look uncomfortable. He wasn't totally devoid of conscience but it was close, which she told him.

He pushed himself up against the headboard, wincing as he pulled his injured leg. "Sometimes it's better not to know the whole truth. I have kept certain things from you to protect you."

Her ire flaring again, she grabbed a towel and hit the mattress with its tail. "Why would I need protection? That's up to me to decide. Besides, I have nothing to hide here. I live an honest and straightforward life."

"Trust me, you're better off not knowing. Everything will eventually come out into the open. I did not plan on injuring myself and ending up here."

"But you did, and I agreed to keep your secret, yet you can't confide in me? It's the height of arrogance."

"I could just call you Miss Nosy for insisting that I share my personal information."

"You came here to deliver horses. As far as I know, there's nothing underhanded about that. A straightforward business transaction."

He had nothing to reply to that.

"Horses are not the only reason you're here."

He didn't deny that, which confirmed her suspicion. "I'm not going to tell you anything at this point, Laura. I'm sorry. Either you trust me, or you don't."

"It's not an issue of trust at this point, and you should not speak of trust. If you trusted *me* —after all, I've shown that I can keep a secret—but you don't. So don't even mention the word again. I want you out of here."

He swung his leg painfully over the edge and stood. Swaying, he steadied himself against the wall and aimed his step toward the door that led outside. She fought her innate sense of compassion, but steeled herself against it. This was not someone she could care for any longer. Disappointment washed through her in the wake of her anger.

How could he have treated her so shabbily? She had believed in him and had started to like him more than she wanted to.

"And don't think for a moment that I enjoyed your amorous advances. You took advantage of me in a weak moment." A wave of anger rolled through her anew. "In fact, your kisses were the worst I've ever experienced."

He gave a whoop of mirth, which infuriated her even more. The cad!

"I take it you're quite experienced in that area," he countered, his arm still braced against the wall as he managed the last steps to the door.

"Yes . . . at least I don't take advantage of people," she cried.

"No, you are honest and good," he said

She couldn't fling an angry retort at that. Her heart ached as she realized she'd cared more for him than she thought. Julian acted cool and controlled, and this man had flirted with her without a care in the world, or any thought to the consequences. She wondered how far he would've gone if she'd let him.

"I don't want to ever see you again," she said as he opened the door.

"A pity. I just about fell in love with you, but the circumstances always appear to prevent any chance at happiness. If conditions had been—"

"Don't even begin. Your character would not change even if the state of affairs did."

He turned to look at her, his face red from the exertion and the pain. "You don't know me well enough to judge what I would do if we'd met in a different situation."

"I don't want to see you again."

"But you will." His jaw jutted out and she knew it would be useless to contradict him. All they did was talk in circles.

"Just go. I don't care if you stumble and fall into the sea."

"How callous," he said, his mouth twisting. He relaxed against the door for a moment before opening it. "I thank you for everything you've done for me. Don't think I didn't appreciate it."

She turned away to hide the tears pushing into her eyes. Misery filled her where anger had boiled recently.

"Good-bye, Laura."

She didn't reply, and when she turned around once more, he had gone.

All at once she began worrying about his wounds, but she reminded herself that they were no longer her business. She left the room without another glance and hurried to her bedchamber. Indulging in a bout of crying, she lay on her bed.

Jane, her maid, looked at her with concern, but Laura waved off any inquiries. "Just find something else to do, Jane. I'm fine."

"Doesn't look it to me, ma'am," Jane said with a sniff.

Laura only buried her head more deeply into her pillow. In due time, she would remember this episode only as something unimportant even if her heart didn't view it that way. It would, though, she consoled herself. She would forget the infamous Mr. Hunt, or whatever his name was.

She must've fallen asleep, because when Jill came into her room, darkness had enfolded the world. A headache pounded at her temples.

"Are you feeling poorly?" Jill asked with concern in her voice.

"Only tired, and my head is aching."

"There's a rumor that a stranger with a severe limp was seen on the grounds earlier, and when two of the grooms rode out to investigate, he had disappeared completely."

"Strider Hunt, or whoever he is, returned here," Laura said, anger creeping back into her. "When I went down to the tower room earlier, he was lying in bed as if nothing had ever happened."

"Of all the gall!"

"I confronted him, but he evaded me, and I still don't know his real name."

Jill sat down on the edge of the bed. "I'm not surprised. He's adamant about hiding his identity and whereabouts."

"I'm sure that everyone knows about him by now. You can't go undetected around here for very long. The village is small, and people have nothing better to do than gossip."

"That's true. This time the constables will catch him."

"But only if he perpetrates a crime. It's not illegal to ride around the area in secrecy."

"I wish Julian and Richard were here. When is Julian coming back?"

Laura shook her head and sat up against the pillows. "I don't know, and it doesn't matter. There's nothing he can do to prevent Strider Hunt's presence."

"Oh, yes. If he catches Hunt trespassing, there will be an investigation."

"Nothing says Hunt is going to sneak around Sandhurst."

"Julian may catch him here. You never know, and remember that you had that break-in when Hunt stayed here, and we deduced that someone was looking for him, which is very odd."

"Hopefully those people will catch up with him," Laura said with a sigh.

"You don't sound too happy about it."

Laura felt her friend's close scrutiny. "I don't give a fig for the fate of Mr. Hunt. May he rot in hell."

"That's a very strong statement."

"One that is heartfelt nevertheless."

Silence fell for a time as they pondered in silence.

"I take it you'll be going back to Eversley soon? You must miss Richard terribly."

"I do, but until this is settled, I'm not going anywhere." Her eyes twinkled. "And I wouldn't miss the tea party at the Hanfields' for anything."

Laura had to laugh. "That'll be the event of the season. Dry crumpets, soggy cakes, stale tea leaves, but the people are good."

"At least you haven't lost your sense of humor."

On Saturday Laura wore a short-sleeve blue muslin gown with a white lace collar and matching sash. Her hair had been tamed into a chignon and a few curls had been coaxed to frame her face in an orderly fashion. Since the sun was beating down, she also carried a parasol to protect her complexion. The day was unusually hot and large storm clouds loomed on the horizon. Fortunately, the Hanfields more often than not served tea in the solarium at the back of the mansion.

Jill looked lovely in a soft green gown, a minuscule lace cap attached to the top of her head. Black curls cascaded from the artful knot under the cap, and she was wafting her painted chicken-skin fan as their carriage pulled up to Hanfield Farms.

In the days that had passed, they hadn't seen or heard of Strider Hunt. It was as if the earth had opened up and swallowed him.

Mrs. Hanfield beamed kindly and took Laura's hands in her plump grip. "My dear! It has been a while, but you look the same, if somewhat pale."

"Thank you, Jenny." She glanced around the yard where zinnias, lupines, and phlox grew in colorful profusion and apple trees held green fruit. The Hanfields may have aspired to gentility, but the estate could not hide the cozy country farm air that prevailed. Laura had always loved visiting because of the variety of animals that lived on the farms circling the main estate.

"We have a litter of kittens. There are goslings and newborn chickens, and a few new calves. Always something for you to see, Laura, if you wish. But you're a young lady now, not the inquisitive child you once were."

"I never tire of newborn animals." Laura smiled and introduced Jill, who immediately became the target for questions about Eversley, the wedding, and Sir Richard. Jenny used to say that if one didn't ask questions, one didn't get any answers.

Squire Hanfield peered at Laura from under the shelf of his white eyebrows. "Do you want to inspect my new horses?" He held up a finger. "I warn you, though, you'll be green with envy."

Laura laughed. "I'll try to contain myself." She followed the squire's bowlegged progress down the path to the stables. He leaned heavily on his cane, and huffed, but no physical limitations would stop him from getting where he wanted to go. She smelled the stables and heard the horses before she could see them. Squire Hanfield was known all over the south counties for his fine horseflesh, and often he had visitors from various parts of England who tried to buy a steed or sell one. The stables were a beehive of activity.

She watched as the grooms rode the new acquisitions around the paddock upon the squire's order.

"Magnificent," she said under her breath. "Utterly superb."

She walked farther down the path to study them more closely. In the paddock behind the first, a colt reared and neighed as if pushed to his limit. It took time and patience to train the young horses. The squire had many hands to help him, or he could not have kept up the size of his stables.

"How beautiful they are," she said to herself. "Incomparable."

She admired the sleek lines of the nearest mare, the small perfect head and the long legs. She would carry those lines into the future, and Laura could not wait to see the offspring that would surely follow.

Again the colt created havoc in the paddock beyond, and over the fence, Laura saw a familiar head. Her knees started shaking. The notorious Strider Hunt!

Anger seized her as she noticed his position. Despite his injuries, he was working with the colt. It was the outside of enough.

"Who is that man?" she asked the squire to see if he knew another name for the scoundrel.

"The trainer? Never saw a better one. That's Mr. Hunt, the owner of Arabian Investments that I told you about. He brought me the Arabians. A fine gentleman to boot." He gave Laura a quick glance. "Do you want me to introduce you? I'm certain you would have many things to talk about concerning horses."

"Oh, no. I have no desire to speak with strangers."

"That surprises me, Laura. He's a horse expert, someone you would enjoy meeting due to your own interests."

"Be that as it may, we need to go back to the house before Jenny finds a reason to berate us for letting the tea get cold."

The squire motioned as if sweeping her comment away. "She's used to my ways. My Jenny has the patience of an angel. She needs that to live with me."

"At least you're aware of your shortcomings," Laura said with a laugh. She noticed her legs shaking and her heart hammering. This would never have happened if she hadn't seen Mr. Hunt. Why he had any kind of impact on her senses was beyond belief. She hated him!

The mare they had admired trotted off to the stables, and Mr. Hunt came into full view, only the fence separating her from him. She started walking back toward the main house, but the squire halted her with his hand on her arm.

"Mr. Hunt," the squire cried out. "I want to introduce someone who shares your interest in horses."

"No! Not now, Squire Hanfield."

But it was too late. Strider Hunt opened the gate and ambled toward them, his leg dragging and his gaze narrowed. He carried his arm in a sling, and a crop in the other. He limp had not improved, but at least he could walk without bracing himself against something. She sensed he suffered a lot of pain.

She grew hot and cold as she watched his approach. He recognized her and his step faltered. He slowed down considerably, as if regretting having stepped forward at all. The squire beamed and introduced them.

Laura bowed her head and hid her hands behind her back as if loath to have him touch her. He murmured a greeting, and she could feel his gaze upon her, searching her mind. She sensed his fear that she had told the squire of their past association, but she would never bring that up. Mr. Hunt might think she yearned for revenge, but she didn't. She was not one to hold a grudge, yet she didn't want to be taken for a fool. He should never think she'd forgotten.

"What a beautiful day," the squire said quickly, as if he felt the tension between her and Mr. Hunt.

"Always," Mr. Hunt said. "In the presence of Miss Endicott, the day would always be lovely."

The squire nudged her arm. "What a compliment, Laura. I don't think I could ever do better than that."

"A lovely compliment, indeed. However, I don't put much store in words. It's action that counts."

The squire peered at her closely. "Is there a hint of bitterness in your voice? I've never heard you convey anything but gracious gratitude to a compliment."

"It depends on how it's delivered and by whom."

Uncomfortable silence ensued. Strider Hunt looked at her, his gaze narrowing with each of her comments. Tension mounted with every breath, and she wanted to hurt him just as he'd hurt her.

"Well," the squire said cautiously, "I think you're the loveliest young lady in these parts."

"Thank you. Your words warm my heart." She gave him a kind smile.

The squire turned to the younger man. "Mr. Hunt, are you getting somewhere with the colt? A more ill-tempered creature I have yet to encounter."

"He has bruises on his legs which make him ornery."

"It's from kicking the box. He gets into fits of rage, and I don't know what to do with him."

"Was he born here?" Laura asked, avoiding Strider's gaze.

"No, I had him from one of my business associates. The man never could cotton to the colt; says he was violent from the start."

Laura listened in her mind. "He's afraid of confined spaces. I believe he was kept in a small dark box and beaten when he acted out his fear. Every time someone comes close with a crop, he thinks he's going to be punished. He panics."

"That's not good." The squire rubbed his chin in thought.

"It will take patience and lots of gentle interaction before the colt understands that we mean him no harm." She pointed to Strider's crop. "Using that will only make matters worse."

"Who says I'm using it?"

She noted Strider's annoyance and reveled in it. "You *are* carrying it, aren't you?" she pointed out.

He couldn't find a suitable reply to that. He gave her a glare that said that she hadn't won.

"I suggest you put it where the colt can't see it, and just walk him around the paddock. Talking to him won't hurt either."

The squire shook his head. "You have strange methods, but I've seen them work. It's as if you get the horse to cooperate rather than make him submit to your stronger will."

"They only resent that," she replied. "Horses are very intelligent—as you should know, Mr. Hunt. I'm surprised you haven't figured out the best way to treat them. You are the expert, after all."

His eyes emitted a beam of anger and his shoulders stiffened.

"You can't expect too much of Mr. Hunt," the squire said soothingly. "He's been severely wounded and is still recovering. That colt is a handful for a healthy man."

"Thank you," Strider Hunt said. "I was just about to—"

"Excuses," Laura said with a sniff. "Anyone can walk that colt around the paddock."

Strider bowed. "I stand corrected," he said, suppressed rage in his voice.

"Mayhap you can try, Laura?" the squire said, his face lighting up.

"Of course," Laura replied. She briskly furled her parasol and handed him that and her reticule.

"You're not dressed for the stable yard," Strider said in protest.

"Pooh, what dust covers my slippers can be brushed off. I don't intend to *roll* in the mud." She didn't know how she could contain so much anger, but she did. She knew she would have that colt eating out of her hand by the end of the session.

They passed through the gate into the paddock. She turned to Strider. "Put that crop where the horse can't see it."

Fuming, he went into the stables and returned empty-handed. The colt stood at the far end of the paddock, his lead trailing on the ground.

She approached him slowly.

"I don't like this," Strider Hunt called out.

"Don't worry, young man. She knows what she's doing. All creatures trust her. It's that kindness that flows out of her. Animals know these things."

Laura focused on the colt, which pawed the ground nervously. She cooed gently and his ears pricked. He followed her every move, poised to bolt at the slightest threat. He was beautiful, his hide a deep chestnut and his mane and tail tawny. The brown eyes held the shadow of fear, and Laura slowed down with every step. She kept talking kindly and the colt stopped pawing. When she bent down to retrieve the lead, she took the risk of having him kick her, but he only stood quietly waiting.

She kept talking to him, moving in closely until she could touch the fine hide and caress the silky mane. He let her. His hide jumped under her touch as if the nerves lay too close to the surface. He neighed and tossed his head, but waited.

She kept talking and felt him slowly relax. The stable hands stood watching, their breaths probably arrested in their throats. She could feel their tension and that of the other two men by the fence. At any second the colt could rear and trample her, but she knew he wouldn't. She knew he was listening and watching, curiosity taking over apprehension.

She stroked his muzzle and kept speaking softly, and then she tugged gently at the lead, wondering if he would step quietly or try to bolt. He stepped quietly, one slow step after the other. While talking to him, she guided him slowly around the paddock, around and around until he tired. She pulled his head down and sensed his surrender.

She asked for a carrot and led the horse to one of the stable hands, who went to fetch the vegetable. For a moment it looked as if fear would take over once more, but Laura kept pulling down the colt's head and he surrendered to her command. With slow movements, she offered him the carrot for his good work, and he didn't hesitate to take the treat.

"I'll be back tomorrow," she said to the speechless grooms, and let the horse go loose. He trotted the length of the paddock as if showing he was glad to be free, yet happy to be where he was.

"I'll leave him out here tonight," the squire said as she joined them.

A tendril of hair had escaped from her arrangement, and perspiration dampened her skin, but elation filled her. Nothing pleased her more than to work with animals, especially with those who had some difficulty.

"Superb," the squire said, rubbing his hands. He turned to Strider Hunt. "Wasn't that a fine exhibition of skills?"

Strider Hunt gave her a dark look and muttered something under his breath. He was not about to acknowledge her successful attempt.

"Give me a few days and the colt will be happy to return to his box without kicking everything in sight."

The squire smiled. "You're a precious gem, Laura." He addressed the other man. "Would you care to join us for tea?"

Strider Hunt looked down at his dusty riding breeches and muddy shirt. "I daresay I'm not dressed for the drawing room."

"We'll be having tea on the terrace."

Strider suppressed a laugh. "That won't make a difference. The ladies would swoon at such uncouth behavior."

"Fustian! We're in the country, not London."

Strider shook his head and glanced quickly at Laura. "I would never presume to push my presence where it's not wanted or does not belong."

"Your sensibilities are acute," Laura said, "but don't look at me. I don't care a fig about your dilemma."

The squire must have sensed the rising tension. He gave them each an uneasy glance. "You must do as you see fit, Mr. Hunt, but I offered."

Strider Hunt bowed. "Thank you again, sir. It's not

my place to sit at your table in my dirt." He nodded to Laura and sauntered off.

Something tugged at Laura's heart and she'd never felt more frustrated.

"Come, my dear. I can't wait to tell Jenny the tale of what transpired here."

Laura could barely tear her gaze from Strider Hunt's back. On the other side of the paddock, she saw a glimpse of the Arabian man, Abdullah, and she wondered where he'd been while she worked with the colt.

The tea party was marginal, as usual. The Hanfield cook had made currant and walnut cake and forgotten to put in sugar, and crumpets, spiced and iced cakes of different designs that were all but melting, but Laura could not taste anything. She ate automatically, not caring what she put into her mouth. She could not get the vision of Strider's face out of her mind. Jill stared at her for a long moment, but she avoided any explanations.

The squire embroidered quite liberally on the story that he told the women. Mrs. Hanfield was duly impressed, but Laura didn't want to get drawn into the discussion of her unusual knack with animals.

"Any gentleman would be fortunate to win your hand in marriage," she said. "Just look at your skills! The man would have the greatest stables in the west counties."

Laura laughed at that. "I am a catch, indeed. Wife-cum-horse doctor and trainer."

"If I were young and unwed, I'd marry you myself," the squire said, and Laura knew he meant it.

Jenny Hanfield slapped his arm good-naturedly. "I'm grateful you're too old, Henry."

"I don't intend to marry to create a great stable," Laura said with a sigh. "The gentleman in question would have to appreciate me for myself."

"That's very proper," Jenny said, straightening her back. "I, for one, do not hold with women who labor alongside the men."

"Be that as it may, Jenny," the squire said, "Laura has special talents."

"So she deserves to marry a very special man," Jill filled in, and cast a meaningful glance at Laura.

Laura smiled joylessly at everyone. Her prospects on the marriage market looked bleak, but she would not bring that up and have everyone speculate about her future.

All she wanted to do was to forget about her future.

Ten

Laura kept training the colt at Hanfield Farms and it responded beautifully to her ministrations. Strider Hunt still worked with some of the other horses. He was overseeing the acclimatization of the horses he'd brought from abroad. Abdullah followed him like a shadow, and sometimes the Arab's sharp eyes made her uncomfortable. He saw and knew too much. She suspected he knew about the confrontation she'd had with Strider before she asked him to leave the Keep.

She was surprised that Strider moved as well as he did. His limp had not improved much, but he moved without stopping, and she wondered if he was fatigued. He had to be, if his pallor was any indication. He avoided her at all costs, and she him, but one morning after she'd worked with the colt, she crossed his path on the way to the main house.

"I take it you're following me," she said tartly.

"You take it wrong. *You* were following me."

"Of all the nerve!"

"I never asked that you would encroach on my territory. You threw me out of the Keep, so please don't rub salt in the wounds with your presence."

"You can just ignore me," she replied. "I'm doing a favor for Squire Hanfield, and the fact that you're still here is not my fault."

"It's not that easy to ignore you when you're flaunting yourself in front of all the men."

Anger boiled within her and she gave him a withering stare. "What infernal cheek! I don't know how you came up with such a totty-headed notion. I don't *flaunt* myself. You can ask the others and they'll laugh at you. You're overreacting as usual. The local men know me as the horse doctor. There's nothing else going on. So if you think I'm not behaving in a ladylike fashion, I think you should stop taking notice of me."

He looked hot and utterly frustrated. His arms looked strong below the rolled-up sleeves, and the bandage on his wound looked old, as if no one had cared to change it since she last did. "It's not easy, Laura, when you're right in my vision every time I turn around."

"I didn't plan it that way, so don't lay the blame at my feet. Besides, I have done or said nothing to provoke your ire."

"Until now you haven't," he said, "but everything you're saying is bringing out my wrath."

"*You* began this conversation, and I'm quite tired of it."

She tried to move around him on the path, but he gripped her arm and pulled her close to his chest. His male proximity made her senses swim and her knees turn soft. Why did he always have this kind of effect on her? He smelled of horses and that elusive male fragrance that was his alone.

When he kissed her hard, she wanted to kick out, but instead, her arms wrapped around his neck in the most intimate fashion and she pressed herself wantonly against him. This was so wrong, but so right at the same time. If she thought about it, she would drown in confusion, not to mention mortification.

He struggled to stay upright and hold them both straight, and Laura sensed that his wounds still ached abominably. Her passionate response to his kiss shook her deeply. When they parted, her heart pounding, they stared deeply into each other's eyes.

"Why?" she whispered, more distraught than she could ever remember.

His breath fanned her face, and he was still breathing rapidly. She could see his heart racing under his shirt. "I can't seem to help myself, but this is lunacy. I'll have to leave the area or lose my mind." He raked his hand through his hair.

She nodded. "Yes." Stepping back, she glanced at the bandage that looked soiled and useless. "How are your wounds?"

"I manage." His voice was curt and labored at the same time.

"You don't." She pulled up his sleeve to reveal the rest of the bandage. "No one has changed this for days."

He only made a grimace.

She took his elbow and forced him back up the path toward the main house. "I'll see to it that it gets changed before I leave here."

He began to protest, but she interrupted him. "Do as I say, or you might still lose your arm."

"As if you cared."

"I don't, but I would be lax in my duties if I didn't bring healing to where it's needed. However much I dislike you, I have to assist you. I have to finish what I started or the care was all for naught."

"Believe me, I am grateful for all you did for me, but there's no reason to continue in this fashion. My wounds will heal at their own pace."

She didn't reply and forced him up the path and into the kitchen where a cauldron of hot water always simmered on the hob. The servants gave them curious stares and halted their chores to watch.

Under loud protests from him, she pushed him down on a chair. He obeyed, but his eyes were dark with rebellion. Perspiration broke out on his forehead. He jerked away his arm when she gripped it to take a closer look.

The kitchen maids scurried away as he swore royally under his breath. Fortunately the imperious cook was snoring in her chair in front of the larder or she might have ordered them out of the kitchen in an effort to protect the young maids' tender ears.

"Leave me alone," he muttered, but she pushed up his sleeve all the way to his shoulder and secured it with a pin from her hair. She noticed the fine material and wondered why he would wear such a good shirt to train horses.

The wound looked mostly healed, but still red and puffy around the edges. She brought a bowl of steaming water from the fire and found a clean towel, which she dipped in the water. While it was still very hot, she folded the towel gingerly, trying not to burn herself.

Under his loud protests, she placed the cooling towel over his wound. It was hot enough to draw more blood to the area of his wound, but not to burn him. His face pale, he glared at her. She pinned him with an imperious glance. "Do as I say, and your arm will be better shortly. Don't you dare move! I'll fetch some plantain from the yard and rewrap your wounds. It looks as if there's still poison under the scab."

"Don't bother yourself with this. I think you're only trying to torment me."

"As I said, I like to finish what I start, and—"

"Stop aggravating me with your virtuousness," he cried, and ripped the towel off his arm. The scab came with it and the wound started bleeding, washing out some of the infection.

Angry beyond words, she pushed him back down on the chair and pressed the towel against the wound to stem the flow. "See what you've done," she said.

"What I've done?" His face filled with outrage. "I was minding my own business in the stable yard and you forced me in here."

A booming voice startled them both. The cook had awakened with the sound of their raised voices and she stood, her arms akimbo and her gray hair sticking out from under her mobcap. "What's going on in *my* kitchen?"

"I'm trying to cleanse this man's wound," Laura explained, "but he's not very cooperative."

"In *my* kitchen?" The cook sounded outraged.

"Yes, in this very room," Laura shouted. "I'm certain Squire Hanfield would not disapprove. In fact, he sets great store on this pitiful man, so I'm doing the squire a service."

"That's a plumper if I ever heard one," Strider Hunt said.

Laura glared at him. "If you don't stop berating me, we'll never get this business taken care of."

The cook stood over them, an imposing presence filled with wrath. "See to it that you do, and quick-like. Or I'll come after you with my rolling pin."

Laura pointed an accusing finger at him. "Hold him down, if need be. I'm going to gather plantain for the wound. Won't take but a minute. Once his wounds are rewrapped, you'll see neither one of us again."

"Hrmph," the cook said, her eyes still bulging with accusation. But she stood over Strider like an avenging angel, and Laura sensed that the older woman had sided with her. Still boiling with wrath, Laura marched outside and gathered a handful of the dark green leaves.

It seemed only moments that she'd been gone, but Strider looked murderous, and she wondered what the cook had said to him. The servant's expression was mutinous and her face red, so Laura deduced the conversation had not been a friendly one.

Laura belatedly remembered the cook's name. This was the woman who had forgotten to put sugar into the currant cake. "Mrs. King, thank you for your help. I daresay we'll manage from now."

"Miss Endicott, it's getting near to dinnertime and I don't tolerate anyone in my kitchen when I create. *No one!*"

Laura nodded. "I understand." She turned to the uncooperative man sitting on the stool by the fire, the towel clamped to his wound. He looked stiff with pain.

"You made things worse," he said, his eyes threatening her with repercussion if she bungled her mission.

"I realize you're in pain, but once this is cleared, you should be feeling immensely better." Without ado, she pulled the towel from his rigid hand, and found that the blood flow had stopped. He grumbled as she mopped up the last and cut the stitches out with a knife, and then put the herb on the wound. Mrs. King provided a roll of bandages, and before long Laura had wrapped his arm.

"How's the muscle?" she asked more kindly after finishing her work.

"'Pon rep, don't mention it."

"And now we're going to change the leg wound," she said matter-of-factly.

"No, we are not!"

"Not in my kitchen, you won't," Mrs. King said,

her double chin wobbling and her eyes bulging with outrage. "I won't have my maids exposed to such indecency." The maids had reappeared, and she shooed them toward the door. "Miss Endicott, I'm appalled at your ill-mannered suggestion. You should be ashamed for yourself."

Annoyed, Laura turned to the servant. "There's nothing indecent about offering assistance when someone is injured."

The older woman pinched her lips and narrowed her gaze. "He said he didn't need assistance."

Strider Hunt started laughing.

"He's delirious," Laura said. "Don't listen to him. The poison in the wounds has gone to his feeble brain."

"Be that as it may, not in my kitchen. Shoo, I don't want to hear any details about your 'exploration' into the medical field, Miss Endicott. 'Tis clear you're not being guided correctly. Your poor mother should be alive. If she were, she would be appalled at your current position, and for all I know, she's turning in her grave even as we speak."

There was nothing that Laura could say to that diatribe. Her cheeks grew hot and she was acutely aware of Strider Hunt's I-told-you-so expression. She wanted to wipe the mockery from his face.

She clamped her hand around his wounded arm. "Come along, we're going back to the stables."

"Dear God," the cook breathed, her eyes bulging even farther. She fanned herself as if the kitchen had turned too hot.

He swore under his breath as Laura pulled him with her out the door.

"What a harridan," Laura said, still angry.

"She has a point. 'Tis unladylike to suggest a tryst in the stables." He pulled himself free, wincing.

"*Tryst?* Of all the silly notions. How could you even suggest such a thing? You know me better than that."

He laughed hollowly. "I'm like putty in your hands."

She pinched his wounded arm, and he cried out. "Laura, your cruelty amazes me."

"I can do something much worse," she threatened, and shoved him into the empty stable. The words echoed in the vast building and the air smelled of dust and hay. "Sit down." She pushed him onto a mound of straw on the floor.

He protested. "I'm not going to pull down my buckskins so that you can stare at my thigh."

"Then I shall cut off the leg."

"No, you will not."

She could see that he would not budge. She sighed.

"By Jupiter, believe me, woman! I'm perfectly well. My wounds are healing nicely, and my muscles are slowly repairing themselves, and all this without your meddling. I allowed you access to my arm—"

"And it needed care badly. I know your leg will need the same treatment."

"I assure you, Laura. If I find the wound festering, I shall take care of it. I'm not quite ready to leave the earth. Common sense says I would care for my body."

"If your arm is any indication, you're not doing a thorough job. But I wash my hands of you. I'll not *beg* you to comply. At least I know I did my best to help you. My conscience is clear."

"The whole world will know about your faux pas in the kitchen. I dare surmise that Mrs. King is not the closemouthed kind."

"Keep your assumption to yourself. I don't need you to remind me about gossip, but as I said, my conscience is clear. I'm not afraid of what people say about me." Still, inside she felt exposed and unsupported. Dratted man! Why would he have to remind her of, or even rub in, her potentially scandalous position. "Besides, if you felt any kind of chivalry, you would do something to protect me."

"Too late now," he said—gleefully, she thought.

"You don't have to sound so happy," she grumbled.

He threw his head back and laughed.

Ungrateful yokel, she thought. "Good-bye, and may I never see you again," she said. "I don't care a fig for your infirmities, and may a horse step on your toes."

"By Jove, how unkind of you."

"Do not speak. If you have more insults to throw at me, spare your breath. You have annoyed me enough for a lifetime."

His laughter echoed behind her, and she wished she'd never set eyes on him. What had she ever done to deserve this kind of treatment? Suddenly a longing for Julian came over her. At least he had the courtesy of a gentleman.

Eleven

Julian Temple might have been surprised to experience Laura's new warmth toward him, but he never doubted his attraction. She had always followed him around like a pet, and nothing had really changed, even if she'd reached womanhood quite some time ago. She was still the affectionate puppy, but now she had allure she'd never had before. He'd been waiting to make his proposal, but something always stopped him as he was about to pop the question.

One of the reasons was the fact that he liked his freedom. Another was Maureen, Lady Penholly. She had female allure, and she kept him very satisfied without the responsibility of marriage. A mature woman knew what she wanted, whereas a young bride would be a lot of work to break in, just like a yearling. He wasn't exactly looking forward to it, even if Laura was a sweet thing.

But he had to think about setting up his nursery, and Laura would be a good mother.

The name of Temple and the Sandhurst title should go on to his offspring, and it didn't hurt that Laura had a comfortable fortune behind her, not to mention the land between their estates. He had the responsibility to increase the value of the estate for coming generations. He wouldn't mind being remembered as the wise and circumspect patriarch of this century. Many had gone before him at Sandhurst, but he wanted to be remembered as someone who made a greater impact on the family name than those before. It was important, more important than anything, because he'd not come into his title lightly. Lots of responsibility sat on the shoulders of a viscount.

He rode up the winding road to Endicott Keep thinking that today would be as good a day as any to propose.

Laura would be ecstatic. Of that he had no doubt. His mother would've approved of her. Not that he'd ever cared about his mother's opinions, but in this it was important.

Laura was not in the Keep. Brumley informed him that he had to look for his future wife in the stables, and Julian resigned himself with a deep sigh. Perhaps Laura wasn't the perfect choice. She had some quirks that were very unladylike, and she always seemed to go her own way, however sweetly. This obsession with animals would have to stop the minute she was promised to him.

She would have to live up to the pride of the Sandhurst name. She certainly did not live up to her own illustrious heritage. If she took any pride in the Endicott name, she should live like a great lady, not like a stable hand.

He steered his steps toward the stables and found Laura throwing sticks for the pleasure of her fat puppies. Those old stable hands of hers, Jethro and Ollie, stood leaning their elbows on the paddock fence and cheering her on, great pleasure on their faces. When they saw him, one of them—he couldn't for the world remember if it was Jethro or Ollie—sprayed a stream of tobacco onto the ground, and they both barely touched their greasy forelocks. The insolence of the cretins!

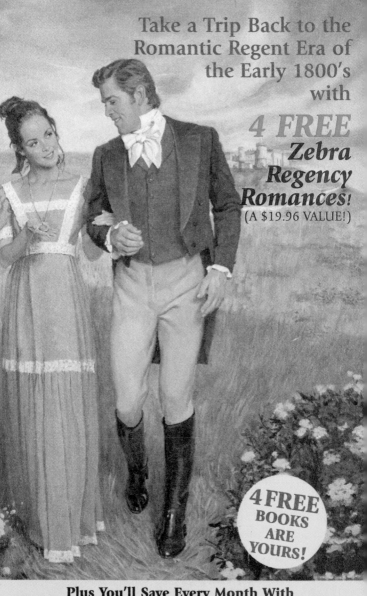

We'd Like to Invite You to Subscribe to Zebra's Regency Romance Book Club and Send You 4 Free Books as Your Introduction! (Worth $19.96!)

If you're a Regency lover, imagine the joy of getting 4 FREE Zebra Regency Romances and then the chance to have these lovely stories delivered to your home each month at the lowest price available! Well, that's our offer to you and here's how you benefit by becoming a Regency Romance subscriber:

- *4 FREE Introductory Regency Romances are delivered to your doorstep (you only pay for shipping & handling)*
- *4 BRAND NEW Regencies are then delivered each month (usually before they're available in bookstores)*
- *Subscribers save almost $4.00 off the cover price every month*
- *You also receive a FREE monthly newsletter, which features author profiles, discounts, subscriber benefits, book previews and more*
- *There's no risks or obligations…in other words, you can cancel whenever you wish with no questions asked*

Join the thousands of readers who enjoy the savings and convenience offered to Regency Romance subscribers. After your initial introductory shipment, you'll receive 4 brand-new Zebra Regency Romances each month to examine for 10 days. Then, if you decide to keep the books, you pay the preferred subscriber's price, plus shipping and handling.

It's a no-lose proposition, so return the FREE BOOK CERTIFICATE today!

A $19.96 value – FREE! No obligation to buy anything – ever.
4 FREE BOOKS are waiting for you! Just mail in the certificate below!

Say Yes to 4 Free Books!

Complete and return the order card to receive your FREE books, a $19.96 value!

FREE BOOK CERTIFICATE

YES! Please rush me 4 FREE Zebra Regency Romances (I only pay $1.99 for shipping and handling).I understand that each month thereafter I will be able to preview 4 brand-new Regency Romances FREE for 10 days. Then, if I should decide to keep them, I will pay the money-saving preferred subscriber's price for all 4... (that's a savings of 20% off the retail price), plus shipping and handling. I may return any shipment within 10 days and owe nothing, and I may cancel this subscription at any time.

Name_____

Address_____ Apt._____

City_____ State_____ Zip_____

Telephone (___)_____

Signature_____

(If under 18, parent or guardian must sign)

Offer limited to one per household and not to current subscribers. Terms,
offer and prices subject to change. Orders subject to acceptance by
Regency Romance Book Club. Offer Valid in the U.S. only.

RN083A

REGENCY ROMANCE BOOK CLUB
Zebra Home Subscription Service, Inc.
P.O. Box 5214
Clifton NJ 07015-5214

PLACE
STAMP
HERE

"Good morning, my fair," he greeted Laura, and smiled. Silently he deplored her careless dress, a dusty old thing of faded muslin, and her slippers were nothing but tatters. Such a disgrace.

"Julian! You've come back from Plymouth," she greeted him, her face breaking into a wide smile.

He noted that her eyes were swollen and red-rimmed, as if she'd been crying. He wondered if she'd been crying for him. Bending over her dusty hand to give her a kiss, he glanced at her expression from the corner of his eye. She didn't exactly look overjoyed, but he could read relief on her face.

"Have you been lonely, my sweet?"

"Er . . . yes, of course. I missed you, but Jill is still here."

"Hmm, she's newly wed and doesn't miss her husband?"

"Of course she misses him, but she's been visiting me. She's my best friend."

"I know." He looked around. Those deuced servants were hanging on their every word. "Let's return to the Keep. I'd like some tea, and it's about time we had a good talk."

He watched her as they walked back to the Keep. She appeared to droop, no doubt about it. Something had happened since he left the area, and he would find out what it was. He didn't like Laura to suffer. In a sense he felt responsible for her, even if he didn't have any warmer feelings for her.

"What has occurred since I left?" He watched her closely.

"Nothing much," she said evasively. "One of the mares foaled—another mare, a real beauty. I predict she'll have the height and the lines for successful future breeding."

"All you ever talk about is four-legged prospects.

You should've been a man and a horse breeder, but in someone so tender as you, it's strange to hear you talk with authority about subjects that are primarily of the male domain."

"Females who tie themselves entirely to raising children and embroidering cushions lose out on many interesting areas. I like to be well-rounded in my education. Besides, I never liked embroidering or watercolors."

"Interests can be developed," he said, annoyed that she had to be so different—and clearly proud about it. Once he'd married her, the music would be different, he vowed.

"Only if there's some modicum of talent," she said. "I've never gotten along with embroidery floss. As soon as it sees me coming, it arranges itself into a snarl of threads that no one can untangle except Aunt Penny."

"Ah. Where is Aunt Penny? She keeps too lax an eye upon you."

"Nonsense. She trusts me implicitly."

"In other words, you do whatever you want to do, whether it's suitable for an unwed lady or not."

She laughed. "You sound more like a disapproving uncle than a daring young man." She gave him a long stare. "You surprise me. You've never censored me before, and I find it uncomfortable."

A flare of anger kindled within him, but he did not continue to berate her. She would soon find out that he would never condone faded dresses and long sojourns with the animals in the stables. She was also much too familiar with her servants. They should be kept in their places at all costs.

"How was Plymouth?" she asked when he didn't reply.

"Noisy and windy. No one of importance spends the

summer in town, so I was eager to return here. But there were some facts I had to find out, business that couldn't wait."

She smiled at him. "I'm glad you're back, Julian."

Her words pleased him, but he wondered if she would be the clinging sort once they were married, and how she would take to London. He would spend a great deal of time there in the future, and as his wife, she would have to become the perfect hostess. He had his misgivings. She might be like a tender flower; once transplanted, she would wilt, or even die. "Tell me, Laura, how would you like to spend some time in London?"

She pondered in silence. "It would be exciting, but I would always long for the open vistas of the sea and the moor. I was never one for noise and crowds."

"No, I can see that."

Uneasy silence fell between them and they stepped into the cool, dim interior of the Keep. Brumley greeted them at the door.

"I took it upon myself to send for a tea tray. It's waiting for you in the front parlor, miss."

"Thank you, Brumley." She led the way to the front parlor and sank down on the sofa. A vase of red roses that she'd cut earlier in the morning glowed on the table in the middle of the room.

She served the tea and handed Julian a cup. A fragrant wisp of steam curled out of the yellow liquid. "I daresay you don't approve. Aunt Penny should be chaperoning me right now," she said dryly.

"It annoys me when you needle me," he replied. "Aunt Penny should, in fact, be here, and I don't support her slipshod ways. She takes her duties much too lightly."

"When did you become stuffy? Did something happen on the way to Plymouth?" she asked.

"I need everything to be aboveboard with my future wife," he said.

The cup rattled as she set it down. "Future wife? What do you mean?"

"You heard me. I think it's time we join forces. You'll become my wife and move into Sandhurst."

He waited for her reply, wondering what level of elation his words had induced in her.

Her jaw dropped and a keen sense of disappointment spread on her face. "Is that all you have to say, Julian?"

He wondered why she had turned so pale, and why she had a horrified expression on her face. "Did I say something . . . ?"

"No, you didn't say 'anything' at all," she replied, her voice trembling.

He frowned. "I believe I just proposed. If I were you, I would be flattered. After all, I'm not a bad catch, and I think we've had an unspoken agreement for some time now. We know each other's quirks. You will, of course, have to shed some of your more hoydenish tendencies, but with my guidance all should go smoothly."

"Hoydenish tendencies?" she repeated, sounding completely at sea.

He nodded. "What do you say? Yes is a good word, I believe."

"Stop patronizing me," she shouted and stood up, her face filled with wrath. "Of all the arrogant—am I really hearing right?"

"Yes, I am proposing—at last. Just say 'yes' and get it over with."

Her face now turned red with fury. "I have no intention of accepting your proposal. Once I thought you would come forth to court me as you led me to believe with your sporadic attention, but I now know that you don't love me."

"Love you? Marriage has nothing to do with love. You're fortunate if you can find love at all in a society like ours. We make do and live an upstanding life."

"I shan't marry you or anyone else if love is not the reason for the union. All such a step would cause is heartache and a bitter, empty life."

He set down his cup. "You have to think about your name and your heritage. That should be your first concern, not some romantic notion of everlasting love."

"I do care about my name, but I doubt I would cause any harm to my heritage by marrying for love. At least the offspring would be raised in happy surroundings."

"You're speaking like an utter fool." He loomed over her. "I suggest you think this over very carefully, and when I return tomorrow or the next day, I don't want to hear any nonsense. I expect you to come to your senses."

He noticed that she was close to crying, and he didn't want to deal with a flood of female tears. The situation aggravated him. How typical of her, or any female, resorting to tears because she didn't get what she wanted. He wouldn't give her any promise of undying love. That would have to be earned.

"I'm leaving now," he said as her eyes flooded. He didn't even peck her cheek in his hurry to avoid the emotional display. Once outside, he drew a sigh of relief.

Laura sank down on the sofa and cried. She'd never felt lonelier, and she swore she would never speak to another gentleman. All they did was hurt her feelings. She'd never dreamed that Julian would be so callous. He'd always been charming and kind, and now that he was planning to take the step she'd dreamed of, he was showing the side of a crusty old curmudgeon.

"I can't stand it!" she shouted between teary hiccups.

The door opened and Jill came inside. "Stand what? I heard voices in the foyer and saw Julian leave posthaste." She sat down beside Laura and pulled her close. "Did he make you cry? Where's Aunt Penny?" She handed her friend a handkerchief, and Laura mopped her cheeks.

"He's just another wretch. I've had enough of thick-headed, pompous fools."

"I can agree with you easily, but I don't know any details." Jill swept back a tear-drenched curl hanging in front of Laura's face. "What happened?"

"Julian finally proposed."

"And you're drowning in tears? That doesn't make sense."

"Not even once did he mention the word love when he proposed. He was matter-of-fact, as if making a transaction with his lawyer. I have never been so mortified. He talked about the union of our lands." She flung out her arm in a gesture of outrage. "Then he had the temerity to find all kinds of faults with my character and my dress."

Jill could not help but giggle. "How very typical. They tend to become very stuffy about their future wives. There can't be any hint of frivolity. Did you accept his proposal?"

Laura looked at her aghast. "Do you have windmills in your head?"

"I thought I'd ask."

"Of course I *didn't*. I told him I won't marry but for love, and he demanded that I think things over and have an appropriate answer for him when he returns. He fled when he saw my tears coming."

"They don't know how to deal with female emotions."

"Be that as it may, I won't marry him. I'm excessively disappointed in him." She shrunk back against the pillows. "I thought he would be different."

"I remember distinctly that you said you never knew what was going on in Julian's mind."

"You're right, but I have known him for a long time."

"He's very good at hiding his true character, and I daresay that if you marry him, you won't be any closer to knowing him."

Laura stared closely at her friend. Her eyes ached and burned. "You're very perceptive. I suspected the same thing myself."

"You need someone who treats you with respect and lets you be who you are. We might not have power over the estates, but at least you should marry a man who appreciates who you are."

Laura nodded. "You're right. Where do I find someone like that?"

"When fate conspires to help you."

"That could take forever. As you know, fate is very fickle."

Jill laughed. "But look at me! I was considered a witch, a veritable freak, but I found the man of my dreams."

"First of all, Richard is a fair gentleman. He would never treat you condescendingly."

Jill said, "Thank God for that!"

They pondered the idea in silence. Laura sighed. "I'm so disappointed. All my life I looked up to Julian and thought he was like the knights of old who rode in on white horses and wore shining armor."

Laughing, Jill threw herself back against the fringed pillows on the sofa. "You're so exquisite."

"That's what they called the fops in the last century."

Jill burst into another blast of mirth. "Your viewpoint is always refreshing, and I know I'm not the only one who thinks that."

"Mayhap Richard has a soft spot for me, but he would be the only one besides the servants."

"Richard is very protective. He would be outraged to hear how callously Julian treated you."

"If you recall, Richard proposed to me by mail, Jill."

Jill grimaced. "I admit it was senseless, but he was only confirming what his father and yours had already settled. Everyone knew it would not be a love match."

"Do you see?" Laura held out her hands as if to prove her point. "No one seems to think that I need to be loved and proposed to in a proper manner. Is it my manner of dress? Is it my strange interests? Is it my gullibility?"

Jill shook her head vehemently. "Anyone who rides roughshod over your gentle sensibilities is a cad of the worst kind. There's nothing wrong with you. In fact, if one of the gentlemen had any sense, they'd see they would be marrying an angel."

"That's doing it a bit too brown, Jill."

Jill shook her head. "Not at all! You're the kindest person I've ever met, and I know I've said that before. You just have to be reminded."

"Perhaps I should put an announcement in the paper. 'Young gentlewoman with quirky interests seeks husband of similar character. Many four-footed friends attached.'"

Jill laughed harder. "I can see the picture now. All your puppies holding on to your gown with their teeth, and kittens climbing up your sashes, Hector the horse chewing on your straw hat."

Laura giggled at that. "You paint the perfect picture. Maybe I should put 'eccentric young gentlewoman.'"

"I would put 'accomplished young gentlewoman, lover of animals' instead."

Laura pondered that and thought it might be a good idea. "I wonder what kind of response I would get."

"No doubt fortune hunters, mushrooms, impoverished younger sons, and opportunists of every kind will respond. The word 'gentlewoman' will draw those types. What we need to do is to present you in London, or at least have a ball in your honor at Eversley. Richard would be pleased to help, and he knows any number of unattached gentlemen."

"I'm tempted, but I don't want to appear desperate."

"I don't know why we've come to this, but Julian's behavior was deplorable."

"We should send him an award for the most churlish behavior of any gentleman stepping forward with a proposal."

"Yes!" Jill said and clapped her hands together in delight. "We can at least spread the rumor."

"No, I don't like to gossip."

"You're right, but it's tempting. I'm sure *he* wouldn't hesitate if the shoe was on the other foot."

Laura heaved a sigh of exhaustion. Her tears had dried up, but the blow of disappointment sat like a weight on her chest. Julian had disillusioned her more than anyone, and from Strider Hunt's deception to Julian's callous behavior, the blows had opened her eyes to the coldness of reality. Romantic notions were the invention of females longing for love, nothing else.

Until all of this happened, she'd lived a life of contentment.

They chatted for another hour, but could not come up with any solutions to wipe away what had occurred. To their surprise, Julian came back to the Keep and stormed into the parlor just as they finished the rest of the cooling tea and cakes.

He didn't even wait for Brumley to announce him.

"What in the world . . . ?" Jill began.

He stood over Laura, who sat on the sofa, and glared at her, red creeping up his skin above the collar. "No sooner do I reach home than I'm assaulted with the foul rumors flying across the county like a plague."

Laura dropped her jaw, and Jill stiffened. "Rumors?" Laura asked, her voice weak.

"About you and that horse trainer who's staying with Squire Hanfield. The rumor is that you were seen kissing him in broad view of every servant on the estate, and that he took off his shirt so that you could see to a wound."

"He did not take off his shirt!" she cried. "I rolled up his sleeve. And he kissed me."

"Same damage," he shouted. "And I heard you wrapped your arms wantonly around him. How could you be so ignorant? Don't you remember anything your mother taught you, however feeble she was? It's simply the outside of enough."

"You would believe gossip before you hear my side of the story?" Laura's face felt tight and hot with anger, and she rose in front of him, not backing off when he took a menacing step forward.

"Just the fact that you would consider touching a stranger wearing only a shirt, let alone kiss him with wanton abandonment in front of everyone, appalls me."

"Wanton—? Of all that is cruel, it seems that everything I do appalls you. I'm tired of your censures, and nothing happened that deserves such a show of anger."

"I'm sure Laura is right," Jill said, her voice edgy. "You have no right to barge in here with accusations,

Julian. I'm surprised you would not show more circumspection. And why would you be angry with Laura without really knowing what happened?"

"Any future wife of mine has to have a spotless reputation." His eyes flashed with wounded pride.

"That wife is certainly not going to be me," Laura shouted. "Not only do I reject your cold, businesslike proposal, but I refuse to take any kind of blame for wild rumors going around the area. You should know better than to listen to them."

"I shall write your cousin in the Colonies. It's about time he comes back and takes the reins of the estate and plants some sense into you. You need a firm male hand to tame your wild and unreasonable behavior."

"I've never—" Jill began.

"Of all the senseless expressions, this takes the cake, Julian," Laura filled in. "I thought you were a generous, open-minded, tolerant kind of man who would not try to change me, but I see that you're just as oppressive as the worst stickler for propriety. I won't have you dictate my life, nor will I continue our friendship if all you want is to berate me and control me." She took a deep breath. "You've shown me a side I don't like, and I won't become your chattel."

His face took on a thunderous expression, and he placed his hands on his hips. "I should take it as a blessing to be released from my duty, but I'm the only one you have to protect you."

"Oh, pooh!"

"You're going down a dangerous road if you invite strange men to kiss you in broad daylight and in front of the whole world. Who knows what you might be inclined to do in the dark, in secret."

Laura's eyes flashed. She'd never been so angry, and she yearned to slap his righteous face, but stopped herself at the last moment. Violence would not serve, and she would not stoop to his level. "You'll never know, will you, Julian?"

"Brava," Jill said and clapped her hands.

Julian looked as if he would take a step to strangle Jill. "Stay out of this."

"I, for one, am Laura's true friend, and I'll stand by her, no matter what. She is the kindest, most honorable woman I know, so how you can march in here full of vile accusations is beyond me."

He opened and closed his mouth like a fish, but no words came out. His rage was such that nothing they could say or do would change his disposition.

"I suggest you leave, Julian," Laura said. "And don't come back until you're ready to apologize for your behavior today."

"Behavior? You're the one who should apologize for *your* behavior in public. By association, I'm tainted."

Jill laughed, and Laura joined in, however shrilly.

"Then I'm surprised you're standing here this moment," she said when she could find her voice.

"Someone has to talk some sense into you." He stalked to the door. "But I see now it was a futile effort." His eyes shot daggers. "Good-bye!"

They didn't reply, and when he left, Laura found that her whole body was trembling. "How could he?" she asked herself as she sat down on the sofa. Her legs could no longer hold her up.

"Because he takes his 'ownership' seriously." Jill sat next to Laura and took her hand. "Don't take on so. He's not worth any remorse."

Laura fought the bout of tears threatening to erupt. Jill was right. Julian was not worth an ounce of distress. "I like peace and harmony. Arguments upset me."

"He's a pompous fool. Tell me, what is the rumor?"

"Julian was right. I went to Squire Hanfield's to work on a horse that is very nervous."

"Yes, you told me about that."

"But I didn't tell you that Strider Hunt has been staying there with his foreign partner. I've tried to stay away from him while over there, but I noticed that his arm wound needed rebandaging. I suggested I'd help him, and he kissed me right there on the path to the main house. He made things difficult for me as I tried to help him, and Mrs. King, the Hanfields' cook, overheard every word, and she was outraged. There's no doubt in my mind that she started the rumor. The only thing that anyone can object to was the kiss, and she did not see that, but she must've heard about it."

"A heap of excitement in a small world," Jill said with a sigh. "My only concern is that you kissed Mr. Hunt. The last I know, you were extremely angry at him."

"I still am," Laura cried.

"But you kissed him, and we don't know any more about him than we did previously."

"I know," Laura replied, filling with frustration. "But you have to understand, *he* kissed *me*, not the other way around."

"Still, your reputation is in shreds, Laura."

"I don't care," she said, feeling miserable inside. Why had she let Strider Hunt anywhere near her? She knew he had no scruples, and she understood about keeping a pure reputation.

"If Strider Hunt were a gentleman, which he isn't, he should offer for your hand after compromising you in such a fashion," Jill said.

"We all know he has no intention of doing that. He's a scoundrel of the worst kind, and even if he were the Prince Regent himself, I would not accept his offer."

"He knew he compromised you, and that really bothers me," Jill said, more to herself than to Laura.

"Don't expect any remorse there," Jill said.

"You're right on that score."

Exhausted, Laura dried her eyes and leaned back against the pillows. What a mess! All she'd done was quietly attend to her business and help another human being in need. This ordeal would make her think twice before she decided to help a stranger again.

Twelve

Jill and Laura rode through the village the following day. People were whispering and pointing, but
Laura held her head high. She refused to hide away
at the Keep and lick her wounds. In her opinion, she
had done nothing. She was still Laura Endicott, and
her conscience remained pure.

At the edge of the village, they saw Tula staring at
them, three days after Julian had come to the Keep
and spewed his accusations. Instinctively, Laura reined
in her mare. "Good morning, Tula." She decided to
come right to the point. "How well do you know the
strangers with the horses? We saw you talking to the
swarthy foreigner in the woods some time ago."

Tula shook her head. "Not well. He was asking me
questions about healing potions. Must want them for
that master of his, the strange Englishman with the
limp."

"Do you know him?"

"He's familiar to me, but my lips are sealed. I shan't
be the one to dig into secrets that are very old."

Laura glanced at Jill, her curiosity tickled. "You
speak in riddles, Tula."

"I have never divulged a secret that was shared with
me," Tula said, her stance defensive. She pulled her
brown rags more closely around her and gripped her
wooden staff with gnarled fingers. Her gaze pierced

Laura's most hidden part of herself, and then Jill's. Laura moved uncomfortably in the saddle.

"I feel things are getting out of hand," Laura said to Jill, sotto voce. "Everyone is acting either secretive or angry."

"You'll be wed before the year is out," Tula said to Laura. "Julian is going to propose. I feel it in my bones, and my bones are never wrong."

"They must be," Laura replied. "Julian proposed already, and if he were the last man on earth, I would never marry him!"

"Hasty denials are childish," the old woman said, her dark gaze pinned unwaveringly on Laura. "You're going to regret your angry outpourings."

"Be that as it may," Laura said under her breath. She addressed Jill. "I'm tired of this. Let's go."

"A true gentleman is coming to your aid," the old witch threw after them.

"She has a lot of gall. I never asked for any information from her, and she keeps throwing Julian at me. He has proved to be a snake."

"Calm yourself, Laura. All this shall come to an end."

"I don't like being the talk of the area." Tears burned in Laura's eyes, but she swallowed hard to suppress her chagrin.

"At least it will make people take a stand for the truth. You know what you did, and if they judge you too harshly, they are not your friends."

Laura nodded, unable to speak.

They rode along the ridge by the sea. The breeze brought the smell of salt to Laura's nose and whipped her already tangled hair into more knots. At least her hat that had been tied under her chin held some semblance of order to her wayward tresses, but she would never look as polished as her friend. No breeze dared to whip Jill's hair into a tangle.

They rode back to the Keep, the summer sun beating down from a clear blue sky. Only a few cottony clouds marred the perfection of that crystal dome. When they rode through the sparse spinney at the edge of the property, they saw a traveling chaise at the front door.

"It's Richard!" Jill cried. She spurred on her mare, which shot forward at the unexpected command.

Laura followed, happy that another friend had come to support her. But Sir Richard Blackwood was a stickler, if a fair one, and when he discovered the truth, he might bundle Jill into the coach and drive off to Sussex to avoid any scandal. He was already inside inspecting some of the luggage the servants had left on the stone flags. His imposing presence dwarfed everything around him, and he looked handsome in a drab caped coat, buckskins, and top boots. His black wavy hair gleamed in the sunlight streaming from the open door. His handsome face and dark eyes lit up as he laid eyes on them, and Laura thought he would squeeze all life out of Jill as he hugged her. Every move showed how much he'd missed her. They kissed quickly, and then Richard came to give Laura a brotherly hug.

"Laura, you haven't changed at all. It's so good to see you."

"You don't know the half of it, Richard, but I'm delighted to see you, too." For the first time in days, Laura could relax. Richard would know how to handle Julian if he returned with hostility. Strider Hunt would never come close to her as long as Richard remained at the Keep. Laura noted her mixed emotions. Part of her so desired to see Strider Hunt again; the other side rejected him without question. He had treated her abominably.

They exchanged news as Brumley brought in tea to the front parlor. The suits of armor standing guard absorbed every word said in that room, but Laura was used to their silent presence. "Have a crumpet, Richard. The cream is fresh from this morning's milk."

He didn't have to be prodded. Richard had a hearty appetite, but then again he spent long hours riding around his estate working on improvements.

"Eversley seems empty without you, Jill," he said.

A new softness had come over his solid features since he married Jill, Laura thought. His new life suited him.

Jill murmured something that Laura couldn't hear. She wanted to leave them alone, but their presence comforted her. "I'm pleased to hear that Eversley is flourishing," Laura said to Richard, and bent off a corner of her crumpet.

"Yes, I believe the estate will prosper with all the innovations."

"I'm so glad you're here, but you might regret your decision when you hear about my latest faux pas." Without ado, Laura launched into the tale of the two men who had turned her world upside down. Richard frowned more every second, his dark eyes flashing. "I didn't mean for any of this to happen."

"You kept a strange wounded man in the Keep secretly?" He gave Jill a quizzical glance. "And you conspired?"

"Mr. Hunt was very convincing when stating that his life was in danger," Jill said, "and he always acted in a gentlemanly fashion."

Laura hadn't told anyone of the kisses that had happened in the tower room before Strider Hunt disappeared.

Richard groaned. "I leave you alone for two minutes and look what happens."

"You knew when you married me that I was far from conventional," Jill said.

"I wouldn't be surprised if you told me you *conspired* with the stranger," Richard said, but he didn't sound too vexed.

"I would never do that," Jill said, her chin jutting out. "What we need to do is to salvage Laura's reputation."

"I daresay not many outside of Cornwall know about her existence. We're far from London here, and the family didn't mix with the *haute monde.*"

"I'm ever so grateful for that," Laura said. "Even if that makes me a country yokel."

Jill and Richard laughed.

"And I don't care what they think about me around here. Life can't always remain dull. Change and upheaval happen. The reason they gossip so much is that nothing much out of the ordinary occurs. I brought them some excitement."

"That's always one way of looking at it," Richard said. "I, however, want to speak with the impudent Mr. Hunt, and I shall deal with Julian, as well. As far as I know, his intentions were pure toward you, but he hasn't said anything to me."

"Yes . . . but I'll have difficulty forgiving Julian for all the hurtful things he said to me," Laura pointed out. "He had no right to lecture me."

"He feels responsible," Richard explains. "Before you know it, your path to the altar at Julian's side will be clear. I'll take care of him."

Laura felt relieved, but Richard didn't understand that she would never marry Julian. He'd killed any feelings she might've had for him.

After an hour, Laura left the newlyweds to continue on her ride. She couldn't stay inside. Despite its enormous size, the Keep made her feel closed in today. After all that had happened, she had difficulty finding peace.

In the distance, the windows at Sandhurst glowed in the sun. The lovely old estate looked as if sunk into a deep slumber full of dreams. Birds flitted from tree to tree in the woods that separated the estates. These were her trees, her land, and she enjoyed coming here with the dogs when she had a chance. Today Leo was following her even though she'd told him to remain in the stables. He'd been out of sorts since his vigil in the tower room ended, as if someone had torn an important mission away from him.

She guided the ambling mare along the thin, winding path. Dappled green light filtered through the crowns of the trees, and the air smelled of wet earth. A squirrel stared at her from the branch of a slender oak tree.

She thought only she and the animals moved on this lazy afternoon, so she was startled when the sounds of movement came from a nearby knoll covered with brambles.

Stiffening, she called out, "Who goes there?"

Nothing.

She repeated her enquiry, and then noticed a set of blue eyes among the leaves. She would have known those eyes anywhere. Strider Hunt, or whatever his name was.

Leo bounded to his side with happy yips, and as she berated him, he ignored her.

Filled with an inexplicable desire for revenge, she stepped forward. She had not seen him since that day when he kissed her in broad daylight at the Hanfield estate.

She noticed he had a spyglass in his hand, and she turned around and looked at the Keep, finding that he could have a perfectly good view of the front entrance with the glass. "What are you doing here?" she asked, angry that he would be lurking in the bushes. Mostly she was vexed with herself for kissing him and listening to his blandishments. He was nothing more than a scoundrel.

"I'm watching birds."

"Don't think you can bamboozle me. Why are you still here?" Her ire rose with his blatant untruth. Bird-watching, indeed!

"I have unfinished business." He looked at her, not at all contrite, she thought.

"I find there's something terribly disturbing about a stranger trespassing and spying on the goings on at my home." She did not slide out of the saddle, and the mare pawed restlessly.

"Bird-watching was never a crime," he said defensively. Gone was the suave charmer she'd seen earlier. He seemed tense and distracted. *I would be, too, if I were hiding and spying in the woods.* She glanced in the opposite direction and discovered that, from his position on the knoll, he had a perfect view of the front entrance of Sandhurst, too.

"What are you really doing?" She sensed a quickening within her and a flutter of fear. This whole situation encompassed much more than she ever imagined. "Tell me the truth."

"I know you saved my life, but I can't explain the whole matter, not yet. There will come a day soon when I'll reveal the truth. I promise, you'll be relieved, and so will I." He rose from his crouching position, and she noted the twigs in his hair and the grass sticking to his buckskins. He looked gloriously male in his loose white shirt with glimpses of bronzed skin in the opening at the neck and at the wrists. His hand closed around the spyglass, and the other, around a cane. He limped forward, and she was happy to see that he walked better.

"Your leg must be healing," she said, suspecting she would never know the whole truth about his life.

"Thanks to you, my sweet. And if you care to know, my arm is much improved since that last herbal treatment. If only I could gain back all of my strength, my life would be good. I still tire easily."

She had nothing to say to that, but his closeness disturbed her. He stood at the mare's head stroking the white blaze and crooning softly in something that might have been horse language. "Don't call me 'my sweet.' I am, however, pleased to hear about your medical progress. With more training, your muscles will recover their former vigor."

He looked at her, his gaze probing the hidden depths of her being. A wave of heat came over her, then a cold chill. She could not understand why his presence had such an impact on her, and she feared the implications of their closeness.

"If you step down—"

"I have no intentions of stepping down, Mr. Hunt! Just stay away from me. It is profoundly disturbing to find you here, and my common sense says you should be reported to the authorities. "

"Don't do that."

"There's something going on that they might need to deal with."

"Absolutely not." He shifted on his feet as if impatient.

"I don't trust you anymore. I used to, but there are too many strange occurrences and unexplained events that I can no longer trust. Besides, you kissed me at the Hanfields', not caring one whit for my reputation. As things now stand, my reputation is in complete shambles, and I don't deserve that. Your behavior tells me you care more for your own gratification than for other people's comfort."

"In other words, I'm a selfish cur." He smiled and shook his head.

"That you are, and more. Dallying with unsuspecting females must be your forte, and when you're finished, you leave."

"How utterly callous."

"There must be a long trail of broken hearts behind you." She clutched the reins hard in an effort to soothe her own roiling emotions.

"Don't tell me I broke yours, because I could not live with myself if I did."

Laura gave an unladylike snort. "Of course not! I'm not a young miss just out of the schoolroom."

"No, you're a beautiful, desirable young woman who needs a family."

"That's neither here nor there. As for that, you did what you could to make sure my name was dragged through the mud in these parts. No one will want to marry me now, not if they have any pride."

"Pride be damned," he muttered. His raised his voice. "Anyone can see that you're a lady of virtue, and whoever can't see that is a nincompoop."

"Convention holds a staunch grip on people's behavior."

"It doesn't mine."

"I know that!" she cried, peeved at his blatant disregard of society's rules. "I can only surmise that you don't know about British convention, but perhaps I'm only making excuses for you."

He didn't reply, something she resented bitterly. At least he could tell her something, but then again, if he planned only to lie, he might as well keep quiet. She was very good at discerning lies, always had been.

"I have no desire to linger here," she said, and pulled at the reins.

He gripped the horse's bridle. "I know you can't

trust me, and I don't blame you, but I assure you, nothing I'm doing is aimed toward causing you any kind of pain. I deeply apologize for my misbehavior at the Hanfields', and I also regret having exposed you to my distemper. It was a singularly trying day, and with the pain in my arm, I had no patience left." He looked at her closely. "Please say that you accept my apology."

She nodded curtly. "I will have to even if every fiber of my being tells me to reject your smooth excuses."

"I think that some part of you believes in me and that I mean you no harm. I would've had ample opportunity to harm you while I rested in the tower room."

"I doubt you would've had any strength to do it. If you recall, you were very weak with a fever." She tried to swallow her disillusionment. "I resent that you would try to pull the wool over my eyes with your statements. I obviously have more sense than to believe your words."

"I would not harm you, not now, not ever."

"Spare me." She wheeled her horse around. "From now on, stay away from my land, or I shall have you arrested for trespassing. I also want you to know that Sir Richard is here to lend his assistance. You won't get past him, so don't try any kind of skullduggery at the Keep. *He* would not hesitate one moment to have you arrested. I will give you one more benefit of the doubt, but they are quickly running out. This is the last time."

He looked uncomfortable. "I . . ."

"Just leave the area. I think you've overstayed your welcome."

"It saddens me no end—"

"As I said, spare me."

His face fell, and she could see his inner struggle.

She wanted to trust him, but she couldn't, not after finding him here. What would he gain from spying on either estate? It was useless to ask any more questions.

"I wish I'd never laid eyes on you," she said. "You've caused me nothing but grief."

"I'm terribly sorry about that."

She'd heard enough. The mare was ready to move and slipped into a trot on the path. Laura could not get out of the woods fast enough. She called to Leo, who followed reluctantly.

Of all the gall, she thought. Sooner or later, someone would shoot the man—in the heart this time. She was tempted to do it herself.

"I know for sure," she said to the mare, "that there was never a question of highwaymen assaulting him. An enemy, someone ruthless enough to want to see him dead, shot him. Strider Hunt would've been dead by now if it hadn't been for the shooter's poor aim."

The mare tossed her head as if in agreement.

"One thing is for sure—if he's ever wounded again, I won't be the one to take care of him. I won't be a fool twice."

The mare must've thought it was a sound idea. She broke into a canter as they left the woods behind.

Thirteen

Jill pulled Richard aside as, through one of the windows, she saw Laura entering the stables. He hugged her close and she reveled in the feel of his strong arms around her. "I worry about Laura," she said into his shirtfront.

"I don't blame you. She's too innocent for this world."

"She would argue about that, and I believe she has a good head on her shoulders. Not much slips by her, but she tends to see only the best in people."

"Which is a credit to her."

"Anyway, I've been asking around in the village about Julian, and it turns out that he's widely disliked. It's whispered that he beats the servants, though it would never be obvious. My experience is that he's quite smooth with the staff and always pleasant in front of guests. The servants are reluctant to speak about him, fearing retribution if he finds out. But I know he broke a groom's arm for not obeying a command, and it's said he put a maid in the family way, and then dismissed her from her post. It's not honorable."

Richard leaned his chin on her head and hugged her even closer. "It's beyond ruthless. It's selfish and brutal. The girl's family won't dare to stand up to him or they'll lose their bit of land."

"I never quite liked Julian. There's something secretive about him, and it would pain me to see Laura tied to such a man."

"It won't happen. I'll see to it, my darling," Richard said with finality.

Jill closed her eyes and her body filled with relief. She'd been more worried than she thought. "I know Laura is very angry with him now, but when he puts on his full-blown charm, she will forgive and forget. That's how great her heart is."

"I know." He released her and looked into her eyes. "What I don't understand is why Julian has so few family members around him. They can't all have died."

"Yes, I believe they must have. Only his grandmother remains, and she's considered an invalid. He claims her mind is gone, but she did recognize Laura when we attended a dinner party at Sandhurst."

"Hmm. She may be able to throw some light on the past. The more ammunition we have against Julian the better. That is, if I need to threaten him to stay away from Laura. I hope it won't come to that."

"We shall contrive something. I want to meet the old woman myself. She must have been quite the lady in her heyday. Laura is very fond of her."

"Pay her a visit when Julian isn't there. You can bring a gift of food or some flowers with the intention to cheer her lonely existence."

"That sounds wonderfully dramatic, Richard. I see a picture of her yearning and longing by a garret window for the lover who disappeared sixty years ago."

Richard laughed. "I can always count on you to invent drama."

"I contrive," she said with mock pride.

At that moment Aunt Penny stepped into the room. She had just returned from visiting her sister. "Ah, there you are, my dears. Has anything happened since I left?"

Jill exchanged an amused look with Richard. "No," she said, "nothing much." *Except for Laura turning down an offer for her hand and then involving herself in scandal.*

"That's good," the older woman said, and sat down with her embroidery. "I would so hate to miss any excitement."

Julian left the area two days later. For how long, Jill could only guess, but they had to strike while the opportunity existed. "Come, Laura, let's take a ride," she said to her drooping friend. "We can stop in to visit the old Dowager Lady Sandhurst. We'll bring an apple pie or something."

Laura brightened. "Yes, why didn't I think of that myself?"

"Because you've respected Julian's desire to keep the old lady secluded. I'd wager she's lonely."

Laura didn't waste any time dressing in her riding habit, and she met Jill at the stables as the grooms saddled their mares. "I haven't seen Julian since we had that falling out."

Jill nodded. "He's not at Sandhurst this morning, so we'll be clear of him."

"He would disapprove."

"Of course he would, but he's not fair to the old lady. Surely he won't mind our showing some neighborly concern."

Laura nodded, but she doubted the truth of that. However, she was eager to see the dowager. Without Jill, she might never have thought of flying in the face of Julian's decree.

Sandhurst looked lovely as it sat like a queen in the midst of the formal gardens. The yew hedges had been clipped to precision, and roses flowered in a border along the front of the estate. The ivy climbed up the walls, as vigorous as ever. Birds sang in the trees and bees darted from flower to flower.

"How beautiful it is here," Laura said, "compared to the starkness of the Keep."

"You have flowers and hedges there, as well."

"But they are dwarfed against the giant walls. No ivy would dare to cover the gray stone there. Sandhurst is so . . . elegant, so peaceful. It's more like a home than the Keep would ever be."

"You sound as if you would like to live here."

Laura gave her friend a quick glance. "I might, but there's no chance of that. Julian lives here, and I won't share my life with him."

Jill kept silent, and they got out of their saddles by the front steps. The butler looked at them suspiciously as Laura enquired after the dowager. She pushed the basket covered with white linen forward. "We thought we might cheer her up with a freshly made apple pie."

"Miss Endicott, you more than anyone would know that the lady doesn't accept visitors."

"Come now, Henslow. We won't leave without at least saying good morning to her. We're only being neighborly."

Henslow shrugged and let them inside. They waited in the hallway while the butler sent one of the footmen upstairs with the message that the dowager had visitors. Hopefully her nurse-cum-maid would not find a reason to object. It depended on how firmly she believed in endorsing the viscount's command.

They waited for a long time, and then the maid appeared at the top of the stairs. "Miss Endicott, I'm afraid my lady is too tired to see anyone this morning. I suggest you leave. His lordship has given strict orders that her ladyship has to rest."

"I understand that, but we don't intend to tire her,"

Laura said. "We just need a moment of her time. I've missed her, and when I noticed after the dinner party that she recognized me, I wanted to reminisce with her."

The maid shook her head. "I can't go against his lordship's orders." On the tail of those words, she returned upstairs.

Laura and Jill exchanged glances. "I don't like this," Laura said. "It's as if he's keeping her a prisoner. "

"I agree," Jill said. She took Laura's hand. "Let's go. Julian is not here to throw us out, and we can always overrule the servants."

Laura followed Jill's quick step up the staircase, and they found themselves in a murky hallway. The green velvet draperies had been pulled across the window at the back, and none of the bedroom doors were open. Laura pointed to another staircase at the end of the corridor, and they hurried across the long carpet, which muffled their steps.

On the next floor they found a suite of rooms, and when they heard voices from one of them, they knew where the dowager resided.

Laura couldn't make out the words, but voices were raised, and she could hear by the dowager's tone of voice that she was complaining. As they moved closer, they listened at the door for a moment before knocking. Laura didn't want to cause any kind of embarrassment to the old lady.

"I don't want to be cooped up here all day," the dowager said, her voice thin and impatient.

"You have to follow the master's orders. He knows what is best for you," the maid said imperiously.

"He thinks he does. I need sunlight on my face and birdsong in my ears."

"She's lucid," Laura whispered to Jill.

"I'm not at all surprised," Jill said sotto voce. "I think Julian is cruel to the old lady."

"She needs distraction and exercise."

Jill nodded. "Let's go inside. If she's as coherent as we think, she'll recognize you."

They knocked softly, and without waiting for a reply, they went inside.

The maid's expression turned outraged, but the old woman stared at them and her face lit up as if given an unexpected gift. "Visitors! It's been an age since I had any visitors." Her wrinkles deepened as she broke into a great smile, and her eyes glittered with something akin to tears.

"Lady Sandhurst, I have missed your wonderful company," Laura said. "I'm Laura Endicott, and this is my friend, Lady Jillian Blackwood."

The dowager held out a paper-thin hand toward Laura. "My little friend! But you're no longer the wee girl I remember."

The maid stepped in between Laura and the dowager. "His lordship—!"

"Oh, go on with you, Allie," the dowager cried out. "Make yourself useful for once. Fetch a tea tray or something."

The maid looked as if she were about to explode with anger, but both Laura and Jill stared at her until she backed out of the room.

"She'll be back with someone who will attempt to throw you out," the old woman said, and patted the sofa beside her. "Sit here, Laura."

Laura looked around the room, which was dusty and filled with the clutter of hundreds of porcelain figurines. No one had cleaned in here for a long time, and Laura made a mental note to remind Julian. The bed hangings were old, faded, and torn in places and the rugs threadbare, as if this room was the last resort of old carpets. The old lady herself looked unkempt, her gray dress bearing food stains, and her white hair a bird's nest of tangles.

"Looks to me that Allie is not very proficient in housekeeping," Laura said aloud.

The dowager didn't seem to notice. "What is new? Is the Keep still standing?"

"Yes, of course," Laura said with a laugh.

"A lot of strange things happened there over the years. There's witchery in your bloodline, and your father came from a long line of warriors. How is he?"

"He has been gone these many years, and Mother died a couple of years ago. She slowly deteriorated and quietly faded away."

The dowager said, "She was never strong."

"But you are," Laura said, and placed her hand on the older woman's thin arm. "You don't look a day older than when I last had a chat with you. It has been a long time."

"Why?"

"I . . . we . . . no one is invited to visit with you. We only came today because Julian is away. He would stop us, you know."

The old woman nodded, pinching her lips into a thin line. "Who is Julian?"

Jill and Laura exchanged surprised glances. "Your grandson," Laura said.

The dowager's hands started fluttering nervously. She pulled at a strand of hair and fingered an old cameo on her collar. "Yes . . ." She glanced nervously toward the door. "Is he here?"

"No, he rode off on business. I'm sure he'll be back shortly," Laura replied.

The old woman shivered as if a dark cloud had covered the sun. Laura sensed that something made her uncomfortable, and Jill nodded as if reading her thoughts.

"A lot of grief has come to the Sandhurst family in this generation."

"Well, yes, his parents are gone, for one. The family is sadly depleted, as Julian does not have many relatives."

"Not much concerns him," the dowager muttered.

"I don't understand."

The dowager shrugged her thin shoulders. "He's mainly concerned about the one in the mirror."

A very roundabout way of saying someone was selfish, Laura thought. And mayhap he was. He had no one to think about except himself. The servants took care of the dowager, and he probably didn't pay her many visits. The realization made her sad, and it was another strike against Julian.

"Surely you have breakfast with him?" Jill asked, her expression filled with disgust.

"No, Julian's life is very much separate from mine. Unfortunately, many are gone. I miss Sabrina and Desdemona, and then there was Daniel, their youngest brother. He was kind to me, the only one of my nephews who cared."

"Did he pass away, too?"

The dowager seemed to think hard, as if the memories resided in a distant fog. "No. Well . . . yes, I believe he did. Ended up in a heap of trouble, which I never believed was his doing. A sweeter boy you couldn't find."

"Julian was older?"

She nodded. "Yes, the older one, but not as kind. Julian's father never got along with Daniel's even though they were brothers. Strange, isn't it? I think they hated each other. Daniel stayed with me for a time, you know.

Those were good years, and my blessed husband lived then. I miss him so."

Her voice petered off. Clearly caught up in the memories, she forgot that Laura and Jill were there. Laura patted her hand as she heard rapid footsteps in the corridor. "We'll come again soon. Now that we know you're willing to receive visitors, I for one will come often."

The dowager smiled, but she seemed lost, as if on a different plane.

"We don't want to tire her," Jill said, and stood.

Laura followed suit, and the door opened. The butler and the maid stood on the threshold, both wearing outraged expressions.

"I uphold order in this household when the master is gone," the butler said.

"Henslow, there's no harm done here," Laura said. "Only a short visit. I'm sure the viscount would not mind."

The butler took on his haughtiest expression. "I'm sorry, Miss Endicott, but I think you should leave."

Laura could tell that his demeanor was triggering Jill's temper and she took her friend's arm. "We're finished. Good-bye, my lady," she said to the dowager. She bent down briefly and kissed her on the cheek.

"Come back," the dowager said wistfully.

"You can count on it," Laura said. She pulled Jill with her, and they left the mansion.

The air outside smelled of warm roses. The sun was beating down on the red ones climbing around the front entrance, and the air hung still as if listening to a storm building in the distance. A headache had begun pounding at Laura's temples.

"I don't know why, but I have the feeling I'm one step behind on everything," she said. "It's as if there are missing pieces in my knowledge, and that Julian knows things about the past that I don't."

"I can understand your frustration."

"For one, he's never mentioned any cousin named Daniel. You would think he would've told me, even if the man were long dead. Once or twice he's mentioned Desdemona and Sabrina."

"Julian doesn't speak of many things unless prodded. He only speaks of the latest news or gossip. To give him credit, I don't know him very well, but those are the only subjects he broaches. And when we came for dinner that night and stood eye to eye with the old lady, he was not pleasant about the situation. He was close to rude with her."

"You're right. It's almost as if he were hiding something, as if it bothered him that people would know that his grandmother is quite lucid at times. I'll visit her again even if I have to tear down the servants' resistance."

"Those are quite formidable," Jill said. "Henslow is built like a professional pugilist. Perhaps Julian keeps him around to ward off enemies."

"Julian has enemies?"

"I wouldn't be surprised if he does. As I've said, there's a side to him that's not too pleasant."

Laura nodded and rubbed her temples. "It's unpleasant to discover new sides to old friends." She glanced up at the sky. "Look at those clouds gathering. We're going to have a giant storm."

They stepped into the carriage waiting by the entrance, and closed the door. Most likely they would be safely back at the Keep before the weather deteriorated.

Fourteen

Laura listened to the thunder and watched the rain beating against her bedroom windows. She had stretched out on the bed with a cold cloth on her forehead after they returned to the Keep. The first raindrops had plopped on the flagstones as they walked through the door, and the storm had increased to gale force since it began an hour ago. The wind squeezed through the cracks around the windows, making an eerie moaning sound. Laura had heard it many times before and paid little attention.

She had grown up in the last week. When beliefs were shattered and truths revealed, one was forced to look at oneself. She had blindly trusted and liked Julian, and just look at how he'd treated her! The anger welled up in her anew, but she knew she was partly at fault. She'd allowed him to carry her along with his smooth talk and promises. In truth, his character held a mean streak at its core, and it hurt to think about it.

"I'm not going to feel sorry for myself," she said out loud.

The wind moaned in response.

"And I'm going to see to it that the dowager is less isolated."

The wind agreed with a deep groan. Laura looked at the window to see if someone was actually standing there, but it was only her imagination.

It hurt to turn her head, and she felt like moaning, too, but instead she gritted her teeth. Anger seemed to be her constant companions these days. She never used to be angry. In fact, she usually woke up with a smile. Most members of her world were prone to smiles.

Gentlemen were difficult. If anything, they did everything in their power to rain on one's inner sunshine, she thought. Selfish, boorish creatures!

The rain kept coming down, the sky turning darker and darker. If only she had a good book to read to take her mind off Julian's uncouth behavior—and Mr. Hunt's devilish smile and flippancy—her afternoon would be less of an ordeal. The reprieve of sleep eluded her.

"Botheration." One of her cats kept her company on the bed, and the warm furry body felt comforting along her leg. Cats brought so much comfort without asking for much in return. In fact, they were much easier than gentlemen.

"Sara, my sweet," she said to the cat and dragged her hand along the soft yellow-striped back.

The cat lifted one green eye and gave her a quick stare, then collapsed back into oblivion. "You don't have problems with gentlemen, do you? You're always perfectly content, and don't give one iota about what the other cats are doing. Most of the time, you scorn the males of your species, and you never seem to yearn for anything."

The cat ignored her completely.

Laura sighed. "What a life."

She must've drifted off, because when she awakened evening had fallen. The storm had abated, and only the occasional drips sounded on the lead casing around the window. She stretched, and so did Sara, her set of sharp teeth on full display as she yawned.

When Laura got up and smoothed down her wrinkled skirt, the cat jumped down from the bed and arched its back. Together they left the room and went in search of something to eat. It was dinnertime; Laura's stomach was telling her as much.

When she came downstairs, she found herself alone. Jill and Richard were still in their room, she thought. Brumley told her dinner would be served in half an hour.

She went to the library to search for a book to read later. The day had turned out to be a lazy one, except for the sojourn to Sandhurst. She still burned with anger when she thought about the dowager's loneliness.

Ten minutes later Brumley announced Julian's presence, and before she could tell him that Julian wasn't welcome, the young man stepped into the library, after elbowing Brumley aside. Julian looked elegant in a black evening coat and a cream brocaded waistcoat; he was clearly about to attend a dinner party.

"What is it that I hear? You and Jill went to see my grandmother against my wishes?" His voice sounded tight with anger.

"Yes, we did," Laura replied firmly. "And I'm glad we did. Your grandmother is a delight, and I don't understand why you're hiding her away in that dusty suite of rooms. What she needs is the stimulation of good company, a chance to talk about old memories. Fresh air."

He looked pale with anger. "That's exactly what she doesn't need! She gets worked up and starts imagining things. It's very hard to calm her down, and then she always catches a cold." He took a deep breath. "I just don't understand your obsession with her."

"Obsession? That's ridiculous. Her name has not

crossed my lips in so many years except for polite enquiry, but when I saw that she recognized me at your
dinner party, I thought it would be only respectful to
pay her a visit." A sense of outrage rose within her that
he would find it unacceptable that she saw an old relative of his. He ought to be delighted that she'd made an
effort to cultivate a relationship with his grandmother.

He couldn't reply to that, and she wondered why
he had changed so much. All she could recall was his
easy banter and his brotherly treatment of her over
the years, but now he'd become pinch-faced and
prone to tempers—all in the last few weeks.

"I don't know what has gotten into you, Julian. I
don't recognize you anymore. You ought to know I
would do nothing to hurt your grandmother."

He flung out his arm in a gesture of frustration. "Of
course you wouldn't, but—"

"But what?" She stared at him hard. "Do you think
I'm meddling, or do you feel I'm putting myself forward?"

He couldn't reply to that, and at least had the decency to look guilty. "Why are you so tense, Julian?"

He flung himself onto the nearest wing chair, a
worn leather item that had been in that same spot for
as long as Laura could remember.

"Anyway, I'm not supposed to speak with you. I'm
very angry at your behavior today and previously."

"I'm having a lot of pressures," he said flatly.

"Financial?" she probed. "Have you gambled away
your estate?"

"No . . . but I'm being hounded." He leaned his
head back and closed his eyes as if to regain his equi-
librium. She wanted to remain angry with him, but
found that she couldn't maintain her resentment.

"Not moneylenders?" That picture was too harrowing
to entertain.

He shook his head. "There's just some old unfinished business dogging me, but I shall prevail. It makes me nervous, that's all." He grabbed the armrests and heaved himself upright. "I'm sorry that I berated you for visiting my grandmother. It's just that I'm protective of her and wouldn't want her to collapse with exhaustion."

"You know I would never do anything to overexcite her."

He gave a small smile. "I know that, but your presence alone is great excitement to her. We can't be too careful."

"I would like to see her again."

"I prefer that you do not." His voice took on that hard edge again.

"Very well," she said with a sigh. She dragged her hand along the dusty spines of the books. "You must miss your cousins. She mentioned Sabrina and Desdemona, who passed on in an accident, an incident I remember vaguely, and then there was someone named Daniel. I don't recall him at all, and you never mentioned him."

"Daniel?"

"Your cousin." She gave him a curious glance. Why would he sound doubtful over the name? Surely he recalled his cousin. "You can't have forgotten that you had one?"

"No . . . of course not." He sounded tense again. "It's just that I haven't thought of him for so long. It's extraordinary that Grandmother would remember him."

"What happened to him?" Out of nothing else but curiosity, Laura wanted to know the truth. It helped her create more of a picture of the Temple family.

"I don't rightly know. What I heard is that he disappeared after shooting someone. Some say it was a hunting accident. Then we received a notice and a death certificate. He evidently passed on in the Orient. A bad apple is what I heard, always into one scrape after another. A disgrace to his family."

"He would have inherited the Sandhurst title."

"A good thing he didn't!" Julian exclaimed. "He would have run the estate to the ground, and he would've ruined the family name. I didn't spend much time with him, as I'm quite a bit older. I didn't have any interest to further our acquaintance."

"You sound as if it happened decades ago, but it can't have been more than fifteen years. That's how long you've had the title."

"That's right."

"When we attended your dinner party, I noticed that you had a row with Squire Norton in the library. Is he the one hounding you? I know he's had some financial difficulties in the past."

"I don't have any business relations with the likes of him." Julian gave her a haughty stare. "What in the world made you mention him?"

"I just now recalled his ill temper and his visit to you, but that's neither here nor there."

"Squire Norton is always in high dudgeon over something."

Laura laughed at that. "There's some truth to that."

"We all have arguments at one time or another. He wants to graze his cattle on some of my land, but I said no. Truth to be told, I've never dealt well with him."

"You rarely see him at any of the local gatherings. I doubt that he ranks high in popularity with anyone around here."

Julian looked toward the door. "Where is your forceful friend?"

"You mean Jill?"

He nodded. "Yes, your guard dog."

"She's with her husband somewhere."

"You mean to say Sir Richard is back here?" He looked incredulous.

"I have no quarrel with Richard. I jilted him, remember? I still like him as a friend."

Julian's eyes turned hard again. "What is he doing here?"

"Perhaps he missed his lovely wife. After all, they have only been married for a short time." She held back that he had arrived because he thought they might need his assistance, as well. "And then there's the issue of recent sightings of highwaymen in the area. Richard wants to make sure we're all safe."

"How thoughtful of him," Julian said scathingly. "I can watch out for you just as easily."

"But you're rarely here," she pointed out.

"I shall fulfill my duty to look after you, but I doubt there's any danger of highwaymen assaulting you."

Laura refrained from reminding him about the break-in; there was no reason to get him involved in anything long since past. She also recalled her meeting with Tula, who still insisted that she would marry a man named Julian. It had to be a mistake. Tula must be getting old and forgetful.

"I'm due at Maureen's in half an hour," he said as he looked at his timepiece, hanging from a gold chain attached to his pocket. "I'm escorting her to a dinner party in Wadebridge."

Laura felt a stab of disappointment that she wasn't going, too, only because she wanted to be part of the local social life. She pushed away the thought. Nothing would change now. Everyone still considered her the odd one, the "witch" who spoke with the animals and mixed herbal concoctions. In reality, she was no different from Tula, except for the fact that she didn't throw personal predictions after unsuspecting riders on the moor. But if she lived long enough in this secluded area, who knows what she might end up doing. She laughed at her own dilemma.

Julian bent over her hand and kissed it lightly. "I'm grateful that we're speaking again," he said.

"I'm still boiling at the callous way you proposed to me, but let's just forget that it ever happened."

He smiled enigmatically. "Perhaps I'll have to take lessons."

No matter how many lessons he took, even if he approached her in a more flowery way, she would always remember his cold proposal.

Richard was coming down the stairs from the upper regions of the Keep when Julian left the library, stepping quickly over the flagstones. Richard thought the man looked pleased with himself, and he wondered what had transpired in the book room.

"Can you spare me a minute of your time, Sandhurst," he asked pleasantly, even if he didn't have any warm feelings for the man.

Julian didn't look too pleased. "Sir Richard! What a pleasant surprise, but I have a prior engagement, for which I'm late."

"I insist," Richard said at his briskest.

Julian looked annoyed, but he followed Richard into the front parlor. The rain had started up again, sending cascades against the windows. The two men faced each other in front of the fireplace, where a fire burned to keep the damp out.

"Is there anything I can do?" Julian asked.

"You can tell me what your true intentions are towards Laura. My wife's account of your proposal made me doubt the seriousness of your offer. I shan't have Laura's name dragged through the mud."

"Of course not!" Julian said, clearly annoyed. "I have no intentions of hurting Laura."

"Then how could you make her an offer she had no choice but to refuse? Ladies have tender hearts; they like a bit of romance, a stream of elegant speech, not ᴀ proposal for a dry business transaction."

Julian shifted impatiently from one foot to the other. "I have every intention of trying again, when she's forgotten about the travesty that was my proposal."

"I don't think it's a good idea," Richard said. "I doubt very much that you love her, and without that, she'll be miserable. I'm not well versed in the ways of women, but I know that much. I want the very best for Laura because she's an exceptional female."

Julian couldn't say anything that would refute that.

"Actually, I'm here to see to it that you stay away from her." Richard stared hard at the other man, challenging him to protest.

"You can't remain here forever," Julian said calmly, a gleam of triumph in his eyes. "What's between Laura and me has been there for a long time. We're comfortable with each other."

"She doesn't seem to convey that sentiment."

"That's because she's miffed with me, but it'll pass. In fact, we had a very good conversation not five minutes ago."

"She perhaps forgives too easily," Richard said. He didn't want to begin an argument that would only end up in more hostility. The peace-loving Laura would not be pleased if he did, but he yearned to plant the man a facer.

"'Struth, I have apologized for my behavior, and that should be enough."

"Devil take it, Sandhurst, just don't hurt her any more. If I hear anything, you'll feel my wrath."

Without another word, Julian turned on his heel and left the room.

Later that night, Laura pondered her conversation with Julian. Nothing had really changed, although he didn't know significant details about his family to still her curiosity. Yet there surely was no reason to know more about the mysterious cousins who had died so young. She couldn't explain her interest.

Her thoughts wandered to Mr. Hunt and a wave of anger came over her anew. He really rubbed her the wrong way, another man with a vague past. He at least was blatantly honest about the fact that he didn't want to talk about it.

She tried to explain to herself why she hadn't told Jill or anyone else that she'd encountered the scoundrel in her woods, but there was no excuse other than her own reluctance.

However, it was highly unlikely that she would see him again. From now on, she would stay away from the Hanfield property. She would hear about it when he was gone.

Fifteen

"Strider" Hunt wiped down his stallion Strider. He'd been riding hard over the moor to get some relief from the pressures of his thoughts. Today had been a catalyst of sorts. He'd cursed the moment when Laura had ridden onto the hill in the woods and spotted him the other day, yet he couldn't deny the dance of his heart in his chest at the sight of her slender form. Her hair had gleamed as if newly gilded; her cheeks had been red—probably from anger or exertion, yet possibly from excitement at seeing him.

She hadn't tried to shoot him—not that she carried a weapon, but she might have concealed one—and she hadn't raised hue and cry. Even if he'd departed shortly after she'd left his hiding place, the constables had not come searching for him at the Hanfields'. For that he was grateful to her.

He couldn't get the memory of her face out of his mind. He wanted to kiss her again. He wanted to hold her body against his and he longed to look deeply into those blue eyes of hers and drown. His breath caught in his throat even though he longed to sigh. He wanted to cry, dash it all!

"Blast and damn," he said to the horse's black, silky coat. The stallion moved sideways as if in response. He did always seem to respond to the smallest cues, and his ears pricked at the minutest of sounds.

It was about time he collected Abdullah and his horse and left the area. Abdullah was increasingly bored with the intermittent rain, so typically English, but he would have to stretch his patience a bit longer. Soon enough, he would be back in the dusty desert under the hot Arabian sun.

"I don't know if I want to go back," he said to the horse. "I've gotten a taste for my homeland, and I don't mind rain sometimes, or gray skies."

The horse gave him a look from those large brown eyes that said he must have windmills in his head.

"I know the moor is not the same as the desert, but in the long run, you might like it. You can run as fast across the moor."

The horse didn't seem convinced as he tossed his head.

"What I want is that blond Cornish goddess in my arms, nothing less, and I'm certain she would never consider moving to Arabia."

The stallion neighed in agreement.

"She does ride a decent mare—someone for you, perhaps." He curried the shining coat until it was dry.

The horse stomped his front hoof repeatedly.

"Temper never impresses the ladies."

The horse nodded, tossing his mane.

"I see that you agree. All's well, then. I shall tell Abdullah that we have come to a decision. Anyway, he scares half the population with his foreign ways. He can leave tomorrow, but we're staying—for good. What I need now is roots, perhaps to get married if the fair lady will have me, and set up my nursery."

Strider looked at him reproachfully.

"Yes, I *know*. Before long I'll have to tell her the whole truth, but I'm reluctant to confide in anyone until this whole unpleasant matter is cleared up."

He finished with the stallion and led him into his

box. The colts he'd been training were just about ready. Time was running out. He washed up and put on a clean shirt in the stable hands' washroom. His wounds, though well healed, ached. He suspected his muscles would never be right again, but he worked every day to stretch his movements, and despite the resistance and the pain, the leg and the arm obeyed him more every day. In fact, he felt damned healthy.

Restlessness gnawed at him and he decided to venture down to the village. He saddled one of the horses that had not been exercised that day and rode down to Pendenny.

The sun was slowly setting over the sea, creating a beauteous sky of red, orange, pink, and pale green. The scene was so lovely it almost caused pain in his heart. Everything about Cornwall made him feel at home, and he longed to experience as much of it as he could. He got out of the saddle and limped over to the local inn. A pint of ale would be just the thing after a long day of work.

Two farmers in brown homespun and hole-ridden caps looked him over as he stepped inside. They touched their forelocks, then went back to their pints. He smelled newly cooked shepherd's pie and turnips, and the sweetness of strawberries, as if someone was making preserves.

He knew the food was good, and decided to eat, as well. He sat at one of the rough-hewn tables. In the corner by the empty fireplace sat a sturdy older man with a long clay pipe in his mouth. Puffs of smoke rose toward the sooty ceiling at intervals, and he looked thoughtful as he stared at the floor.

Something was bothering him, no doubt about it. Just as Strider thought as much, the gentleman looked up and stared. He nodded. "Good evening."

"A good one it is, indeed. The sunset dazzled me."

"You're that Strider Hunt fellow who works with the horses at Hanfield Farms?"

"You're right, but you have the advantage of me."

"Yes, I apologize. I'm Squire Norton, from Bodmin way. I had business in the area and decided to stop here for a meal. The cook here is the very best."

Strider laughed. "So I've heard. I'm here to sample it myself."

A buxom serving girl wearing a faded yellow gown and a mobcap came to take his order, and then went back to the kitchen.

"Do you mind if I join you?" Squire Norton asked.

"No, I would enjoy your company."

The squire rose, walking stiff-legged across the uneven plank floor. "Your reputation with the horses precedes you, young man."

Strider smiled. "Thank you. Do you need any help in your stables?"

"At the moment, no. My horseflesh is docile, and most of them are rather long in the tooth, just like myself."

"I could help you find some good mounts to purchase."

The squire shook his head. "Oh, no, my finances are not such that I can spend any on horseflesh, but thank you for the offer."

Strider realized the deep creases between the man's eyes came from his worries, and if one looked closely, one could notice that the squire's coat and buckskins had seen better days. When the food arrived, he ordered a pint for his companion, and the squire lit up. "Thank you, Mr. Hunt."

"How about some food, as well?"

"I just finished my supper. That shepherd's pie is delicious."

Strider sniffed the steam of potatoes and meat

curling off the plate. "It smells very good. My stomach is growling ominously."

The squire laughed, his rotund form shaking. He had combed his gray hair into an old-fashioned queue at the back, and Strider saw that that the man had been handsome in his younger days.

"You'll be staying or leaving?" the squire asked.

"I plan to stay. This is my home, but I had forgotten all about it."

The squire's blue eyes narrowed, and he stared at Strider for a long time. "You're a young man and could not forget that fast."

"Not so young, I'm afraid."

"You look . . . um, familiar somehow, but I swear I've never seen you in these parts before. Were you ever in Bodmin?"

"Possibly a long time ago, but I don't recall." He sprinkled some salt over his food and ate with pleasure. He realized he was very hungry. The ale foamed as he tipped the wooden tankard to his lips.

"There's something about your face," the squire said, and pointed the stem of his pipe at Strider. "A family resemblance. It is as if I know you."

"No . . . I don't know."

"Don't you have family in the area? If you don't, what's the point of settling here? You want to be close to your family."

Strider nodded. "Aye, I don't have a family, but I have met a lady . . . someone who has caught my fancy more than I thought possible."

The squire's eyes grew round. "A lady? Well, well, well." He dragged hard on his pipe and took a swig of ale. "And who might she be?"

"Miss Laura Endicott."

"Miss Laura?" The squire looked uncomfortable for a moment, and his gaze raked over Strider's simple garb. "I daresay you set your sights high. Miss Laura is the sweetest imaginable, and I would marry her myself, but she's . . . er, well, highborn. I don't want to cause you any disappointment."

Strider laughed. "I can easily understand your concern, Mr. Norton."

"How do you plan to win her hand?"

"By courting her ardently."

Again dismay covered the squire's features. "I realize she has no family to protect her, but I daresay her friends will be very opposed to the match and warn you off. No insult intended, but can you afford to support such a lady? I don't want to even mention your birth, as I respect all men, be they humble or highborn."

"I don't think she cares about lineage," Strider said. "She's a very simple person despite her heritage."

"You're right on that score, but a lady is a lady, and she has certain obligations to fulfill." He pinned a sincere glance on Strider. "I have to be blunt here. She won't marry a horse trainer, no matter how humble she is."

"I see." Strider knew the man was talking common sense, but he could not get Laura's sweet face out of his mind. "My business has been very successful; I'm not lacking in funds. And my horse business abroad is doing very well."

"That does you credit, and I'm a good judge of character. I daresay you're more gentlemanly than many so-called gentlemen I know. I just had an encounter with one who calls himself a lord. He's a mean one if there ever was."

Strider nodded. "I have experience in that area, too. We deal with all kinds." He looked at the squire closely. "Is he by any chance Lord Sandhurst?"

The squire's jaw dropped. "How did you know?"

"I've seen you a number of times in the area, but never at the Hanfields', and the only nearby gentleman is Lord Sandhurst." He didn't add that he'd seen, through his spyglass, the squire storm out of Sandhurst on two occasions.

"You must be a mind reader."

"Only making accurate deductions, Mr. Norton."

"Needle-witted young man, aren't you?"

Strider laughed. He liked the squire and wished to manifest a friendship with him. He could use all the support he could get at this point, and he enjoyed talking with this man.

"Would you mind if I ask you about your problems? I might have some solutions."

"Young man, you're kind and thoughtful, but you don't know me at all." He put down his pipe and leaned his head in his hands.

"Sometimes strangers are good confidants. There's no emotional attachment."

The older man sighed deeply. He seemed to deflate more with every breath. "My estate has not supported the family—I have four daughters, you know—and my lands are barren. If it weren't for my sheep, we would not have food on our table. Two of my daughters are still at home, unable to find husbands. My oldest married clergy; my second is married to a poet, impoverished, of course." He brightened. "You're a sharp and pleasant young man, how would you like to marry my little Mary?"

Strider laughed. "That's a solution, but as I told you, my heart is already given to Miss Endicott."

The squire's face fell. "Yes . . . but will she accept you?" He didn't wait for an answer. "If she doesn't, you know where to find me. Mary is a delightful young lady."

"Yes, thank you for the offer. If my romantic luck runs out here, I shall seek you out."

The squire's shrewd gaze searched him. "You really believe there's a chance with Miss Endicott?"

"Hope springs eternal. She has given me no hope, but I don't give up easily."

"That's a credit to you, young man. Perseverance is a virtue."

"Perhaps your lands can be improved."

The squire shook his head. "I've tried everything, and you need money for improvements."

"I could perhaps lend you a sum—after I inspect your lands. I have lived in arid places and there are ways to improve the yield of crops, or turn to other kinds of farming. I have some experience of this."

"Yes, but borrowing money is what brought me into trouble in the first place. I've been borrowing for years, and however much we turn the pennies, I can't seem to get free of my debt. My lender is happy to keep me at his mercy. When he calls, I have to step in. Some of the assignments are rather distasteful."

Is that lender Julian? "That sounds like extortion. You could perhaps borrow from another source and get out from under the burden this man puts on you."

"I wish, but there are other . . . well, issues involved."

"Yes? There has to be a way out. You're talking about oppression."

The squire heaved another sigh. He looked pale, as if the burden bleached all life out of him.

"Bluntly," Strider continued, "you're being black-mailed."

The squire put up his hands as if to ward off the word. "It's too strong of an accusation. I have been in such a quandary for years now." He sounded tired and disheartened.

"You can stop this by letting the truth come out."

"And lose face? If my wife finds out that I've been borrowing funds all these years, she'll be mortified. She comes from a very proud Scottish family, you know."

"You've only done your best to support your family in style. Nothing wrong with that, surely?"

"No . . . but I have my pride."

"Sometimes pride causes more trouble than standing up for the truth does." Strider leaned forward. "I tell you what—I shall clear your debt with this gentleman, and you shall pay me later, when you get yourself back on your feet. I won't pressure you in any way."

"You cannot be serious." The squire's eyes lit with new hope.

"I am. What is the sum?"

"Five thousand pounds, plus interest."

"Hmm, a large sum indeed, but I know gents who lose that much or more on the gaming tables in one night."

The squire nodded. "Yes, I've heard of that, but I was never a gambler, only a family man." He pointed at Strider. "I know who you remind me of, the old Lord Sandhurst, the one of the other branch of the family. He died young, but a kinder man you couldn't find. He was generosity personified." The squire scratched his head. "You even look like him a bit, the same proud nose, the same bearing. He had dark hair, too."

"Didn't know him," Strider said flatly.

"You would've liked him. It was a sad day when he passed away so young."

"Was he married?"

"Of course. His wife Cordelia produced three children for him, two girls and a boy. All gone, alas."

"There must be a family curse."

The squire chuckled. "Probably caused by one of

the Endicotts. You might've heard the legend that one of Miss Endicott's forebears was a witch, some foreigner from a far-off country. She married an Endicott forefather, but didn't last long on these shores. Probably didn't like the dampness of the sea."

"Very possible," Strider said, sadness lodging in his heart. He hadn't known any of these people, but they had been of the same blood as he. Not the Endicott witch, but his roots went deeply into the rocky soil of Cornwall. He wanted to confide in this earnest old man, but couldn't find a way to utter the words that meant so much to him.

And how could he prove his claim? All papers had been destroyed, all the people gone. He had hoped to find something that would work in his favor, but everything, everyone was entrenched in their lies— lies that had become truth with time. He couldn't bear to see that others had milked every reward from that which was his, while he had to struggle for every penny gained on his path. Not that he minded the experience. It had made him grow up fast and taught him quickly about the ways of the world, but fairness had not been part of it.

"Life is never fair, is it?"

"A more common belief you cannot find, or a truer one." The squire leaned back in his chair and sucked on his empty pipe. "I have a sense that you haven't told me everything. Since you've been so kind as to help me, I offer you the same. Mayhap there's something I can do for you."

Strider looked at the older man, searching for any signs of mockery, but found none. "I believe I've found a new friend in you, Squire Norton, but I doubt very much that you can help me with my dilemma— unless you are Merlin the wizard, himself."

The squire laughed.

Strider smiled. "Well, are you?"

"That I am not, alas. But I have a lifetime of experience, which is nothing to sneeze at. I've had my moments of brilliance even if they've been few and far between. But who says lightning can't strike again?"

"You're right on that score."

The squire's gaze narrowed and he pointed at Strider. "I know that smile. I know who you remind me of."

Just as he gathered his breath to explain, the wind caught the opening door and slammed it against the wall, interrupting all conversation. Three people entered. Strider's gaze ran to the lady at the front, and his heart skipped a beat. Laura looked stunning in a green riding habit with gold braid. Jill and a male stranger followed. Lady Blackwood's husband, Strider thought.

When they laid eyes on him, a thundercloud gathered in the room.

Sixteen

"'Pon rep, I didn't expect to encounter them," Strider said under his breath.

"Miss Endicott is a vision in that green velvet," the squire said. "'Tis a mystery why she hasn't married yet. Has her eye on that scurvy Sandhurst, no doubt. All women fall for a charming smile and an elegant figure."

Strider was speechless.

"She would be better off with you, if you are who I think you are," the squire said. He smiled. "Damme, but you've come back from the grave."

"She hates me," Strider murmured as Laura's gaze blazed with anger.

"You! What are you doing here?" she asked, her back straightening as she looked down at him.

He wanted so much to stand up and gather her into his arms.

"It's a public house, if I'm not mistaken," he replied, and leaned back in his chair, stretching out his legs. He'd be damned if he'd let her get the better of him. She could not dictate his actions. "I'm having my dinner in peace with Squire Norton. No crime in that, surely."

"I think we should leave," she said to Jill and their male escort.

"Not at all," the man said. "As he said, it's a public inn, and I'm thirsty after our ride."

The gentleman sized Strider up with his dark gaze, and gripped the ladies' elbows. "Come, there's a private table by the fireplace." He lowered his voice. "Who is he anyway?"

"The so-called Strider Hunt. We don't know who he really is, but he put Laura's reputation in jeopardy," Jill explained. She looked at Strider with anger, too. "You should be ashamed of yourself, sir!"

"My conscience is clean," Strider replied. He glanced at Laura. "And I'm not trespassing on anyone's land."

"Should I call him out?" the gentleman asked.

Laura shook her head vehemently. "There's no reason to put yourself in danger over this. The man has no scruples, and I would not want to be the reason for a sword fight."

Strider stood and addressed the nincompoop. "I find it highly provocative that you would discuss me amongst yourselves, and that you would broach the delicate matter of a duel in front of the ladies. You can speak to me face-to-face like a man and introduce yourself. As far as I know, I have no quarrel with you."

"You're right," the stranger said, and crossed the floor after he made sure Laura and Jill sat comfortably at the table. "It was remiss of me, but I was somewhat taken by surprise." He stood in front of Strider, who realized instinctively that this was an honorable man.

Strider said, "I'm trying to live my life peacefully, and I'm sorry if I did something to endanger Laura's reputation."

"I am surprised you know her at all," the man said, clearly trying to make the connection as he eyed Strider's simple clothing.

"This is a small community. You're liable to encounter any number of people. Strangers don't remain strangers for very long."

"I presume you haven't been formally introduced, so any liberties—"

"I have no intention of embarrassing Miss Endicott further, and I apologize deeply for any transgressions she perceived." He threw a veiled glance at Laura. She hadn't fought him when he'd kissed her; in fact, she'd wrapped her arms around him, but he would take the blame. "If it will make you feel more comfortable, I shall remove myself from your vicinity. You can drink your ale in peace."

"Thank you. I'm Sir Richard Blackwood, Jillian's husband. I am very fond of Laura and will do anything to protect her."

"No need to. I'll go now."

Squire Norton huffed at that, as if irritated that his chat with Strider was cut short.

"Don't worry, Squire. We can continue this conversation some other time."

"It was getting very interesting." He pointed at Strider. "Dash it all, but I want to speak with you. 'Tis urgent."

"All in good time, my friend." Strider turned to the other gentleman. "I shall remove myself from Laura's sight, as I don't wish her to experience any unpleasantness."

The stranger's stern facial expression hadn't changed, but he nodded curtly as if deciding that a duel was not necessary. "That's very good." He gave a stiff bow and returned to his flock. Laura looked pale and worried, and Strider's heart ached. He tried to catch her eye, but she refused to look at him. Sighing, he bowed to Squire Norton.

"It was a pleasure. I shall meet with you shortly." Strider longed to speak with Laura, but there was nothing else to do but to leave. Sir Richard would see to it that he had no chance to converse with the fair lady.

An hour later he sat at the top of the ridge that bordered the sea and looked through his spyglass at the Sandhurst estate. The time was coming.

He could see Julian's traveling chaise in the drive, but no one moved around it. He couldn't tell if Julian was coming or leaving, but if he remained long enough on the ridge, he would find out.

Riding closer, he cut through the Endicott spinney hoping that no one would see him. If Laura did, she would call in the authorities as she'd threatened. He didn't blame her. He would be angry, too, if someone who had kissed him wouldn't reveal her true identity.

Why did life have to be so complicated? He hadn't planned on getting shot and meeting Laura Endicott. He removed his foot from the stirrup and stretched his leg. It ached like the devil, but had certainly improved greatly in the last week. His arm had regained a lot of strength, if not full movement.

"Cursed nuisance."

He rode slowly to the back of the Sandhurst estate, and stopped behind a large stand of lilacs. If someone discovered him, he would be exposed, and then he would have to explain. But he had no proof, and the authorities would be prone to listen to a viscount who had the support of his peers.

What he really needed was a witness. He'd contacted many in the area, but most of the men who had been involved in the past were dead, from old age or other calamities.

He looked up at the façade and noticed a woman standing in the window at the top floor. She had white hair, and he knew her, but he couldn't approach her. Ducking behind the lilacs, he prayed that she hadn't seen him.

He would have to leave before someone could raise hue and cry.

Riding back the way he'd come, he got back on the path on the ridge. He still hadn't found a way to confront the issue for which he'd come to Cornwall, but he would fall apart if he didn't address the problem soon.

He couldn't go back to the Hanfields now. Too many knew of his whereabouts.

If he didn't reveal his purpose soon, his life would be at an end. But Julian would not win another time. The frustration of the wait was tearing him to pieces, but without a witness or some document to prove his case, he could not proceed. Maybe Squire Norton would know something, or somebody. *I will have to confide in someone soon, no matter what happens,* he thought.

He looked out at the glittering sea as the dissatisfaction washed over him. Would this issue ever work out to his liking? Too much time might have passed already.

His reverie was interrupted as another rider came toward him on the path. His breath caught as he realized it was Laura.

Torn, he wanted to follow his first instinct and turn around on the path. He didn't need any more reprimands from her, but the other side of him drank in the sight of her and didn't want to leave, no matter how many times she yelled at him.

"Are you following me around?" she asked, her face pale and her posture straight as a rod.

"It looks as if you're following me." He braced his hands on the edge of the saddle.

"Why would I do that? I'm trying to get away from you." With those words, she wheeled her horse around and headed toward the Keep on the other side of the spinney.

"Then why do we constantly run into each other?" His horse followed the mare.

"You're everywhere at once." She sounded more annoyed by the minute. "What do I have to do to get away from you? I will be the first to cheer when you leave."

They reached the spinney as his anger rose within. He rode up beside her and gripped her arm. "Be honest, for once! I have no doubts that you loathe me, but I also know you have deeper feelings for me—just as I do for you."

She stared at him openmouthed, her blue eyes glittering with fire. "Perhaps you're right, but that doesn't mean I can acknowledge those kinds of feelings. It would be wrong, as you're a man I can't trust. I don't want to be reminded of my own humiliation, or my stupidity." She tried to tear her arm free. "Just leave me alone!"

He let go of her, and a long silent moment passed between them. The whole universe listened, it seemed.

Before he could find a reply that would make everything right between them, the whole world exploded around them.

A shot. Someone was shooting at them.

Something whistled by his ear, and he could feel the sudden draft and the iciness that ran through him. He threw himself at Laura, dragging her out of the saddle and pushing her to the ground in the tall grass. As he looked frantically around between the green clumps for the attacker, he could feel her squirm under him to get free.

"Shhh, don't move, Laura. Someone is using me for target practice."

"Again?"

He nodded, his body going hot and then cold as tension tightened up his muscles.

"Lie still, or you might get shot," he hissed.

She stopped struggling, her chest heaving under his. Filled with fear for her more so than for himself, he kept parting the grass and looking around. He didn't see anyone. The horses had skittered off after the shot and were now grazing at the edge of the spinney. He could see no sign nor hear movement from the perpetrator.

His horse looked up once toward the trees, his ears pricking as if listening to movement. Strider looked in that direction, but everything remained quiet.

He slowly rolled off Laura, but held her back with his hand, afraid she would bolt and reveal their whereabouts.

"Let me go. It's you they are after, not me." Her eyes had darkened with suspicion. "You must have done something terribly wrong to have enemies who want to kill you."

"If you want to believe that, I can't convince you otherwise, but remember there are two sides to every coin." He reached out and pushed a tendril of blond hair from her face.

"What's the other side?" she asked after a lengthy pause.

"That I might know something that would cause someone to desire to see me dead."

"That's nothing but flummery. Why would someone want to shoot you here? We don't even know you around here. To this area you're a stranger. I could understand if you've made enemies, the way you treat people, but we don't have any murderers among us."

"So you think."

"In your opinion who is it—if I might ask?" Her

voice had taken on a righteous edge, and he hated her mistrust.

"You won't believe me if I tell you."

"What makes you say that?"

"I don't want any more derision from you. I've had enough to last me a lifetime."

She turned her head in the grass and stared at him. Overcome with a desire to kiss her, he stared back, but he was too tense to move. If he did, he might draw his last breath. He was not going to lose everything again, not after all the trouble he'd taken to return here.

"Secrets," she said, "ever more secrets." She thumped her fist into the ground. "I shan't talk to you anymore."

"Let's just lie here in silence and hope the perpetrator has left, which I'm certain he has. He doesn't want to get caught, but I also think he knows his shot missed his mark."

"So he'll try again. I hope he does," she whispered.

"How callous you can be." He was filled with disappointment.

"My experiences with you keep deteriorating, and I suspect you're about to show your true colors any minute now. My cynicism increases accordingly."

He looked at the clouds scudding across the sky. "That is understandable, but save your judgment."

The horses both stopped grazing and the sounds of hooves through the underbrush came to Strider's ears. He raised up on his knees, hoping he would see something that confirmed his suspicion, but only the trees rustled. That familiar frustration ate at him. He stood and looked down at Laura. "Stay here. Don't move for another ten minutes. If you do, you might die." Not waiting for a reply, he rushed through the grass to where the horses stood and leaped into the saddle of his mount. If he got as much as a glimpse of the perpetrator, he knew he could catch him. His horse was faster than anyone else's.

Filled with regrets that he'd lost Laura's trust, he set off through the spinney, knowing that every move might be his last.

Laura watched him go. She had not obeyed his command, but while she wasn't worried for herself, she was extremely worried for him. She shouldn't be, but she couldn't help her feelings. Tears burned in her eyes and she swallowed hard; why did she have feelings for someone who sought to deceive her and take advantage of her at every turn? She got to her feet, noticing the mud on her riding habit. He had pulled her hard out of the saddle, and her body ached, but she had no broken bones. He had genuinely wished to protect her, but anyone who wasn't a complete scoundrel would do the same. She shouldn't be so eager to find excuses for him.

She didn't feel that going back home would improve her mood, and she had no desire to be the recipient of Jill's pitying glances. She loved her friend, but ever since Richard had arrived, Jill was concentrating on him—which was wholly understandable. It also brought home to Laura how lonely she felt.

She rode toward Sandhurst. Julian wasn't there; she'd seen him leave the estate, riding, a traveling coach following. Perhaps he was escorting someone, but whom? She didn't care—another mysterious man doing his mysterious things. Julian never was an open book, but then again he'd never deliberately deceived her.

The estate sat quiet amid fragrant flowers in the weakening afternoon sun, which would set shortly.

Laura didn't know why she had chosen this route, but something drew her to Sandhurst.

As her mare ambled up the drive, she looked up at the facade, admiring the roses that bloomed in profusion. The sun reflected in the windows, and she noticed movement in one of them on the uppermost floor.

"It's the dowager," she said to herself, surprised.

The old lady waved, and she waved back. Drat it, she didn't care what Julian had said about her visiting the dowager. It was clear the old lady could use a short visit. She got out of the saddle and tied the reins to a bush by the front entrance. This time she wasn't going to argue with Henslow; she would just walk in.

Which she did. The hallway lay in shadows and silence reigned in the house. Like a thief, she sneaked up the stairs and knocked quickly on the dowager's door. She knew the old lady wouldn't deny her, so she stepped inside.

The dowager still stood by the window and clapped a hand to her mouth as she recognized Laura. "You . . . came back."

Laura smiled and hugged the frail older woman, who smelled of violets and dust. "I'm Laura, remember? From the Keep."

"Ah . . . yes, the young lady." She touched Laura's hair, tears in her eyes. "The golden-haired one." She seemed very distracted, and Laura wondered if this was her true condition. The dowager smiled and pulled Laura to one of the sofas.

"Sit down, my dear. You're not eating well, are you? I'm going to invite you to one of my famous feasts. I'll see to it that you eat right."

Laura laughed. "That's very thoughtful of you."

The dowager chuckled. "I like you, Miss . . . ?"

"Laura." She glanced around the room, noting that

none of the dust and clutter had moved, but she hadn't really expected it. "Where did Julian go?"

"Julian?" The dowager shrugged her thin shoulders. "You never know where that young man travels. A very slippery fellow—always was."

"Why?" Laura wondered what the old lady knew.

"He's never been one to stay at home—likes the glitter of the capital."

Laura nodded. "Yes, I've seen that."

"And he has the funds to live well." The dowager rubbed her forehead as if to clear her thoughts. "I saw Daniel earlier today."

Laura stiffened, taken by surprise. "What? Your grandson who disappeared?"

The dowager nodded. "Yes, he's older now, but he's here. . . I think." She nervously fingered the lace at her throat. "I'm so . . . befuddled."

"Did you see a ghost?" Laura asked gently and placed her hand over the dowager's paper-thin one.

The old lady grasped her hand and held on. "No . . . no ghost. He was outside, in the bushes. I saw him looking at the house."

Laura could barely breathe. "What did he look like?"

"Dark-haired and broad-shouldered. He has that open, friendly face; that hasn't changed. He looked up at me, and then ducked behind the trees. I waved, and I don't understand why he didn't come up to see me."

Dear God, she's talking about Strider, Laura thought, shaken. "Are you sure you saw him?"

The old lady nodded. "Yes . . . the dear boy was here, wasn't he? I saw him clear as day."

"Tell me, do you remember what he was wearing?"

"Oh dear, a coat I'm sure, and a . . . white shirt. No neck cloth, which I thought very uncouth."

Strider had been wearing a blue coat and a white shirt, without a neck cloth. "What was the color of his coat? Do you recall?"

"Yes . . . blue, I think." She wrung her hands. "I would like to see him. Would you find him for me, Laura?"

Laura nodded. "I think I know where he is. If he has returned to Sandhurst, he's truly the viscount, isn't he? Julian would not want him to come back, would he?"

The dowager straightened her back and spoke with conviction. "Julian was never the true viscount in my opinion. He's been a usurper. Never belonged here, even if he is my grandson."

"What would happen if this becomes common knowledge?"

"What?" the dowager asked, clearly confused again.

"That Daniel is not dead. Everyone thinks he died in foreign parts."

The old lady nodded. "'Twas a foul day when they brought the news of his demise."

"The *false* news," Laura pointed out. "Someone was spying on him abroad."

"It . . . yes, I believe so." The dowager squeezed her arm. "Can you find Daniel for me? I shall see him before I die, and the truth shall be revealed. I cannot wait to see him and hold him."

Laura felt weak with shock. Strider Hunt was Daniel Temple. If this became common knowledge, Julian would lose his title and all the privileges. He would not like that, but what would he do to Daniel, or Strider, if he knew his true identity? Perhaps he already knew? Someone had tried to shoot Daniel twice—but no, Julian could not be that cruel. Or could he? Confusion fought with common sense, and the urge to find out the truth became overwhelming.

"Lady Sandhurst, don't tell anyone that I was here. I'm going to find Daniel for you and bring him back here."

"Bless you, my dear. I never thought I'd see him again, but there he was, plain as a pikestaff."

Laura wasn't sure what to feel. Part of her was elated to have found out the truth about Strider Hunt at last, but what if the dowager had seen a dream only? Until she had talked to him, she would not be able to trust, even if the old lady had described him correctly. This was too great to bear, she thought. How would she find Strider Hunt—or Daniel, if it really was he who had returned?

What if someone had managed to shoot him since the shot behind the Keep? What if Julian, or someone Julian had hired, had tried to kill Strider for the secret he carried? Could Julian be that cruel. She didn't know him any longer.

She gave the dowager's hand a squeeze. "I'll be back soon. With Daniel."

The dowager smiled as if wondering what had just transpired.

Laura waved and ran out of the room, her legs wobbly. So much had happened in the few minutes she'd spent with the dowager. If Daniel really existed, he would throw the whole world upside down in these parts. The scandal would reverberate all the way to London. Julian would not be able to stand against it.

She looked around as she went out into the gathering dusk. The roses still sweetened the air and peace lay like a blanket over the estate. Would the status quo be broken? she wondered. Would the news change the very fabric of life here? She had no answers to that and she didn't wish pain on anyone. She felt for Julian, as well as wondering if he had gained his position by scheming.

Her breath trembled, and her knees wanted to give out. It was with difficulty that she managed to get into the saddle. Her mare felt her nervousness and tried to bolt, but Laura gained control in the last moment.

She would return to the spinney. If Strider were there, she would find him. The stand of trees could hardly be called a spinney, let alone woods. She wasn't afraid for herself, but she wondered if she would find Strider wounded in a meadow again. The thought made her cold, and she shivered. When had he become so important in her life?

It had happened the first time he kissed her in the tower room. His kiss had melted all of her defenses, and she'd tried to put them back up, but nothing had worked. She'd only lied to herself, and to Jill.

But Jill *knew*. They had kept the lie alive because his love was a travesty that could only ruin Laura's life. But if he truly were Daniel? What then?

She shivered, not knowing how to think or what to feel. All she wanted was to find him and talk to him. This time he would not be able to circumvent the truth, and she would discover his motives. Thoughts raced in her mind and her hands clutched the reins, tight and achy. Her gaze darted from left to right, before her and behind her, but there was no sign of Strider.

She rode the length of the ridge and headed toward the moor. Perhaps he'd returned to Hanfield Farms, but she doubted it. He wouldn't rest until he found the person who had shot at him among the trees—and missed, thank God.

"Where is he?" she asked the air, but got no reply.

The mare headed of her own volition toward the Keep. Perhaps he had decided to hide in there? It would be the perfect hiding place, but if he stayed concealed, he could not confront his ill-wishers.

She could see no easy solution, and obviously neither could he. When they had been shot at, he'd said he needed proof, or a witness. That could be what he'd been looking for. She reached the Keep and left the mare at the stables. Running, she went into the tower room from the secret back entrance, but the room lay in empty shadows, goose down everywhere.

He hadn't gone into any other parts of the Keep; someone would have detected him, and he didn't want that.

No, he wasn't hiding. She went through the house and ran into Jill coming down the stairs dressed in a ruby red dinner gown, a silky paisley shawl over her shoulders.

"There you are, Laura. I looked into your room, but didn't see you." She looked closely at Laura, who knew she must appear disheveled and distraught.

Laura drew a deep breath to steady herself. "I'm just about to change now."

Jill gripped her arm as she tried to move past. "What is going on?"

Laura shrugged. "Nothing." She didn't know how to confide the immense new development to her friend.

"Don't lie to me," Jill whispered fiercely.

"Let's go to my room," Laura said. She would have to confide in someone, and Jill was her best friend. She closed her bedroom door firmly behind them and took off her somewhat muddy hat. Shaking out her hair, she sat down on the window bench.

"Tell me before I expire with curiosity," Jill demanded.

"I went to see the dowager again. Julian wasn't there. She had the most extraordinary information."

"You know she might not be all there at times."

Laura nodded. "She was mostly clear today. She claims she saw Julian's dead cousin Daniel this afternoon."

"What?" Jill's dark eyes widened in surprise. "She's filling your head with balderdash."

"I asked what he wore and what he looked like, and she described Strider Hunt perfectly. Furthermore, I saw him riding along the ridge, and he was wearing what she described. 'Tis quite uncanny, but it would explain why Hunt is lingering around the area, and there may be a deeper reason why he was shot in the first place. Someone wants him dead."

Silence hung heavy for a moment. "Julian," Jill whispered.

Laura nodded, tears pressing into her eyes. "It's too much to comprehend. If Strider Hunt is Daniel and he's reinstated as Viscount Sandhurst, Julian stands to lose everything."

"But why hasn't he come forward?" Jill paced up and down the room.

"He'll have to explain that himself." Laura smiled at her friend. "Thank you for listening and not berating me."

"For all I know, you have windmills in your head, but you are my friend." Jill went to sit down next to Laura and took her hand. "You must be very upset by this whole debacle."

Tears swam in Laura's eyes at the concern in her friend's voice. She wiped them away with a gesture of impatience.

"I don't blame you," Jill continued.

"Yes . . . well, it shouldn't affect me in any way, but it does. I never dreamt that something like this would happen."

"Julian will be shocked, of course," Jill said. "He'll be beyond himself with fury."

Laura nodded. "I suspect he already knows. I have the worst feeling in my stomach."

"You care about Strider Hunt more than you're willing to admit," Jill said softly. "I don't blame you for that either. He's a delightful man, but until we know the whole truth about this, you can't let the guard down around your heart."

Laura dried her nose on a handkerchief. She couldn't stem the flow of tears streaming down her cheeks. "Do you think we'll ever know the whole truth, Jill?"

"If there is a truth to know, we will. There's always the chance that the dowager saw a ghost, you know."

"I'm well aware of this, but Strider Hunt wore the clothes she described, and . . . and . . . well, when I tried to get away from him at the ridge above the sea, someone shot at us from the spinney."

Jill stiffened. *"What?* This is now a matter for the authorities," she said without preamble. "I shall have Richard contact Bow Street and lay out the whole. Perhaps we can capture Strider Hunt and hold him prisoner until the law can look at the matter in detail. That way we can keep him safe also, if someone is trying to kill him."

"He wouldn't take well to such treatment," Laura said with conviction. "He abhors confinement." She sighed. "Anyway, just look at the situation. Why would he remain here if there wasn't something more than the horse business?"

"You're right." Jill stood. "I shall broach the matter with Richard immediately, and he'll know what to do."

"I hope they won't be too late," Laura said. "Strider's enemy is relentless."

"The situation will eventually come to a head, and

the truth will come out. If he is who we think, he'll be able to prove that to the authorities."

"I beg that he does."

"He'll have some papers to prove his right," Jill said.

"If he did, what has he been waiting for?" Laura stared at Jill. "He had no reason to wait if he could prove his claim."

Jill sighed. "He's walking a precarious path at best."

Seventeen

Richard was livid. "You could've died, Laura!"

"Whoever was shooting didn't aim at me," she said in a small voice. Laura had never felt more vulnerable and exposed.

"I told Mr. Hunt to stay away from you or have a taste of my wrath, and then you go and meet him secretly behind my back."

"I did no such thing, Richard. I was riding along the sea minding my own business when he appeared on the path."

"A big victorious grin on his face, no doubt." Richard inserted a finger under his neck cloth as if it was too tight. Despite his thunderous expression, he looked elegant in a black evening coat and cream and green striped silk waistcoat.

"I did nothing to encourage him," Laura said defensively. "I tried to avoid him and then the shot rang out."

"Excuse me, ladies, but I'm going to write a letter to a friend at Bow Street and send it out tonight by special messenger." He bowed and left the room before they could comment.

"I'll feel better when the Runners arrive to look into the matter," Jill said. "I don't like it that someone with murderous intent is free on the moors. Perhaps Julian sent those men to break into the Keep and look for Strider Hunt."

Laura only listened with half an ear. "Where do you think Strider is? I would like to go to his side."

"And expose yourself to more danger? Of all the harebrained ideas," Jill said, and stood over Laura, who sat on a straight-back chair in the front parlor. "You are to stay right here."

"He needs someone in his time of danger."

Arms akimbo, Jill said, "Of all the silly notions! What could you do? Stand in front of him as a murderer aims a pistol at him?"

"Of course not," Laura said, her anger igniting. "I would not put myself in danger."

"Wherever he is there's danger, so if you join forces, you accept the possibility of getting killed."

Laura tried to swallow her rising frustration. "It's not easy to sit and wait."

"No, but that's what ladies do. We wait for news and suffer unless there's absolutely no other way than to confront the danger. In this case, I'd say you have to wait and suffer."

Laura squirmed on her seat. "I detest the inactivity, and Richard is so . . . so overbearing."

"He has to be, since you're not willing to listen. He cares about you and wants to protect you."

Laura sighed. "I know. I'm sorry. I have no patience, and I want to know the truth."

Jill bent and kissed the top of her head. "Yes, I understand, believe me. My patience is worse than yours, but in this case, I'm siding with Richard. He'll get to the bottom of this."

Laura nodded. "Yes, he's been of great help."

When everyone had gone to bed that night, she sneaked out of the Keep. She'd tried to sleep, but as soon as she closed her eyes, she saw—through her inner eye—Strider lying bloody in a field somewhere, and she had to be at his side. Why, she wasn't quite sure, but her heart fluttered madly every time she thought of him. "This is what love must feel like," she said to herself as she pulled her gray serge cloak closer around herself.

She stopped for a moment as the thought went through her and came to full realization. Yes! That was the truth. Love had assaulted her. She'd fallen in love with Strider Hunt right at the beginning, but she hadn't known it. The feeling was so different from the one she'd felt for Julian. With him there had been more of a sense of youthful admiration.

"I'm in love," she said to the night. Her heart hammered uncomfortably. What if she was too late to tell him about her feelings? What if he didn't care? He had to; he just *had to*. Any other possibility was unbearable.

She decided to ride around to the familiar haunts again, and crossed the village. She looked into the stables at the Duck and Arrow, but saw no sign of Strider's horse. He had tethered him somewhere, but not at the inn. The candles had been blown out for the night, and everyone slept. The silhouette of a cat slunk by, and the howl of a dog rose toward the silent sky, but otherwise she was alone.

At the outskirt of the village she halted the mare and turned toward the light breeze coming off the sea. It cooled her hot face, but did not bring peace of mind.

With a sigh of defeat, she rode back toward the Keep. She couldn't very well go knock on doors to find Strider. At the edge of the village, she saw a human shape, bent and shrouded in a shapeless cloak. The mare took a fright and skittered sideways, but Laura pulled on the reins.

"Who goes there?" she asked, trying to keep her voice calm.

"I would ask the same of you," a raspy female voice answered her.

"Tula? Is that you?"

The shape came closer. "You ride in the night where danger lurks?" the old witch asked.

"Just as you walk without any protection."

"You're looking for that young man, the stranger. I know you are." Tula came closer.

Hope lit within Laura's heart. "Do you know where he is? Please tell me."

"Why such foolhardiness? Why such hurry? Do you want to end your life before your time?"

"Of course not," Laura said impatiently. She stared at the old woman in the dark. Tula reminded her of a juniper bush—limbs incredibly tough, bendable yet almost impossible to break; sharp needles that pricked if one came too close; and berries that were small and insignificant, yet offered a powerful stomach remedy or could be made into wine. Tula had all that knowledge.

"Come with me," the old woman commanded.

"Is he with you?"

Tula shook her head and stomped her gnarled staff in impatience.

"I don't have time, Tula."

"If you don't take time, you shall have none left," Tula said, making Laura more confused than ever. "Come with me now."

Laura knew she couldn't deny the woman's request. Silently, she aimed the mare into the woods beyond the village. Tula's cottage lay deep within the trees, invisible from anywhere except from the narrow path that led through the woods. The rough building had never seen a coat of paint, and the interior was dark on a sunny day. Yet tonight it was inviting with the fire in the grate and the candles lit on the clumsy table.

Laura slid out of the saddle and tied the horse to a tree branch. "Did you know I was coming?"

Tula nodded. "My poor dog. She needs your help, and I knew you would come, so I waited by the road."

Laura saw the dog on a threadbare rug in a wooden box. She sank to her knees and examined the panting dog that was in the process of birthing a litter of puppies. The white hide with brown spots was gray and damp with perspiration.

"She's been struggling for hours," Tula said, real anxiety in her voice now.

"One is breech," Laura said. "Get me a bowl of water and some soap. I shall help her."

Tula hurried to the stove.

Laura glanced at the two pups already born and now sucking greedily at tits. "The puppies are awfully large. No wonder she's having problems."

Tula looked worried, a stark contrast to her usual belligerent expression. "Will she die? Mandy is my best friend."

"Mandy is a strong dog. She'll survive this. I'm going to try to turn the puppy around." She washed her hands and went to work with soapy fingers. With utmost care, she managed to turn the puppy around enough to get a grip on the body. It took eons to gently extricate the puppy, and Mandy could only lie there and pant with exhaustion. The little body didn't move.

"I'm afraid this one is dead," Laura said as she extricated the puppy.

Tula nodded and dried her eyes with a grimy handkerchief.

Laura felt for more puppies, and prayed this was the last. Mandy didn't have any more strength to deliver. They sat and waited for an hour. Mandy stopped panting, and a gentle peace overcame her. She must have known the ordeal was over.

"I would feed her some good beef broth as soon as she's willing to eat something," Laura said. "At least she has two healthy pups." She watched as the puppies sucked greedily, their tiny tails like corkscrews on their backs and their chubby hind legs digging into the rugs.

Tula put away her handkerchief, and Laura washed her hands once more. She wrapped the dead puppy in a large rag and Tula carried it outside.

"A cup of tea would be just the. thing," Laura said when Tula came back inside.

The older woman went to the cauldron on the hob and ladled up hot water into a teapot. Throwing in pinches of tea leaves, she then set it down to steep. She found two mugs and set them on the table. Laura went to sit on one of the wooden chairs.

"Thank you, Miss Laura," Tula said, her voice soft and so unlike her usual one.

"I'm glad I could be of help. It takes patience and faith to assist in a birth like this. Mandy is a terrier mix, I believe—very strong dogs."

It had started raining outside, and the wind whistled in the trees. Storms worked themselves up over the sea, making sudden assaults on land. Laura looked toward the door. Branches scraped against the wood, and her imagination played havoc with her mind. What if someone was after her, not just Strider Hunt?

"Don't be afraid," Tula said. "I always know if someone is about to approach the cottage."

"How?"

"I just *know*. You have that same ability when you use it, Miss Laura."

Laura nodded. "I'm afraid anyway. There is someone riding with evil intentions tonight."

The older woman nodded. Limping slightly, she

fetched the teapot and served the tea. "Yes . . . there's a man with two faces."

Laura immediately thought of Strider Hunt. "I believe Strider is innocent."

"I'm not talking about him. You have to look further, to the Sandhurst estate."

Laura stared at the witch. "I see." She realized Tula was reluctant to mention Julian's name, as he was a powerful man in the area. "I went to see the Dowager Lady Sandhurst today," Laura said. "You must've known her in the older days."

"Yes, she is a woman who demands respect. Always honest and kind. That young man is destroying her."

"How?"

"By keeping her confined to those rooms. She needs variety and company; she's not an invalid."

"You're right. I don't know why Julian over-coddles her."

"She's one of the last who knows the truth."

"About Julian, about his cousin." Laura took a deep breath. She badly wanted to unravel the mystery.

"She knows what transpired that day long ago."

Laura was now even more confused. "What do *you* know, Tula? If you're hiding something, you have to come forth. We have called in the authorities, and Bow Street Runners will be here in a couple of days if they travel post. What do you know about Daniel?"

"So you've found out that he's back, then?" Tula grumbled as if reluctant to speak about it. "The dowager had those two boys of hers, and their offspring were as different as night and day. Daniel and his sisters were engaging young people, always had a kind word as they rode by. It was a pity when they all passed on. Julian was an only child, and spoiled accordingly."

"Julian can be both kind and charming," Laura defended, just to be fair.

"When he wants to be."

"The dowager claims she saw Daniel earlier today."
Laura looked expectantly at the older woman to see if
she would corroborate the story. After all, she'd spent
time with Abdullah and must've come in contact with
Daniel.

The witch sat down with a heavy sigh and sipped her
tea. "Aye . . . the poor man. I don't see how he can
prove his innocence. It is a desperate act to come back
here. Julian won't give an inch, we all know that."

"Daniel is in great danger." Laura's heart started
aching at the thought. "I'm out tonight looking for
him to warn him about Julian's murderous intent."
She clutched the warm mug with both her hands.

Tula closed her eyes and muttered something to
herself. She sat in silence, as if looking deeply into
herself. "I see much danger—someone will be hurt.
I see an owl, bringer of messages from the dead.
Someone will die before this is over. A man—a young
man."

Laura shivered with foreboding. "Is there a chance
for Daniel to claim his rightful place?"

"If he doesn't die. I don't know who will."

Laura didn't want to hear more, but she stared as if
mesmerized at the older woman. Tula opened her
dark eyes and looked straight into Laura's soul.
"You're still going to marry a man named Julian."

Laura shivered. "That's nonsense. I'll never wed
Julian, not if he were the last man on earth."

Tula nodded. "My spirits don't lie."

Awkward silence fell, and Laura didn't know
whether to be annoyed or hopeful. She got up and
went to examine the dog. Mandy looked much better,
her warm brown eyes bright and friendly. She slapped
her tail against the rugs and gave one of the puppies
an experimental lick.

The puppy whined, and then busied itself with the tit.

Tula stood beside her. "These will be brutes when they grow up."

Laura laughed. "They have all the signs, don't they? Good hunters, no doubt."

Tula touched her arm. "You'd better leave now. This is not the night to be gallivanting about the moor. Danger abounds."

Laura shivered again, and fear gripped her middle. She looked toward the door just as a knock sounded. Tula started, her face growing pale. "You didn't sense someone coming, Tula?" Her hands started shaking. "Who could it be?"

"Someone looking for a secret love potion, perhaps," Tula said, and set her teacup on the table. She went to press her ear to the door. "Who goes there?"

The wind was hissing outside, but there was no sound of voices or movement.

Another cautious knock sounded, and Tula opened the door a crack. An eye gleamed in the opening.

"Oh, 'tis you," Tula said, and opened the door wide.

In limped Daniel. His blue coat had been torn and he had mud all over his breeches. His face looked haggard and dirt-streaked, and his hair hung limp and muddy over his ears. He stopped abruptly as he saw Laura.

"Daniel," she said lamely.

His gaze narrowed, and his whole body stiffened. "You know?"

Laura nodded. "I found out today, or just let's say I put two and two together after a conversation with the Dowager Lady Sandhurst. She saw you behind the lilacs at Sandhurst today."

He rubbed his chin as if in deep thought. Laura wanted to go to him and hold him, but it was out of the question after all the animosity that had passed between them before.

"Yes . . . I was afraid she saw me. I so longed to go to her, but it'll have to wait. Julian will never accept my presence."

"Stands to reason. He'll lose everything," Laura said.

"As I lost everything—and almost my life. I did nothing to deserve this treatment. My whole life was stolen from me, but I created a new one. Still, it was never the same."

He limped to a chair and Laura saw how tired he was. She served him tea out of the pot and set it before him. "Drink."

"Is your horse outside?" Tula asked.

He nodded, too tired to lift his head.

"I shall go and hide it," she said, and wrapped an old brown shawl around her head. After giving Laura a glance of caution, she left the cottage.

Laura sat down across from Daniel at the table. They stared at each other as if hard put to find a point of conversation.

"Perhaps you can explain everything now that I've figured out most of it myself. I do resent that you didn't trust me enough to confide the truth."

"I *couldn't* trust you! You're too close to Julian, too close to the whole situation."

Laura took a deep breath. "I told Jill about my conclusion, and Richard has sent for the Runners. They'll get to the bottom of this."

"What?" He leaned forward, his body tense as a bow. "How could you?"

"If you're truly Daniel, you'll need the authorities to protect you." Laura felt weak with worry. Clearly he was angry with her.

"I can't prove anything as yet," he cried. "Why did

you meddle? I have to find proof, witnesses. This is no light matter."

"They might be able to help you."

"The Runners will believe Sandhurst before they believe me. Julian *is* the viscount in the eyes of the world. They don't know he's a killer."

"A killer?" Laura already knew Julian was capable of violence, especially if he had to protect his turf, but she wanted Daniel to explain.

"He gained the Sandhurst title through death," Daniel said, his voice tense. "But I can't prove it."

Laura digested this explosive piece of information. "You mean he killed those many years ago, when you disappeared?"

Daniel nodded and his lips turned down at the corners. "And I was blamed for it. I have lived with this for a long time. At first I only longed to kill him, but all I want now is justice. Julian is nothing, and he'll return to nothing." He threw edgy glances toward the door. "That is, if he doesn't kill me first."

Laura wanted to walk to him and hold him, but at the same time she felt as if she didn't know him. On top of that he was angry with her for calling in the authorities. "To make any claim legal, the authorities will have to be involved."

"Yes . . . but I wanted to wait until I have solid evidence." He pushed his hands through his hair. "Do you know how difficult it is to accuse a peer of the realm of any criminal act? You could hardly get him tried in front of a jury if he retains his title."

"But he won't, and then he can be tried. I still don't believe that Julian could murder someone."

"He's a very cold character under all that charm."

Laura felt cheated. All her life she'd looked up to Julian, and mostly he'd treated her with cheer and appreciation. "Only this spring he gave me a beautiful painting of a horse, a Stubbs, no less."

"He gave you expensive gifts while Sir Richard was courting you?" Daniel gave her an incredulous stare.

"He has always been my friend. That didn't change when I got engaged to Richard. He never showed any kind of jealousy or underhandedness."

"By Jupiter, that's a great blessing."

"Don't be sarcastic . . . Daniel. 'Tis strange to speak your real name. I got used to Strider Hunt, but I realize it was ridiculous to call you that."

"It gave me a certain sense of freedom," he said with a crooked grin.

"Daniel Temple."

"Viscount Sandhurst," he filled in.

She was both happy and sad. Happy for him that justice might be done, sad that someone she'd called her friend had sunk as low as Julian. If Daniel was right, Julian had carried this for as long as she'd known him.

"We went out fox-hunting that day so long ago. I remember it clearly. The air held that crisp sense of autumn, and the fallen leaves crunched with frost on that morning. All the colors of red, orange, brown, and green were covered with silver rime. My breath stood around me in a cloud, and the other members of the hunt wore thick coats, gloves, and scarves. It could've snowed that day, but the sun crept over the horizon onto that deep blue, brilliant sky. It was one of the loveliest days I've ever seen, and it was to end extremely badly for me."

"You went with the hunt, obviously."

"It was my first official fox hunt. I was fourteen and rode a spirited mare that liked to jump all the obstacles. I liked the chase, and I've always been interested in horses."

"I would've saved the fox and hid it," Laura said with a laugh.

"I take it you've never hunted."

"That's correct, and I never will. I'd rather save lives."

"We rode out, horns blaring, dogs baying. The fox was a red streak against the backdrop of the forest. Everything went well, I kept up with the hunt, and our friends were proud of me. I spent most of the time off at school, so this was a treat.

"Then something went wrong. Shots that should not have been fired, were, and one of the hunters went down. A wealthy man from Hampshire, but I don't recall his name. It all became a blur. Julian was riding in behind me and accused me of shooting the man. I was holding my rifle because it had almost slipped out of its straps—one had broken after close contact with a tree. "

"Was the hunt called off?"

He nodded. "There evidently were witnesses who saw me shoot, but I don't remember anything. All I could see was the horror of the accusation. I was taken back to the estate outside Wadebridge. Someone contacted the authorities and I was to be taken away to the nearest gaol, but Julian bundled me off in the dark of the evening and put me on a ship in Plymouth. 'Don't ever come back, or you'll die.' Those were the last words he ever said to me."

"But he couldn't have become the viscount unless you were dead."

Daniel nodded. "There were attempts on my life, but I always escaped. I suppose he produced a document at some point, because I heard he took my place only one year later. My contact in London informed me of the goings-on, and Julian took the London scene by storm." He sighed. "Julian always liked the glitter, but could never afford it—until he gained Sandhurst. He was young and strong and clever."

"It sounds as if he had it planned all along. How evil." Laura could not shake the cold in her bones at his tale.

"Julian is successful because he only cares about himself, and he knows exactly what he wants."

"To think I expected to marry him," Laura said with a shudder.

"Well, you didn't know, until now."

"The whole thing leaves me cold. I have allowed a thief and a cheat into my house all these years."

"Don't berate yourself. You truly didn't know, and Julian is quite pleasant—on the surface. He would not harm you, unless you stand between him and the source of his comforts."

"Sandhurst."

Daniel nodded. "Yes, Sandhurst supports him handsomely, and he's been biding his time waiting for the right time to set up his nursery. He must know that I survived the assaults, and has been lulled into security since he never heard from me."

"Yes, and now that you're back, you are threatening his very existence. He's the one who shot at you in the meadow and almost killed you. And this latest attack . . ."

"His informants must have informed him I had returned to England. He probably had spies meet me at Plymouth. Then he followed me, ready to kill me at the first opportunity. He's not a very good shot, but he was going to hunt me down like that fox so long ago. In the end, the truth will win."

They stared at each other for a long time, and Laura feared for their future. He leaned forward and gently took her face between his hands and kissed her. This was not passion; there was no demand on her to respond, only endless tenderness. It melted her last stand of resistance, and softened every tension until she could barely remain upright on the stool.

"Thank you," he whispered against her lips as the kiss ended, "for listening."

"I support the truth," she whispered.

"Do you believe me?"

She nodded. "I do. Julian has lived a momentous lie; his greed knows no bounds. I'm sorry for his small-mindedness, but I rejoice in your strength. You need every help you can get, and I for one support you."

He dropped his head down and sighed. "I wish the circumstances were different. I want to court you as befits your station; I want to start over completely."

"All in good time," she replied. She paused for a moment. "I still wish you had told me the truth."

"I knew you were close with Julian and I wasn't sure I could trust you."

She nodded. "That's understandable."

"But you saved my life, in more ways than one."

A sound by the door alerted them, and Laura stiffened with fear, but it was Tula returning from her mission. "No one is sneaking around these parts," she said, frowning, "but there's evil afoot—close by."

Laura felt it, too. It was as if the very air was hushed, listening to what was to come. Waiting never was easy.

Eighteen

"You'll have to hide until the authorities arrive," Laura said to Daniel as they huddled in front of the fire with Tula. "Then we'll have to prove that you are who you say, and allow the course of justice. Meanwhile, we'll have to act as if everything is normal. I'll return to the Keep, and I won't breathe a word."

Daniel squeezed her hand. "I won't sleep a wink worrying about your welfare. What if Julian figures out your connection to me?"

"He won't."

"Don't be so sure. He's bound to have heard the rumors about us."

"Yes, of course, but there's nothing he can do about it, and Richard is there to protect me."

Daniel closed his eyes and sighed. "*I* should be the one to protect you."

"As I said, I'm safe. 'Tis you we should worry about."

"Julian will grow more dangerous every day as you elude him," Tula said, "but you have a safe place here for as long as it lasts. The viscount will come searching here when everything else fails, but he's afraid of me and my 'powers.'" Tula cackled, her dark eyes flashing with mirth. "Basically he's a coward and always will be."

Laura stood. "I have to go back now. If someone discovers that I'm gone, Richard will turn the whole village upside down to find me."

Daniel hugged her hard. "I'm loath to see you go."

"We have no other choice."

Laura swept her cloak around her and thanked Tula for the tea. The night felt damp and empty after the warmth and intimacy by the fire. Sometimes the world outside could be a very vast and lonely place. She rode silently through the village, looking left and right for movement, but nothing stirred. It was as if all life force had left the area. She reached the Keep without mishap.

After she went to bed, she tossed and turned for hours before she could find a comfortable position. Leo shared her bed, but he only made it more difficult to move. He refused to budge.

Her mind tried to digest everything that had happened, but it was too big a piece to chew. One thing she believed: she'd fallen deeply in love with the mysterious stranger who was no stranger anymore. "I love him so much," she told Leo, who snorted in his sleep.

The cats at the foot of the bed didn't seem to care at all.

The morning came with sharp sunlight and blue skies. The air held a nip that spoke of an imminent autumn. Laura dressed in a narrow, dark green dress with a pleated bodice and matching spencer. It was the first day this season she'd worn something with long sleeves, and she wished the summer had lasted longer.

Her head was filled with cotton yet weighed more than a large boulder, and she didn't feel fit to deal with the day ahead. Her limbs heavy from the lack of sleep, she went downstairs. She didn't have any desire to chat with anyone over breakfast, but her need for aloneness was squashed as both Jill and Richard sat at the table in the dining room, plates of eggs and bacon in front of them. The room smelled of fresh coffee and newly baked bread. She didn't feel much like eating, but had to or she'd feel light-headed in an hour—which might not be a bad solution to the boulderlike problem she currently suffered.

All she wanted was to be alone.

"Good morning," they greeted her in unison.

She replied, but could not dig out much enthusiasm.

"You don't sound very chipper this morning," Richard said, smiling brightly.

Curse his happy face, she thought uncharitably. She put some buttered toast on a plate and Brumley served her coffee. She thanked him and dismissed him. When he'd left the room, she asked, "Have you heard from the Runners, Richard?"

"'Tis too soon. They'll be here the day after tomorrow at the earliest."

Laura's spirits fell even further. Two days to wait were two days too many. She didn't know how she would get through them, and then there was the issue of proving Daniel's rights to the Sandhurst estate.

Jill looked at her curiously, and when she opened her mouth to speak, Laura made big eyes at her and she paused. "Nice weather," she said lamely. She stared at Laura as if trying to read her mind.

"Have you seen Julian this morning?" Laura asked when she noticed that Richard was wearing riding clothes.

"No . . . and I don't really want to run into that blighter," Richard said. "Nor do I want to see that other 'admirer' of yours. It's the outside of enough that you would surround yourself with such ramshackle here-and-therians."

"If you put the blame onto me, I shall leave the room," Laura said, steeped even more in weariness.

"I'm sorry, that was not my intention," Richard said, and forked up some scrambled eggs.

Jill stared even more intently. "Are you feeling poorly, Laura?"

Laura shook her head. "I don't need coddling, but thank you for your concern. I just had a turbulent night—bad dreams," she lied.

Jill only pruned her mouth in disapproval, and Laura knew the questions would rain over her as soon as Richard left the room. *Two long days.* How would Daniel stay concealed? She might hide him here, no one the wiser.

The thought brightened her, but she didn't like to deceive everyone. However, this was a life-and-death situation.

Richard left with the excuse that he wanted to read the news sheets before taking a ride, and Laura found herself alone with Jill.

"Well?" Jill demanded. "What are you hiding?"

"Nothing." Laura knew her voice didn't hold conviction. "Nothing at all."

"You're protecting that scoundrel, Strider Hunt." Jill set her teacup down. "You're walking on a very narrow edge, Laura."

"No."

"Spare me."

Laura realized it would be useless to lie to Jill. "I have discovered something very disturbing." She paused and found the words very difficult to bring out. "I'm deeply and totally in love with that . . . scoundrel."

Jill slumped in her chair. "Oh, dear. I hoped it wasn't true."

"I can't help myself."

"I know he's very charming, but what if he can't prove his claim? What will you do?"

Laura could not speak as tears clogged her throat.

Jill placed a hand on Laura's stiff shoulder. "All

shall be well. I don't wish him evil; I just want you to be happy."

Laura put down her napkin and fled the room. Jill spoke her name, but Laura ignored her and raced across the foyer, only to career straight into Julian. His chest was as hard as a wall. *What is he doing here?*

"Laura, my dear, what is ailing you?"

Laura gulped, fear making her stomach wrench. "No-nothing," she stammered. She wiped her eyes quickly. "Why are you here?"

"I heard about the shot that was fired behind the Keep yesterday and came to investigate. I worry about you."

"Who told you?"

"One of my grooms. He also told me you'd been at Sandhurst right before that happened. Did you come to visit me?"

"Perhaps," Laura said, unable to come up with a different reply without lying.

"You knew I had left for the day, didn't you?"

Laura shook her head. "I knew no such thing. I saw your coach, but it's frequently parked in front of the house. Besides, I was taking a ride for relaxation without any specific goals."

"You went into the house?" He sounded like a member of the Inquisition.

Laura decided to lie. It would be her word against whoever had seen her at Sandhurst. "I went 'around' it," she said, which was true, too. "Then I rode along the ridge. Why are you interested? You've never berated me for crossing your lands before."

"I care about you, and worry about you riding alone. I've been hoping to patch up our friendship and move along into better relations. No crime in that surely, and if you have poachers on your grounds, they'll have to be discouraged. I can help you with that, and I want to."

Laura twisted her handkerchief between her fingers. "In truth, I don't know what you're talking about. Someone said they'd heard a shot in the woods, but that means nothing. Everyone hunts around here. We hear shots every day."

"Not on private property, unless they've been invited."

"There are any numbers of farmers who hunt for rabbit around here, as you well know. Could've been one of those. I really don't worry about it, and they have my permission."

He sighed, and she noticed how drawn and anguished he looked. It was clear he hadn't slept much. If he'd been hunting for Daniel all night he must have been exhausted. "You don't appear in good spirits, Julian." She aimed to avert his interest in her toward other things. "Did you sleep poorly?"

"Many things on my mind." He clearly didn't want to elaborate, but she knew he was thinking about Daniel.

"You are afraid, aren't you, Julian."

He paled visibly. "What are you talking about?"

"You haven't seemed at ease for a long time. You travel back and forth; you can find no peace at home. Perhaps you have financial problems, I don't know, but problems you do have."

He pinched his lips together into a hard line, and he looked at her with such coldness that she shrunk back. "What do you know about these things, Laura?" he replied, his voice hoarse. "You work with your animals and you don't care what happens to the people around you. A rather lopsided view of the world, don't you think? I tried to woo you, to bring a bride to Sandhurst, but you turned down my offer with serious animosity."

"Because you treated me with complete inconsideration. I don't want to speak about the issue again, as it's not important. My mind hasn't changed, and I'd like to stay cordial due to the fact we live so close. However, what goes on at the Keep is no matter of yours. Furthermore, I live my life as I please. You're not one to dictate to me what is right or wrong."

He made a derogatory sound, and she whirled around and ran up the stairs. "Good-bye, Julian."

She stopped at the top and stared down at him. He stood motionless and his gaze held such strong dislike that her legs began to tremble. He had never had any tender feelings for her at all, she realized. It had all been a lie. "Don't come back here, Julian. You're not welcome."

He stomped out of the house and slammed the front door. She was shaking, and she knew Julian did not feel any regret. He could raise a pistol and fire at a person without feeling any remorse. The knowledge made her blood run cold. How naïve she'd been to think that Julian would be a potential husband. He would've made her life miserable.

She shivered. Two long days before they could bring out the truth.

"You'd better enjoy your status, Julian—it'll soon be taken away from you," she whispered as she went to her bedroom to change into her riding habit.

She wrote a note to Daniel and decided to find Tula. She didn't dare to ride up to her cottage lest Julian had someone watching her, but she would ask one of the hands at the inn to deliver the note. She begged Daniel to hide at the Keep where they could keep the enemy out. If he could, he would join her, of that she had no doubt. She wrote with her heart in every stroke of the ink, but she didn't dare say too much. The note might fall into the wrong hands.

That night she waited eagerly by the tower door. His old bed awaited him—now feather-free—but he didn't arrive. She waited until three in the morning, falling into fitful sleep on the lumpy mattress, but no knock on the door awakened her. With every minute that passed, she grew more apprehensive. Had something happened to him, or had the note been intercepted? One of the stable hands had accepted her money eagerly and run off to deliver the note.

"Daniel, where are you?" she whispered, her tension rising. Had someone waylaid him?

Daniel had received the note and decided he couldn't spend one hour more away from his beloved. Hiding at the Keep was not a bad idea; no one would think to look for him there. The dogs would raise the household, though, and he hung back at the rear of the property. A few lights lit up the windows at the Keep, telling him that people still moved about. Which was Laura's room he had no idea, but he suspected she was holding a vigil in the tower room where they had first gotten to know each other.

He inched forward, all the while keeping an eye on his surroundings. His senses on high alert, he knew that Julian and his men were not far away. He'd managed to elude him for this long, but his grace period was running out.

He saw well in the dark, and if someone were heading toward him, he would notice.

Nothing moved, and he decided to make a dash for the door. *The dogs be damned,* he thought, holding his breath as he crept along the wall until he'd reached the door. He knocked, hoping his instincts had told him right, that Laura was waiting for him in the tower room.

He knocked again, this time a little harder. Something rustled in the shrubs nearby and he twisted his head to see if anyone had approached. The vegetation moved slightly, and he sensed danger. He stood exposed against the wall.

Just as he'd decided to take cover, the door creaked open. Laura emerged, silhouetted against the feeble light from a candle inside. He pushed her back and followed, closing the door quietly behind him and locking it.

"What's going on outside?" she whispered, her eyes huge with worry. She looked paler than he'd ever seen her.

"Nothing that I could see," he said, and stroked her hair.

"If the Runners respond to Richard's request, they'll be here in two days. Meanwhile we have to make sure Julian doesn't find you. I suggest that you hide here."

He nodded. "This is the last place he'd look."

"Let's not underestimate Julian. He's a very shrewd man, and dangerous at this point."

Daniel nodded. He could not find an argument against it.

"If Julian was the one who shot at you that first time in the meadow, why has he waited so long to hunt you down?"

"Honestly, there's a chance that highwaymen set upon me. I'll never know for sure. I had left my luggage with Abdullah, but I had some funds that disappeared, and a fob watch. I did not travel with an abundance of funds as I expected to gain from the sale of the horses." He pushed his hands through his hair and sat down on the narrow bed. "I just don't remember, because pain such as I've never known overcame me."

"You didn't see the perpetrators?"

"Everything happened so quickly. Two men came across my vision—a blur really—and I knew no more until I opened my eyes and you were there."

They sat next to each other in silence pondering the events that had brought them to this point. Daniel finally turned to Laura. "I wish we had met under different circumstances." He touched her hair and her cheek with his forefinger. "You saved my life."

"Some day I might need your help," she said, tears rimming her eyes.

He wiped them away. "Don't fear. This matter with Julian will be cleared up, and we can begin a new life."

"I don't understand how he could live to hurt people. His whole life is based on a lie."

"His choice, my dear. The truth will out, always. Light will shine in murky corners, be it now or later."

"I believe that." She leaned into his hand and kissed it.

He breathed deeply, experiencing the exquisite sweetness of her love. He'd never felt anything like it, and the depth of his own love almost frightened him. At this point most everything seemed unattainable, but he had to persist, had to believe what he had just stated to her: the truth would come out.

"I have another ally," he said, "a trump card, you might say."

Her eyes filled with curiosity. "Who?"

"My old nanny. I don't think Julian has 'disposed' of her, as he didn't know her. I was five when she left. Lives with her daughter outside of Bodmin."

"We might need her to testify that you are who you say you are."

"Unless my grandmother is lucid. The authorities will believe her."

"Unless Julian can convince them otherwise. I don't put anything past him at this point."

Daniel nodded, feeling the surge of frustration returning. If only he could find someone, anyone, an independent witness who would stand up for him. "I worry about my grandmother. Julian wouldn't harm her, would he?"

"I highly doubt it. There's no love lost between them, but he's not that cold-blooded."

Daniel gave her a long look, and saw that she shivered in fear. "I don't believe that either," he said hastily, as he didn't want Laura to suffer such anguish. If the dowager were the only witness, Julian would not hesitate to eliminate her. Daniel knew that, but he didn't want to believe it.

The distant sound of the dogs giving warning came, and Daniel stiffened, bracing himself against a possible conflict.

Nineteen

Nothing happened, and that night Daniel tried to relax, but his body felt tighter than a bowstring.

"You have to go to the harvest fete in the village, Laura. I'll fend for myself," Daniel said the next morning. He'd spent an unbearable night on the narrow bed, one ear open to strange sounds outside, but no one had approached the door.

"I forgot all about it." Laura looked as if she had not slept all night when she entered the tower room early the next morning. She brought in a covered basket with fruit, bread and cheese, and bottles of lemonade. He drank thirstily, the tart, fresh taste awakening him. He wished she'd brought some coffee, but someone might have noticed.

"I don't want to go," she said. "I can claim a headache."

"No, I need you to spy for me, find out what Julian is doing." He rose with difficulty and took her into his arms. "I'm burning inside with frustration. I would like to meet him like a man in the dueling field, but—"

"Duels are illegal. Besides, you need to prove your authenticity in front of the world."

"You go with Jill and Sir Richard. At least I'll know you're well protected. That bulldog of a man would not let anything happen to you."

Laura smiled. "No, he wouldn't. He can be tedious

at times, but he's reliable." She looked at her watch, pinned to her bodice. "Tomorrow the Runners will be here. The wait is unbearable."

"Until then, you might as well take your mind off things. It will make time pass more quickly." He held her, knowing he didn't want to let her go, but she would be better off with something to distract her mind. "Go now," he said, and kissed her temple. He inhaled her sweet fragrance and closed his eyes. He would hold her scent with him while she was gone.

She reluctantly went to the door "I'll be back as soon as the fete is over."

The selfish part of him wished she could stay, but it was better he suffered through the waiting alone.

"Bring me some taffy," he said, forcing a smile to his lips. He longed for her already.

She blew a kiss at him and sneaked through the door, closing it softly behind her. He could not help but feel a strange premonition, a helplessness, as she left his sight. He had promised to stay here in the safety of the Keep, but the inactivity was driving him insane. He paced the room and knew that he couldn't fulfill his promise to her; he had to leave. While everyone spent the day at the fete, he would try to see his grandmother, and possibly deal with Julian.

Unable to wait any longer, he cautiously opened the tower door and peeked outside. Nothing but the grass moved at the back of the property, but it wouldn't surprise him if Julian were lying in wait somewhere. Looking left and right, he crept out of the Keep and ran for cover.

Laura had no desire to partake in the harvest festivities in the village, but the Earl of Larigan had invited them to a picnic in a meadow on the road out of Pendenny. It was on land that one of his sisters owned, a small property near the village, but she hardly ever traveled down to visit from Scotland, where she lived. Sometimes the family used it as a hunting lodge, but the only one who loved Cornwall was the earl.

Jill looked fetching in an Empire-cut dress of sprigged muslin. Her white parasol had a ruffle along the edge, as did her poke bonnet. Laura had dressed in a pale blue dress with lace trim and a wide straw hat, and she wished she could have stuck her arm under Daniel's as she followed Jill and Richard, who walked closely together and whispered secrets to each other.

They rode in an open barouche to the village. The sun shone from a clear blue sky, and the breeze played in the flowers and trees. The day was pleasantly warm, and the earth smelled of leaves and moistness as the barouche pulled in under the wide canopy of an oak tree. Other carriages had thronged to the shade, but the occupants had already mingled with the revelers in the village.

People milled on the main road. Stalls with all kinds of wares lined the road. A cacophony of scents assaulted Laura's senses. On the air wafted the temptation of toasted chestnuts, sweet rolls, apple pies, and mulled wine. Newly picked apples gave out that crisp smell that heralded autumn, and farmers' tables were stacked high with them. Plums and pears fought for space, as did taffy in paper cones.

People thronged to the inn, where a whole pig was roasting on a spit in the yard, and ale foamed out of barrels into tankards with a speed that made Laura dizzy just watching. Stable hands and footmen elbowed each other at the tables as they exchanged stories and raucous laughter. Joints of meat steamed on platters and mounds of turnips and potatoes towered in bowls.

You would never go hungry in Pendenny if you had coin to pay for it, Laura thought and smiled. Yet, the villagers were known for their hospitality.

"I shall enjoy a tankard of ale," Richard said as he eyed the ale with evident longing.

"We'll go to the milliner's stall," Jill said. "I could use some new ribbons. Come, Laura." She threaded her arm through Laura's and pulled her to the table filled with handkerchiefs, ribbons, fans, lace fichus, and fancy hats on stands. "You're so quiet. What's the matter?"

"I have a headache," Laura lied, as she was unable to come up with some other excuse.

"You've looked long in the face since I last spoke with you. I'd say you're worried about the man with many names."

"Desist, Jill," Laura said, and poked her friend in the side.

Jill pulled her fingers along a satiny length of blue ribbon while the young girl behind the stall looked on. "You don't suffer from headaches, my friend."

Laura didn't argue. She picked up a beaded reticule in black and white and asked for the price. Touching the tassel at the bottom, she said, "I wonder if Julian will be here."

"I haven't seen him; he has a lot of things on his mind, I'm sure." Jill fished some coins out of her purse and handed it to the merchant. "Laura, that reticule is a gift from me to you. Mayhap it'll cheer you up."

"Oh no, I couldn't take it," Laura said and tried to put the reticule back.

"Nonsense!" Jill shoved the article back into Laura's hands and pulled her away from the stall.

Laura clutched the gift to her bosom. "Thank you."

"Perhaps it'll help you to forget that foreign scoundrel who took such great advantage of you."

"I can never forget him, and when truth comes out, he'll be my neighbor," Laura whispered. "That's why I'm asking about Julian; if he has his way, Daniel won't live to see the end of the day."

Jill looked at her for a long time. "I know, and I suspect you know where Daniel is, which makes this a very dangerous business—for you."

Laura didn't reply.

"I won't let you out of my sight until this whole debacle is over," Jill said. She looked for Richard. "We'd better wait for him. He's talking to someone at the inn." She shaded her eyes with her hand. "It looks like Lord Larigan. The picnic starts in an hour."

"I'm sure Julian was invited," Laura said. "I wish he would come so that I can keep an eye on him."

"You would act as a human shield if anyone threatened your beloved Daniel, wouldn't you? No thought at all for your own safety."

"As far as I know, it'll still be perfectly safe to attend the picnic." Laura felt as tart as one of the new apples.

Jill heaved a sigh of frustration. "If only I'd known!"

"You wouldn't have come here," Laura filled in.

They looked at each other and started laughing. The laughter brought a wave of relief to Laura, and she began enjoying the fete. Everyone had seemed happy except herself until she got this reprieve.

They visited a stall with sweetmeats, and Laura purchased sugarplums and taffy for Daniel as she'd promised. She would've given him the world if need be.

The memory of his sweet kisses and tender hands made her ache with longing.

Richard waved at them from the inn, and they turned back their steps. Arm in arm they joined him, and Lord Larigan greeted them with a smile and a bow. Everyone in the village knew his imposing figure and friendly face, and not five seconds went by without someone greeting him or calling his name over the crowd. Besides being a peer of the realm, he took his office as the local magistrate seriously. The lowliest thief had stood in front of him at the bench, but he was known never to judge people unfairly. Some he had sentenced still gave him cheerful smiles and waves from the crowd.

"A good turnout," he said and rocked on his feet. "My servants are setting up the picnic, so you're welcome to join us now. I can always produce a bottle of claret and sherry for the ladies."

Richard offered each lady his arm, and they walked away from the main road with Lord Larigan. Two footmen followed with a basket of purchased fruit and sweetmeats.

"I don't know if you've read in the news sheets that the highwaymen who have plagued the moor are now in custody. Their hanging is assured," Lord Larigan said. "The militia has scoured the area for the criminals since the rumors of their dastardly robberies started flying, and finally caught them red-handed."

Thank God, Laura thought. Daniel had spoken the truth, then, about possibly being assaulted by highwaymen. This was confirmation.

"We're grateful for that," Richard said. "The roads will be safe at last."

The earl nodded. His wispy white hair gleamed in the sunlight and ruffled in the breeze. "If only we could recover what they stole, but that's not possible."

"They shall steal no more, we'll have to be grateful about that," Richard said as they walked into the meadow.

Tables had been set up under the trees. Pristine tablecloths covered their surfaces and bottles of red wine had been uncorked to air and stood waiting as the lackeys placed glasses, plates, and silverware on the tables. The scent of smoked duck, beef, and fresh bread filled the air. Laura greeted several of the guests: Maureen, Lady Penholly; the vicar, Squire Norton; and the Hanfield family. She sidled up to Squire Hanfield, who had accepted a glass of claret from a servant.

"How are your horses, Squire Hanfield?" she asked.

"Very well, and the colt you gentled is exceptional. I knew it had good bones and a good personality under all the unruly temper. A sweet-goer all around." He smiled with pleasure.

"I'm glad to hear it. I left on a somewhat awkward note," she added to find out what the squire thought of her "scandalous" behavior with Daniel in the Hanfield yard.

"Don't mention it. That young man, however clever with the horses, took advantage of you. No blame should be put on your plate."

"I was afraid everyone would cut me when I 'dared' to show my face in public."

"This is not London," he said with a chuckle. "I don't think anyone has judged you too harshly."

"What happened to . . . er, Mr. Hunt? Did he go back to his foreign home?"

The squire glanced at her shrewdly. "You cared about that here-and-therian, didn't you? I haven't seen him since he finished with the horses. Some say he was a villain; I don't. I quite liked the man—always ready to give a helping hand."

His words warmed her heart. "I'm surprised he didn't tell you where he was heading next."

"I'm certain I'll see him at the horse races next," the squire said, and greeted another gentleman.

Laura left his side and drifted toward Maureen, who was laughing uproariously at something Squire Norton had said.

"My dear," Maureen said, and slung her arm over Laura's shoulders. "We all heard that you stepped out of your shackles," she said loudly, and Laura wished she'd gone to speak with someone else. "I'm glad you dared to do something . . . er, shocking, to enliven your life."

Laura felt heat rise in her cheeks. "I did my part to expand the gossip stream."

Maureen laughed. "How very excellent." She glanced around the gathering crowd. "Tell me, is Julian coming?"

A frisson of fear went through Laura. "I . . . don't think so. You know Julian, always busy with his mysterious trips." He was probably even now sending out his spy network over the area to catch Daniel.

"Ah." Maureen's eyes were veiled, and Laura sensed something. Disappointment? Did it matter to Maureen where Julian spent his days? Perhaps there was more to his life than she ever suspected.

"He was invited," Maureen continued. "I saw him last night, so he's about."

"Lord Larigan might know," Laura said, not wishing to encounter Julian.

Laura moved away from the older woman. Maureen and Julian had a special connection and Laura sensed what it was, but she pushed away the thought. The understanding made her feel only disgust. A cloud settled over her, and she longed to return to the Keep. She suspected that Daniel would not be able to remain unoccupied for very long. He would put himself in danger.

Fear coursed through her and she gulped down the sherry that one of the footmen had offered her. If anything happened to Daniel, she didn't know how she'd be able to go on. He mattered more than the world to her.

* * *

Daniel managed to get to the stables at the Keep without intervention. Two old grooms looked up from a game on an upturned bucket between them. One of them said, "Ollie, look, 'tis that wounded gent that Miss Endicott cured."

"Aye, 'e's on the mend all right, but don't walk good at all."

"I need a horse—quick. I have to find Miss Endicott posthaste." Daniel thought it would be the only command that would make them obey, and it did. Jethro saddled a large tawny gelding as he muttered something under his breath.

"She's in trouble then?" the man named Ollie enquired as he led the horse outside by the bridle.

Daniel shook his head. "No, I just need to see her."

The older man leered. "I see. She's ignited yer tender feelin's, then? I understand. If I were younger and 'ad somethin' to offer, I'd ask for 'er 'and meself."

Daniel chuckled. "I'm glad to hear that you appreciate her."

He rode off, keeping to the shelter of the trees as he headed toward Sandhurst. If Julian wasn't there, he might try to see his grandmother. She would be one who could support his claim, and he knew she would be happy to see him. He prayed all the excitement wouldn't kill her.

He approached Sandhurst slowly, and when the estate came into view, he tethered the horse behind a stand of trees and sneaked from one shrub to the other to stay concealed. He saw no movement at the estate, and with any luck, Julian had joined the fete, though he doubted it. More likely, Julian was scouring the area to find him.

The estate sat quiet in the midday sun. He saw two

gardeners in the distance, but the stables were quiet.
If he could let himself in through a side door, he
might be able to evade the servants and make his way
to his grandmother's rooms.

He got inside unseen and went up the narrow corridor that led to the main house. This had once been
his home, and a sense of longing for long ago happiness came over him. Nothing much had changed.
The old furniture and art were the same, but the gold
velvet drapes looked fairly new. Everything looked
polished and well taken care of. Julian took pride in
his ill-gotten heritage.

He heard voices and fled into an open linen closet
and prayed that it wasn't the housekeeper coming for
supplies. Just as soon as he'd pulled the door shut,
women walked by, chatting about the fete. He heard
them giggling as if they'd partaken of too much wine
in the village.

He continued on his endless journey up the stairs
without encountering any of the footmen, thank
goodness. Grandmother had stood in the back window at the very top. He searched his memory for the
location of her rooms, and pressed his ear to several
doors before he heard any sign of life.

His heart hammering, he waited and listened. The
old creaky voice must belong to his grandmother, he
thought, and then a younger female voice responded.
She didn't sound very enthusiastic, nor did she have
much to say.

He would have to enter. The servant would have to
be persuaded to stay in the room. She probably would
out of pure curiosity once Grandmother caught sight
of him.

Holding his breath, he opened the door and
stepped inside. "Good afternoon, Grandmother," he
greeted her, his hands perspiring as he closed the

door behind him. His old wounds ached like the devil, but he walked forward.

She sat in a shaft of sunlight, still regal, but her hair hung in disarray, and her lips drooped as if sadness had weighed them down for a long time. Her gaze pinned on him, focused, and filled with awe. "Daniel!" She rose with some difficulty and came to embrace him.

He held her tightly and tears burned in his eyes. "It's me. I'm back, Grandmother."

"My dearest boy! You've risen from the grave; I knew I saw you the other day."

He held her until his arms ached. She trembled with the excitement of his appearance.

"You'll have to help me, Grandmother. You'll have to tell the authorities who I am so that I can reclaim Sandhurst. When I do, you shall be freed from these rooms."

She sank down on her chair, crying. The maid stood by, her mouth wide open in shock.

The door opened behind him, and as he turned, he came eye to eye with Julian.

Twenty

Daniel looked down and saw the pistol in Julian's hand, aimed right at his heart.

"I knew you would come here sooner or later. You couldn't stay away, could you?" Julian looked pale and thin, as if he'd lost many pounds overnight.

"Why should I? This is my home."

The animosity hung dense over the room.

"Now boys, don't fight as you always did," the dowager said tremulously. "You're grown now. You can both live here in peace, can't you?"

The enormity of that suggestion, so filled with forgiveness, was a testimony to his grandmother's great compassion and tolerance. Yet he didn't feel compassionate inside, and forgiveness lay out of his grasp.

"I alone live here," Julian said, his voice harsh with anger. "Under no circumstances could I live with Daniel."

"But he's the only real family you have, Julian, besides me."

"Be that as it may, his fate was sealed many years ago, when he left the area."

"Against my own wishes, I might add," Daniel pointed out. "You thought I'd died, but I'm a survivor. I don't give up."

"I see that. It was, however, bacon-brained to appear here today."

"Sometimes we have to take chances." Daniel moved ever so slowly toward Julian. Afraid that the pistol might go off and hurt someone innocent like his grandmother, he made sure he stood as a shield to her.

"Don't move. Don't underestimate me. I will protect my position, and I command you to come downstairs. This is not the place for the reckoning."

"I agree," Daniel said, struggling to keep his anger under control. "Let's go downstairs."

"We're going much further than that," Julian said. "You won't be coming back."

The dowager wailed behind them, and Daniel wanted to hold her. "Don't cry, Grandmother. I'll be back."

Julian snorted, and Daniel walked before him downstairs, feeling the cold barrel of the pistol in his back. The servants had made themselves scarce, and Julian demanded that he walk outside. A traveling coach with four horses waited by the entrance, door open. If Julian forced him into the coach, his life would be over. The only other person in sight was the coachman sitting on the box. Voices came from inside the house; the servants were coming. He had to act now.

Without thinking further, he whirled around and glanced his forearm against the pistol so that it flew. Julian must have pulled the trigger instinctively. The pistol went off with a deafening blast, frightening the horses. They bolted, pulling the heavy carriage down the drive. The bullet dug into the dust at Daniel's feet.

At the same moment, Daniel aimed a hard blow to Julian's face with his good arm. Julian staggered back, but he didn't go down. Daniel attacked again, this time punching Julian's jaw with immense force. As Julian fumbled around, Daniel fled as fast as his injured leg would allow him. He hurried around the corner of the house and into the thick hedge of lilacs. The branches hampered his movement somewhat, but he desperately pushed through.

He heard Julian coming behind him.

The gelding. He needed to get to the horse. If he managed, he would have the advantage. Though his leg burned like the devil, he rushed through the formal garden, jumping the low hedges. Julian shouted and swore behind him, gaining speed.

Daniel launched himself in among the trees, startling the gelding. He groped for the reins among the leaves, and managed to free them. Climbing with his good leg, which trembled with the exertion, he swung into the saddle.

Julian just reached him as he kicked his heels into the horse's hide. Daniel cursed as Julian managed to grab hold of his leg and slow the gelding's progress through the grass. Daniel tried to shake off his cousin, but his bad leg was going numb with the pain Julian was causing.

Julian hung on even as the gelding started galloping out of fright. With sheer force, he clung to Daniel, gripping his coat and twisting it. He tried to drag Daniel out of the saddle, but Daniel clenched his knees against the horse and wrapped his hands around its mane to hold on.

"Let go, you idiot!" he shouted. "We'll both plunge into the sea."

"I don't care at this point," Julian shouted back. "You've destroyed my life."

"You destroyed mine."

The gelding was headed in the direction of the village, not the sea. He stopped abruptly as they reached the lane, kicking out. The strain must have prompted him to halt his progress and try to throw off both men.

Daniel went flying over the horse's flanks, and Julian fell below. He shouted in pain, and Daniel could not speak as the wind was knocked out of him. The gelding trotted off.

No additional pain that might herald a broken bone assaulted Daniel, and shortly he sat up, shaking his head. A group of onlookers had stopped. Julian lay motionless in the dusty road. A burly farmer started hoisting him onto a cart filled with apple crates, and Daniel followed.

"Nasty spill there," the farmer said.

Daniel could only nod, totally exhausted. He borrowed a piece of string from the farmer and tied Julian's hands. He hardly managed, as his own hands trembled so much they barely obeyed him.

"That's Lord Sandhurst," the farmer said, suspicious now. A group of people had gathered around the wagon, and Daniel could hear the distant clamor of the fete.

"Take us to the village, please."

"What do ye aim to do with him?" the farmer asked, peering at Daniel from under a tattered straw hat, his brown hair lanky and his lips brown with tobacco.

"I need to speak with the authorities."

"Not a good day for that, surely. They are all at the festivities."

"Then we're going there." Daniel breathed hard and clutched his leg as pain rolled through his body until cold sweat covered him. Perhaps his wounds had reopened. Perhaps he would faint. The clamor of the day went in and out of his consciousness, and his head spun. He braced himself against a heavy crate.

The farmer grumbled something and got up on the box of the wagon. "Lord Larigan, the local magistrate, is there. He'll sort this out; I don't want to be in the middle of this."

Daniel sighed with relief. "I don't know Larigan, but he's the right man. He might even remember me."

The farmer gave him a suspicious look over his shoulder. "Ye're a barmy one, aren't ye?"

Daniel threw a glance at Julian, who was waking up, groaning and cursing. "No, he is." Julian was covered with dust and one of his hands was bleeding.

The wagon moved with a jolt and the onlookers dispersed. They passed people on foot, who pointed and stared at the man stretched out on the wagon. Everyone knew Lord Sandhurst, and it was a most scandalous event that he would enter the village trussed up and filthy. No one paid any attention to Daniel except for a few glances of derision.

He felt exposed, but at least there would be plenty of witnesses to hear his claim. The throngs thickened, and in the distance he saw tables set up under some trees in a meadow. The people at the tables looked well dressed, and by the appearance of the servants, the host was wealthy.

"That's 'im," the farmer said, pointing at a tall, white-haired gentleman.

"Lord Larigan. I remember him vaguely," Daniel said more to himself than to the farmer.

The nag pulled the apple cart up on the grassy verge that bordered the lane. Everyone in the party stared. Daniel caught a glimpse of Laura, who jumped up, threw down her napkin, and came running toward him. He noticed that she was on the verge of crying, and his heart twisted with concern.

She reached the cart as he was slowly sliding off the bed. Immediately she became aware of his pain, and she reached out to help him. He gratefully leaned on her shoulder as he got off.

Julian struggled to his knees, evidently just as beaten

by the gelding's flight across the fields. He moaned, his head hanging and his hair in wild disarray. Clumps of mud stuck to his elegant blue coat. He saw Daniel with his arm around Laura's shoulders and his eyes darkened with anger. He tried to wrench his wrists free.

"What is this spectacle?" Lord Larigan asked as he hurried forward, Jill flanking him on one side and Sir Richard on the other.

"This kindly farmer assisted us to the village," Daniel explained. He took a deep breath. "I have a claim that I want everyone to hear."

Silence hovered for a moment, then Julian shouted. "All he'll give you is lies! Don't listen to the madman."

"Sandhurst, I won't have my gathering interrupted with melodramatic spectacles," the earl said, his eyebrows pulling together in anger. "If you're inebriated, I suggest you return home."

"You need to hear this, Lord Larigan, and then you can decide what to do," Daniel insisted.

"Tell him quickly," Laura whispered.

Daniel pointed at Julian. "This is my cousin, Julian Temple. I'm Daniel Temple, the real Earl of Sandhurst. He's an imposter."

"What?" Lord Larigan looked suspiciously from one to the other, his eyes popping.

"He's a liar," Julian said hoarsely. He jiggled his hands to try to get out of the cord that bound them. "Help me with these." He held out his hands to the earl, who immediately ordered one of his servants to cut the cord.

The farmer watched with unbridled curiosity. Julian flexed his hands to get the circulation back, and struggled off the cart. He stood next to Daniel. The knot of onlookers grew every moment.

"*He* is the liar here," Daniel replied. "He's lived a lie for the last fourteen years."

Julian flew at him, but two strong footmen went into the fray and separated the men. Daniel could barely stand. New pain coursed through him from the blows Julian had delivered. He leaned against the cart, and wished he could pull Laura close, but Jill had forced her to move to the side.

"My father was the Earl of Sandhurst before me. I was accused of killing a man at fourteen and bundled off to India to save my life—by that man." He pointed at Julian. "I left with only the clothes on my back. He took my place."

"'Tis said you died in foreign parts," the earl said. "Sandhurst must have proof of that."

"I do!" Julian cried.

"Anyone can make up proof," Daniel shouted. "He paid well for it, no doubt."

The earl crossed his arms across his middle. "And you?" he said to Daniel. "Can you prove your claim?"

"I have no papers, but my grandmother recognized me."

"She does not have all of her faculties," Julian said.

"Yes, she does," Laura blurted out. "She's as lucid as you and I, and you've kept her locked up to keep her from speaking about the past."

"That's nonsense," Julian said with a sneer.

"You need an impartial witness," the earl said. "But I shall speak with the dowager myself."

"If you ask, she'll testify that I have a red birthmark on the back of my left thigh," Daniel said. "If I'm an imposter, it's not something I could manufacture."

The crowd cheered at the mention of bare body parts, and Daniel cursed under his breath.

"That's right," the earl said.

"I swear he's lying," Julian said, pale with anger. He struggled to get away from the footmen, but they wouldn't budge.

A commotion at the back parted the crowd surrounding the wagon, and a gentleman stepped forward.

The man was rotund of body and round-faced, his gray hair thick and tied back in an old-fashioned queue. He gave Julian a glance full of anger, but also fear. Then he faced Daniel, who recalled his name, Squire Norton.

"I can testify that this gentleman is right." He pointed at Daniel. "I personally don't know him well, and I know nothing about the birthmark, but this . . . scoundrel"—he turned to Julian—"took the gentleman's place. He has blackmailed me for years. I had borrowed money from him before the incident that made him the Earl of Sandhurst, and he swore he would ruin me if the truth came out. I have a large family to support." He took a deep, raspy breath. "Well, I'm tired of carrying the yoke of his oppression."

Julian screamed in anger, but Squire Norton continued. "Fourteen years ago, we all went to a fox hunt that went sadly awry." He pointed again at Daniel. "This young man was accused of shooting another member of the party. I saw with my own eyes who pulled the trigger that day—Julian Temple. He saw his opportunity to wrest the Sandhurst title from his cousin. How anyone can act in such a craven manner is beyond me, but I've seen his coldness over the years, and his refusal to ease the payments of my financial debt to him." He paused. "Daniel was persuaded that he would hang if he stayed in England, and Julian bundled him off on a ship bound for the Orient. One year later, he stepped into the title with the false claim that Daniel had died."

Daniel could not remember a time when he'd felt more grateful. "I don't know how to thank you," he said, his voice cracking.

"This is a very serious matter. It'll have to be looked into carefully," Lord Larigan said thoughtfully. "Meanwhile, you two will be locked up."

"You can't be serious," Julian shouted. *"I am the Earl of Sandhurst."*

No one replied, and the onlookers were giving him a wide berth.

Richard stepped forward. "I was aware of this man's claim," he said, and looked at Daniel. "I've sent for the Bow Street Runners, and I'm certain that they'll help with a thorough investigation."

"I had help after I was left homeless and penniless," said Daniel. "You can contact Mr. Ashley at Ashley's Bank in London. He can verify that he took me in, as I was lost on one of his ships."

"You have no papers to support your claim?" the earl asked.

Daniel shook his head. "No, but I have no doubt that every detail can be proven."

"God bless the real viscount," someone in the crowd shouted.

"I daresay my testimony is quite valuable," Squire Norton said, puffing himself up. "I have suffered for years under that man's tyranny." He gave Julian a dark look. "I can produce threatening letters and accounts to prove my point."

"Hmm," the earl said. He turned to the footmen. "Escort your prisoner to the gaol and see to it that he's locked up. I'll have to explain to the local constable."

The men bound Julian's hands again even as he struggled and let out a foul string of obscenities. The crowd parted and jeered as they jostled him down the lane toward the village center.

Daniel shot a glance at Laura, who returned it full of love.

"If what you said about your birthmark is true, you'll have to show it to me—and later to the Runners."

The crowd cheered again.

"Not to you, you idiots!" the earl shouted. "I don't believe something like this would ruin my picnic."

"I'm at your service, my lord," Daniel said.

"I know you won't leave the area until this matter is cleared up. You are free, but if I find out that this is nothing but a Banbury story, you'll be severely punished. I'll see to it personally."

Daniel nodded. "I know." He straightened himself. "Also, my nanny will recognize me."

"Hmm, yes, I daresay she will," the earl said. "She'll know about the birthmark."

Daniel nodded eagerly, but the earl walked off with a wave of his hand.

Laura ran to Daniel's side as the crowd dispersed. "You couldn't wait in the tower room, could you?"

"I was going insane in that gloomy silence. I knew everyone was out celebrating."

Jill and Richard joined them. "I have no doubt you're speaking the truth," Richard said, "but I still disapprove of the way you treated Laura in public."

"I know I acted in an ungentlemanly fashion, but I shall redeem myself. I promise." Limping heavily, he pulled Laura away from the crowd and under the wide canopy of an oak. "My darling," he whispered. "I want so badly to talk to you, in private, but this will have to do."

"You're in excruciating pain, aren't you?"

Daniel nodded. "But not half as much as I would be if you refused me. Laura, I love you more than you can ever imagine," he said against her forehead. "I want to fall to my knees, but I can't." He tilted up her face. "This will have to do for now. Will you marry me? Will you become Lady Sandhurst and live in my much smaller house?"

She smiled. "Yes, and yes."

"Once this dashed leg has healed I shall get down on my knee and do this correctly."

"Everything becomes correct when there's love involved. I have one request," she said, a warm light in her eyes as she pressed close to him. "What about my animals?"

"I accept them just as I accept you, my darling. They shall all be at the wedding. I might even ask Hector to stand up for me."

"That would be a 'horse tale' for many years to come." Laura kissed his lips with great tenderness. "I love you so much. Just so that you know, Tula told me on several occasions that I would marry a man named Julian. Naturally I thought it would . . . well, be Julian."

Daniel smiled and pushed back a wayward tendril of her hair. "That's understandable. Just to let you know she was right, my middle name is Julian."

Her eyes widened in shock and as the crowds cheered, he kissed her until he lost track of time and space.

Epilogue

The Dowager Lady Sandhurst described the exact location of Daniel's birthmark, and several officials witnessed the authenticity of the mark. It had also been recorded in the family Bible, something that further strengthened Daniel's claim. What made the real difference to show Julian's ruthless character were Squire Norton's letters and accounts; evidently Julian had forced him to pay thousands of pounds in interest over the years or he would've revealed to Norton's wife the truth of their financial situation. The squire never disclosed to anyone that he'd witnessed Julian shooting the hunter at the fox hunt, as he feared for his own life. After all, he had a large family to support. However, it was a great relief that he could testify to the courts about Julian's perfidy.

Daniel also found his old nanny, who gave further details of marks on his body that supported his claim.

Lord Larigan and the court decided that Daniel was in fact the real Lord Sandhurst.

Julian changed. During the proceedings he looked haggard and his eyes blazed with hatred. Laura could barely watch him, and she suffered the loss of his friendship, which had always been there. But the trait that destroyed any kind of compassion for him was the fact that he'd cold-bloodedly killed that hunter so long ago, and lived with that on his conscience without any regrets at all.

If found guilty of murder, he would hang despite the fact that he'd been born an aristocrat. Then there were the claims of blackmail and harassment. Squire Norton would see justice affirmed.

Laura knew that Julian would be punished, and she would never see him again after the trial.

But love had entered her life, more so than she ever thought possible. She was now Lady Sandhurst after a beautiful autumn wedding at the chapel at the Keep. Her animals lived in two places; the dogs had made quite a path between the estates, and Hector sometimes broke out of his pasture and munched on the borders in the formal garden at Sandhurst, but there was no talking to him. He did as he pleased, stating seniority, and everyone fell into step behind him.

When Laura was expecting her first child, Daniel's leg had healed until he walked almost without a limp. The servants had accepted the new viscount without demur, and the dowager now walked wherever and whenever she wanted, usually sticking her nose into matters that didn't concern her.

But at Sandhurst, love prevailed, in every corner of the house, in every blade of grass, even in the wind, and in every stitch that went into the baby's clothes. Most of all, it grew in the residents' hearts.

Historical Romance from
Jo Ann Ferguson

Discover the Romances of
Hannah Howell

WILL SHE BE RULED BY THE FATES...

Much to her family's chagrin, Miss Laura Endicott believes she is descended from an ancient line of witches. Accordingly, she's ready to accept a wise woman's prophecy that she will marry a man named Julian, and nurses a *tendre* for the neighboring viscount— Julian Temple, Lord Sandhurst. She refuses to see that he is the worst sort of rake, until she discovers a wounded stranger in her meadow, and soon it's clear that someone is looking for this mysterious gentleman, with malice in mind...

...OR BY HER HEART?

Daniel has returned to England, determined to clai[m]
title and reveal the deception lurking on the Sandl
Although love forms no part of his plan, Laura's nu[r]
warm beauty, and gentle compassion are quite irres[...]
more alarming then, to hear that this trusting youn[g]
promised to wed self-serving Julian Temple, whose [...]
best questionable. Somehow, Daniel must avert a w[...]
match, and prove to Laura that true love is indee[...]

Visit us at www.kensingtonbooks.com

ZEBRA
U.S.$4.99
CAN $6.99

ISBN 0-8217-7524-3

PRINTED IN U.S.A.